ARCHIVIST

ARCHIVIST

By Corryn Anderson

ARCHIVIST

Written by Corryn Anderson

Edited by David Gatewood

Cover, interior design, and interior formatting by Corryn Anderson

Awkward Apostrophe Publishing

6707 16th Terrace N, STE 352, Saint Petersburg, FL 33710

ISBN: 978-0-9905671-0-3

First Edition

Printed in the United States of America

Twitter: @CorrynAiyana

Give Feedback At:
Email: CorrynAiyana@gmail.com

PUBLISHING

For Tyler,
Because being the best partner one could ever hope for has not always been easy with me, but you still somehow manage to exceed all expectations,

For Angel Lee,
For teaching me how to let the stories inside me shine through,

And, of course, for all those who have supported me beyond measure in this endeavor:
James, Julia, and Brenden Anderson,
Sheila Kittle and Maurice Van Zoolingen,
James Swinehart and Rhonda Winters Swinehart,
Tyler Johnson,
Rebecca Vogel,
Katie Montes,
Cheryl and Danny Kittle,
Terri La Rue and Keith Faison,
and Steve and Emily Pedlow.

Love you all.

Jonathan Augustus Gregory began writing three days after the total loss of London. He did not stop until sixty-four years later, on the day of his death at his home in Complex 441.

Part One

The Thief and The Boy

1

Michael Driftveil—thief, coward, prisoner—thought he was being tricked.

"Excuse me?" He almost laughed, sure that he must have heard the Judge's sentence incorrectly. They couldn't have assigned him such a massive task for such a small offense. His charges had been downgraded! He was supposed to go to a work camp—the cell warden had told him so. But as he looked around him, all he saw in the unsmiling faces of the few in the room was boredom; there was no trace of hidden mirth, no secret desire to let him in on the joke. His mouth ran dry as he considered that maybe he hadn't heard incorrectly at all.

"I'm to *what*?" His face went pale and he felt as if he might vomit.

The young man sat, shackled. He stared up disbelievingly at the woman who had just read off a few lines of text from an ancient screen, shattering his life in a matter of seconds. He tried to catch her eyes. He *knew* that if the woman really saw him she would realize the mistake, re-sentence him; but she wouldn't look anywhere near him.

After a few moments of silence, dread clawing at Michael's chest, the frail creature shifted uncomfortably on her perch above him and triple-checked the monitor.

"That's what it says."

She spoke slowly, her words creaking out painfully from between her teeth, as if her voice had been begging her to give it a rest for years. Michael's eyes traveled down to the chain around her neck, secured to the aging Judge module and the red, oozing skin underneath. Fleetingly, he wondered how long ago she had been assigned as Voice to this unit, and how much time the poor thing had left. *How big must your lie have been,* he marveled, *for them to have put you here for so long.*

She cleared her throat, winced, and spoke again, her eyes dragging across the words on the screen. "'Jonathan Augustus Gregory did not stop writing until the day of his death, sixty-four years after the Loss. Please report to the Archives to begin reading his contributions by sunrise tomorrow.'" She stopped reading and looked at him briefly before flicking her eyes away. "A vehicle will be available to transport you. You may wait outside your hut tomorrow morning until it arrives."

"Please." He gaped at the Voice, begging her. "Please, check the Judge again! It's got me confused with someone else. That's not right—that's too much. Was it input correctly? *Theft!*" But his two Minder escorts were already unhooking the links that secured his restraints to the Sonicrete floor, snatching his arms and driving him from the sentencing chamber. "I was charged with *THEFT!*"

He struggled against the two giants, his arms crushed in their grasp. Angry sounds rose from his throat, but the Voice had already moved on to the next case. Michael twisted his neck and looked back, and saw a small, starved-looking child being lifted into the hard chair he had just occupied. The child's escorts were just as mean and wicked-looking as his own. The Judge began its mechanical whirring again, calculating this child's fate based on a formula some stranger had typed up over half a century ago.

Just before the doors closed heavily behind him and his escorts, Michael looked back into the chamber once more, his eyes and voice both begging for mercy, as if the sound of his rising distress would change the Judge's computation and the sickly woman would call him back in. The Voice's eyes darted to him nervously. Michael saw pity, and dared to hope.

But then her dull eyes slid back to the module, the old doors swung shut, and Michael knew he was worse than dead.

His escorts ushered him down the Law Building's corridors, and after several minutes of being dragged along roughly, he forced himself to stop pulling away from them, to stop the humiliating whimpers coming out of his throat uninvited. His body still twitched, wanting to flee, but Michael knew he wasn't going to get away. And even if he did, miraculously, manage to break free of these great, hulking mountains of human flesh, Michael had no doubt they would run him down and tear him in two.

Michael's mind spun. Sixty-four years. Sixty-four *years.* Something had gone wrong. The Judge had miscalculated. Surely what Michael had done didn't warrant slaving through sixty-four years of another man's life—not even if the charges *hadn't* been downgraded. One last whimper squeezed its way from between his teeth.

The two thugs led him down a final hall and plopped him down into yet another hard chair. This one was molded from Sonicrete and was attached to the wall, growing straight out as if it were a tumor. One of the seemingly genderless escorts kneeled down before him and secured his chains through a loop embedded in the floor between Michael's worn boots.

"You stay here," the thing said in a voice like grinding glass, glaring with red veined eyes. The thug's breath reminded Michael of shit. "You wait."

Michael felt very small then, as if he were being chastised by his mother. As the two Goliaths turned and left him on the unyielding chair, he didn't even think of disobeying.

Michael Driftveil waited.

The walls around him were the same pale pink as the rest of the Law Building, a shade that was characteristic of Sonicrete set too quickly. Bereft of any decoration or break in the smooth walls, the uniformity was maddening. When he couldn't stand the color anymore, Michael bowed his head and stared at his clothing, loathing it, but hating the pink more. *Grey,* he thought with mounting horror. *They dressed me in grey.* He realized the implication. *They've known where I was going the whole time.* He retched.

The pants they had kept him in for days had dried porridge crust on the left knee, a remnant of dinner from two days ago. There was a wrinkle on his thigh that looked a bit like how he remembered his grandmother if he squinted and turned his ear down to his shoulder.

The shackles around his wrists were old and nicked; maybe once they had been polished and bright, but it had been a very long time since anyone without weapons clearance had seen new metal of any kind. Michael had certainly never seen any. His hands were grubby, and black grime was caked under his nails. They hadn't allowed him a bath in the week since they had found him hiding in the mud under a cart. While he hadn't seen his reflection in a long while, he expected that he looked just as filthy and deranged as he felt. Michael hoped he'd be able to get clean clothes, *green* clothes, from Supply before he had to go to the Archives. He shivered and felt bile rising in his throat again. *This is insane,* he thought.

After what seemed like hours of memorizing the wrinkles of his clothing, he heard footsteps and turned his head to look down the long corridor stretching away to his right. A woman was heading toward him, her sky-colored skirt swirling around her ankles, and the heels on her shiny boots clacking down the hall as she crossed the distance swiftly. She held something in her hands.

Michael exhaled a shaky breath he hadn't known he'd been holding, and felt a surge of relief stab through him. Maybe someone had figured out their error, and they'd sent this woman to come get him and bring him back. He got a little dizzy from breathing too quickly at the thought.

"Hello?" he called to her. "You're here to take me back down? There's been a huge mistake." His voice was shrill, and he cursed himself.

If the woman heard the strain in his voice, she did nothing to let him know. As she drew closer, Michael could see that she was older, but composed and healthy, neat grey hair pulled back from her face with elastic. She didn't look at all affected by the elder rations, even though she was certainly over sixty-five. In fact, she looked almost overfed, her cheeks round and full in her stern face. *Only senators get to eat so well.* His stomach growled at the thought of food.

"Look," he said, louder. He decided that she must not have heard him on account of her age. "That Voice told me that I was to report to the Archives on a big job, but I knew that couldn't be right. I only took a few supplies to supplement the equipment on the farms." That was only a partially a lie, but he wasn't about to tell her what had really happened. If he did that they might revoke the lesser charge, but then at best his position would be only marginally better. "The Judge has ordered me through several decades of journals. That's a mistake, right?"

The woman was right beside him now, and her face wasn't reassuring. He smelled something sweet, but there was something else underneath it that was making him gag, something rotten. The smell was coming from her.

"Driftveil, yes?" Her voice was soft and high, at odds with the rest of her.

Michael nodded, looking up at the woman helplessly.

"My name is Coleman," she said. "I work the Archives. There has been no mistake. You are assigned to J. Gregory's documents. You know how to read? Hold out your right arm."

"But—"

"Your arm, Mr. Driftveil. Please do not make me call the escorts back. I hear those two are up for contract review this month. Something about sending a prisoner to Medical." She paused, studying him carefully. "We'd hate for that to happen to you, wouldn't we?" She arched a grey brow.

Michael couldn't tell if she was bluffing or not. After calculating the risk and not liking the end result, he held out his arms—as best he could with his wrists still shackled together.

Coleman grabbed his right arm and swiftly pushed the metal cuff as far down onto his hand as she could manage, ignoring his wince of discomfort. Michael saw the thing she had been holding now, a slick black box the size of one of the inventory binders they kept on the farms. She carefully lined it up so that the thin edge traveled down Michael's forearm from his wrist to his elbow, and then she pressed a small button on the side.

Michael yelped as a sharp pain lanced through him. He jerked away from Coleman and hugged his throbbing arm against his body.

"If you try to remove the tag yourself, before your sentence has been completed, we will know. You will be punished, and you will be punished swiftly."

With horror, Michael looked down to see a worn metal plate embedded into his arm, anchored by what felt like barbs all around the edges, the skin around it already red and angry. After a beat, blood welled up around it, flooding into the grooves around the edge, and a red light at one corner flicked on, flashing. There was a chirping noise, and an identical light on Coleman's box started blinking in time.

The plate had words stamped into it. At one time the letters painted black, but now only flakes of old tint remained. The metal was so scratched and dingy that Michael could make out only one word, the largest on the plate:

ARCHIVIST

2

Coleman had left without another word, her smart shoes clicking on the Sonicrete as she strode down the corridor, obviously satisfied that Michael would recover from the shock and pain of the tagging on his own. He couldn't even look at her as she walked away, too focused was he on this violation of his body.

Just looking at the plate made Michael feel violated and ill, and his arm pulsed in pain with the rhythm of his too-quick heart. Spots appeared before his eyes. *They can't do this to me.* But they could, and they had, and before too long someone was before him, unlocking first his left wrist, then his right, and pushing him from the Law Building and out into his complex. Not once did Michael look away from the horrible thing that was now a part of him.

Michael didn't know how long he stood at the side of the road, numb, not noticing the people who grumbled and pushed him out of the way as they hurried home or to work or to pick up their children at the schoolhouse, but eventually the sky fell dark around him and he began shivering in his thin, dirty clothes. He needed a new set, and then more to take with him.

An old, hungry-looking woman approached him cautiously, she herself shivering in soiled clothes. She touched his arm and Michael jerked back, hissing.

"Mind the Minders, dear," she said quietly, with pity in her eyes, before looking pointedly across the street.

Michael followed her gaze and saw the two she was referencing, standing at the corner and peering at him with interest, guns gleaming on their hips.

Michael nodded thanks to the old woman and started the long walk back to his hut, acutely aware that his right arm was heavier than it should be. Despite the cold, the skin around the plate felt like fire, and Michael had to keep himself from clutching his arm to his stomach to hide the marker from view.

After a quick stop at his hut for clothing tickets— it occurred to him that this bare Sonicrete structure he had spent most of his life hating now seemed like paradise in comparison to where he would find himself the next night—Michael dragged himself to Supply, a big stone building in the center of the complex.

He cringed when he saw that the man behind the counter was Jonah, because wasn't that the best luck? This meeting was doomed from the start. He almost turned around and left without trying, but instead he took a deep breath and surged ahead. He tried to not to draw any attention to the plate on his arm, moving as casually as he could, although his neck grew hot and he felt ashamed.

Although Michael tried to hide his embarrassment, Jonah must have seen that something was wrong immediately. The man had a nose for any kind of trouble, even if most of it was imagined. This, though, was not imagined. He knew Michael was up to something. Jonah narrowed his pale eyes in much the same way he had done for the last decade whenever he saw Michael, but his expression was now tinged with an extra dose of suspicion.

"Michael." Jonah nodded politely enough, but his voice was cold and curt. There was no point in pretending that Jonah had any fond feelings for the man standing in front of him.

Michael nodded back and plunged his left hand into his pocket, pulling out the tickets. He held out the little scraps of colored rough paper that had spent years shoved underneath his mattress, hoarded quietly for such an occasion. (As if he had ever dreamed in a million years he would have to purchase extra clothes for a trip to the Archives!) His fingers were trembling as he tried to smile at Jonah with a cheer he didn't feel. "Hi Jonah, could I have five sets? Green, you remember. I'm stocking up."

The old man's eyes moved coolly to the extended tickets, his own hand at first stretching out to accept them. Then, inevitably, Jonah's gaze caught the grey fabric laying across Michael's shoulders, and his eyes trailed down to the plate on Michael's other arm, held close to his side in an attempt to hide the evidence of the thief's sentence. The man froze.

Michael's smile faltered only slightly. "Oh, it's nothing, really. Just a misunderstanding. I'll get it sorted out soon." He laughed hollowly. Even to his own ears, he sounded pathetic. Like a dead man, only worse.

Slowly, Jonah retracted his hand, a furrow appearing between his unruly brows. Michael's chest grew tight.

"I promise you, it's all wrong. They charged me with taking a couple of shovels without authorization. I didn't realize I hadn't signed them out, that's all. They're going to fix it soon. Probably tomorrow. I'll have them take off this nasty plate immediately. Honestly, I can't believe they could make such a mistake—that Judge has to be recalibrated or decommed or something—but it's going to be one heck of a cool scar, I tell you." Michael forced a laugh. "Of course, I'll keep it bandaged up when I go to see Lily so she doesn't get spooked. But yeah, it's all a big mistake."

Michael could tell that the babble pouring from his mouth was only digging him in deeper. The frown on Jonah's face grew as he spoke, but for some reason he couldn't stop talking. He wanted to explain it all away, to make the other man believe his half-lies and sell him the clothing. But most of all, in that moment, Michael wanted to be absolutely sure that Jonah wouldn't go home and tell Lily that he was a criminal. It wouldn't do.

"You're not going to see Lily, Michael." Jonah's voice was hard and quiet, leaving no room to argue. Michael tried anyway.

"Now, wait a minute—"

"No."

Michael felt the air leave his lungs in a whoosh, his mind turning. After a minute, he shook his head. "I don't want to fight with you. Just let me have the clothes, please. We'll discuss it later, after this is all sorted out." He knew it wouldn't *be* sorted out, but somehow letting Jonah know that he had lied was much less appealing than just running with the fantasy that he would wake in the morning and everything would be okay.

Jonah still didn't take the tickets.

Michael was growing agitated. "Jonah, come on now. I need some new sets. I'm tired and I have work in the morning. Just give them to me so I can go home and sleep. Please?"

"Go home, Michael." Jonah's lip curled in disgust, his old leathery face wrinkling up like an empty grain bag. "Archivists don't wear green." And he walked away from the counter into the back room.

Michael stood there, dumbstruck, still holding out his tickets. He could see the clothes behind the counter, stacked up neatly by size and color. He could just climb over and take them. Hell, he could even leave the money on the counter, so he wouldn't even be stealing them. It would all be perfectly legal. It would. But despite his brain's best efforts to rationalize the theft, Michael couldn't make his feet move forward. Instead, he turned and left the building, full of shame.

I'm a coward, he thought bitterly as he walked back to his hut. *I should never have asked. He has to take my tickets. I should have demanded that he help me. I should have just taken the clothes.* But the thought sat like a stone in his stomach. If he had taken the clothes, Jonah would have known that he really was a thief. Jonah would have known that he had lied.

I should just go see Lily. His stomach turned over in anguish. Without a doubt Jonah would be sending a runner to the other side of the complex, to Jonah's and Lily's home, to let her know not to let him in. And there was nothing he could do about it. Lily might as well have been a hundred miles away. Michael tried not to weep. *I am a coward*, he repeated in his mind, the words bouncing off his skull, battering his brain like hail. *I am a coward. I am a coward. I am a coward.*

The remainder of the night was spent lying on the bare cot, trying to sleep. Once, twice, three times, Michael got up, thought of sneaking over to the other side of the complex to leave a note for Lily. But each time, before he had even made it to the rough wooden door that didn't quite fit the doorway, he gave up and sat down, shaking. There was no one to say goodbye to anymore, unless he counted the cat that begged for food outside his hut some mornings. Somehow Michael didn't really think the cat would miss him.

The next morning—the morning he was to be moved to the Archives—Michael sat waiting outside what had been his home. He hadn't needed even half the full night they had given him to clear out his belongings and pack them up. His two changes of clothes, a blanket, a few mementos—all were shoved into a single crate, which he now sat on as he waited for his transport.

It was strange to be vacating the space he had occupied for so long. Now that he was being relocated, the ugly, hastily molded and set hut would be assigned to someone else. He wondered if he'd ever see the hut again. Would he even recognize it if he did?

The sun was far from being up yet, and it was cold. Michael bounced his knee, his breath steaming from his mouth, and gazed out across the complex. It was nestled in a valley between two hills, tall fences all along the perimeter. To keep out what, Michael didn't know. The hill to the east had the farms terraced into it, forming thick steps of vegetation. Did they know he wouldn't be coming in this morning to help tend to his section?

He sighed heavily.

Here and there, people would be moving within their own huts, just getting in from the late shifts at the hatchery or looms or the import house. Mostly, though, the complex was asleep. Hundreds of identical little huts were clustered on this side, all the homes for single citizens set pink and sloppy by someone who wasn't paid enough to care about curing the Sonicrete properly. On the other side of the complex were the family dwellings, married couples with children, real buildings of stone and brick. That was really what the people in the complex strived for: to save up and get married and have a child so they could be rewarded and escape their pink coffins. To get out of the huts and start living with a real space of their own.

There had been a girl, once. She and Michael had whispered to each other in the dark about getting their own house, with pretty red brick and a kitchen and windows where she could set a pot with flowers, like her mother had. But she had gone, and he had ached and been angry. And then the anger had turned to grief, and he'd never thought about moving to the other side again.

As Michael looked out across the complex, there was something hard and painful in his chest.

The cart they had sent to transport him was motorized, and Michael hated it immediately. As it pulled up in the dark, making a god-awful racket that ruined the still night, he stood up from his crate. The driver pulled up close and motioned through the dirty window for Michael to put his crate in the back, and as Michael moved to do so he was surprised to see a cloth bag already occupying the space. When he walked around to the passenger side, he caught a glimpse of a woman asleep in the back seat, her leg propped against the door and an arm thrown over her eyes. Michael hadn't realized another prisoner would be transported with him. He pulled open the door, listening to the angry creak of the cold metal, and slid into the front passenger seat. The driver didn't speak to him, so Michael said nothing.

Within minutes they were traveling up the hill, skirting the edges of the farms and approaching the fence. The driver nodded to the guard at the gate, and Michael looked back through the side mirror to the reflection of the valley. It was too dark to see anything, so he imagined the way it looked just before sunset, when his body was tired from working all day and his mind was weary: pink and yellow and purple playing over the huts and houses, the sun falling behind the peak across the way.

Then they were through the gate and the valley was lost behind the crest of earth.

They rode in silence until the sun began to rise above them, the rays of light slipping above the long hummocks that dominated the area. Somewhere, he'd been told, there were other complexes, hidden between the hills just like his home, but he'd never seen one. There had never been any visitors. For the most part, the complex you were born in was the one you served until you died, until they buried you behind the west hill—*To watch God's sun set, always*, the chaplains said. The only time you left was when you were removed for punishment, like Michael was now. He swallowed thickly at the thought.

He knew that the hills radiated from the crater, like ripples around a water droplet in a pond, but Michael had never strayed far enough from the complex to ever grasp just how many ridges there actually were. Up and down they went, driving over hill after hill after hill, toward the place where Michael would die. After riding for nearly three hours, the back-and-forth swaying motion made him close his eyes tightly, afraid his stomach would empty itself of what little it held. He had only been in a motorcart a few times in his life, the last time being when he was very small. The driver sitting beside him snickered when Michael groaned and held his head in his hands, his elbows propped on his knees.

"You'll get used to it," the other passenger in the cart said quietly. Michael glanced back at her from between his fingers. She was awake now, small and dark, still sprawled out in the back seat. "It really is much better when they're maintained properly. Not as rickety."

"I keep it maintained just fine!" the driver snapped.

"I don't ever want to be in one of these again," Michael whimpered as a wave of nausea rose up over him.

The passenger shrugged. "Lots of long hallways in the Archives. You'll be back in one sooner or later. I'm Mary." She held out her hand expectantly.

Michael only looked at it, weary.

Mary sighed and dropped her hand. "Friendly, aren't you?"

"I'm not supposed to be here."

"Right. Okay." Her voice was flat with disbelief. Michael scowled.

"Crater's coming up," the driver grunted, and Mary sat up straight quickly, looking out the window.

"This view . . ." she said. "Hey, puke boy, have you ever seen it?"

Michael shook his head in his hands, keeping his eyes closed. Mary punched him and giggled manically.

"Hey!"

Michael sat up, irritated with the small woman, but she was climbing up into the front and practically pressing her nose against the windshield.

"You don't want to miss it. *Look.*"

Michael looked. As the small cart crested a hill, Michael's eyes widened further than he thought possible, and he sucked in a breath.

Before them, the hole opened up like a colossal mouth. It was a gash in the earth so immense that Michael couldn't see the edges of it—just miles and miles of dead space reaching up at them. It seemed to swallow light, and his eyes began to water as he struggled desperately to find something to focus on in that dark. There was nothing, he knew. To call it a crater was disgraceful; it was a void.

"It's been almost eighty years and we still can't grow anything within a hundred miles of this place," Mary whispered, as if she were afraid she'd wake it.

Michael felt like he was being pulled in, but he couldn't stop staring. It had him, and he wasn't going to be able to get out. It was eating him. Michael wanted to scream.

Mary looked at him, her eyes wide and bright in her round face. "They called it DeeSee."

3

Michael started shaking as the motorcart pulled up to the gate. A female grunt with a harsh face emerged from the squat guard tower and waited for them to roll up, waving her hand in an odd rolling motion. When she had deemed them close enough, she held out her hand like a wall. *Stop*, the hand said. The driver rolled his window down with the hand crank and held out a badge, which she took from him and studied carefully. Her eyes slid back and forth between the picture on the badge and the driver's face.

"I've got Mary with me, and a Michael Driftveil," the driver said when the woman made no move to let them through the gate.

The Minder clicked her tongue absently before stepping back into the post and picking up a phone.

"Oh, for fuck's sake," the driver grumbled, slamming his head back onto the headrest. "The hell is wrong with her?" He started drumming on the steering wheel impatiently.

The tower was little more than a shack; it looked to Michael like it had been slapped together with scraps and then patched and repaired so many times it didn't quite remember what it was supposed to be in the first place. It was a sad little building with no true identity.

"Calm down," Mary said. "If you cause a scene she's going to think you're up to something. You'll get us all shot."

Michael made a choking noise, but the driver snorted a laugh. Mary chuckled and punched Michael's arm again, but he was too focused on the guard to protest. *It was just a joke, Michael*, he thought to himself. *For god's sake, calm down.*

The guard spoke into the phone for an awfully long time, and Michael chewed his lip, worrying that something had gone wrong. He couldn't calm himself down. The guard didn't look happy. Michael's blood was rushing in his ears again, and he hated himself for it.

Eventually, the grunt stepped back over to the cart and handed the driver's badge back to him. "Was that really necessary?" the driver complained. "You know who the fuck I am, Julie. Christ."

The woman, Julie, shrugged and waved the driver through. Michael thought he saw a smirk cross her tough face as the cart pulled away and through the gate.

The cart lurched along loudly, and they headed down a slope and into the earth, past a huge metal and Sonicrete door that swung open for them slowly, and into a grey cavern. The walls and floor were smooth and even. Michael was just glad they weren't pink.

The motorcart did much better on the Sonicrete floor, the easy terrain keeping the cart level, and it no longer sounded like it was going to shake apart. The engine rumbled and echoed in the wide corridor, and they drove past door after door after door, each painted with a large yellow number. Finally, they turned and pulled into a cavernous room, the ceiling arcing high above them. There were rows and rows of motorcarts here, but the room was so large that Michael thought it must have been designed for something more than simply housing carts. He wondered what it was built for, all those years ago before the Loss. He tried to remember what he had learned as a child, but he knew it was pointless—he had always been a very poor listener.

The driver pulled to the end of the line and switched the cart off, the monstrous grumble of the engine ceasing, leaving Michael's ears ringing with emptiness. He immediately missed the deep cacophonous sound of the machine—the silence was so much worse.

"End of the line, bud." The driver grinned at Michael, tilting his bald head to the side and popping his neck.

Michael stared out the grimy, dust-scratched windshield, not wanting to move. Once he left the cart, he'd officially belong to the Archives, and he was still hoping there was a way to get out of it. Truth be told, he was still hoping it had been a joke. A terrible, mean-spirited joke that Michael would never forgive someone for. *If this is a joke, I promise I'll never think about stealing anything ever again. I won't go out to the hill. I promise. Please, please, please.*

"Hey," the driver said when Michael didn't budge, "it's time to get the fuck out of my cart. Get your shit and leave."

"Don't be a jerk, Alex." Mary was leaning over the back seat and grabbing her cloth bag. To Michael, she said, "You don't even know where to go, do you?"

"No . . . They just said—I mean, 'Report to the Archives.'" He felt his face flush hot, embarrassed at how sharp his voice had become.

Mary, to her credit, didn't laugh, though he did see a creasing at the corner of her eyes that hadn't been there before. Michael was grateful that she was trying.

"See? Give the guy a break." She kicked open the door and crawled out. The driver popped his neck again and stared right back at Michael.

Michael took a breath to steady himself, then climbed out of the cart. What he really wanted to do was to run screaming under another cart, hide there until they pulled him out from under it like they had over a week ago. But instead he forced himself to relax. He was here now, and there was no way out until he was done. His only option was to complete the assignment as quickly as he could.

I just have to be sure that I'll still be me at the end of it.

He pushed that thought to the back of his head. *Nothing to do now but work until they let you go*, he reminded himself. He wished he believed they would release him quickly.

He grabbed his crate out of the back, a splinter immediately lodging itself in his palm, and rushed to follow after Mary, who was sauntering down the aisle like she owned the place.

"So, what did you do?" she called back at him over her shoulder. "Kill someone? Rape? You don't *look* like the scum they normally send up here."

Michael shook his head, knowing she couldn't see him. "I stole."

Mary whistled low. "What did you steal, the president?"

"No. I told you, I don't think I should be here."

She shrugged and continued walking.

"Yeah, Coleman didn't care either," he snapped at her angrily. Why didn't anyone *care*? He could explain away everything, but no one would even listen to him.

The small woman stopped and turned to look up at him. She studied him for a moment, then asked, "Coleman saw you?"

"She tagged me." He waved his right arm vaguely to illustrate, the red light blinking steadily.

Mary's eyes narrowed down to slits, and she was chewing on her bottom lip.

"What is it?" He was irritated with her, hungry, and lightheaded, and she was just looking at him like he was a complicated math problem.

Finally she shook her head and turned to leave again. "Let's go. Breakfast is soon, and you need to be assigned."

He grumbled, but trudged after her, her long black braid swinging back and forth like the pendulum on a clock, ticking down the final moments of Michael's time as one, whole person.

"You seem like you've been here before," he said to her, after they'd walked for a minute in silence.

She laughed airily. "Well, of course. You're very observant, aren't you?" She spoke so joyfully that the words didn't even sting.

They passed through a grey door and entered into another long, wide hallway. It seemed much bigger now that he was on foot. Mary didn't try to fill the silence that had fallen between them, so he just listened to their steps echo down the hall. They didn't meet anyone else in the corridor, passing only the endless doors with their yellow numbers. Behind some of the doors Michael could hear people crying. His fear came back to sit like a stone in his throat.

The facility was like a maze. Mary navigated expertly through nearly identical hallways filled with doors and yellow numbers, but Michael was hopelessly lost. If his life depended on getting back to the motorcart, Michael thought, he most certainly would die right then and there.

At last Mary led him to the end of a hall, and entered a door numbered 0001. Michael looked around in confusion, hesitating before following her inside. The other doors on this hall were numbered in the 300s.

"Michael!" Mary called from within. He scrambled after her, not wanting to be left behind.

It was another cavernous room, like the one the motorcart had parked in, but if anything, this one seemed to be even bigger. Most of the room was caged off behind a tall wire fence that stood behind a massive wooden desk. Michael stared at the desk, a rich red wood that seemed impossible. It was clearly old, but it was polished to a beautiful shine. He traced the grain of the wood with his eyes, and realized that it seemed to be one continuous piece. Had there ever been trees so big? Growing *here*? What had been done to them? Michael wondered why anyone would cut down a tree like that, just to make something as mundane as a desk. This whole building seemed stark and cold, and then this desk . . . whoever it had belonged to, they certainly didn't have any say in how the rest of the building had been designed.

Behind the desk, the caged-off area was packed with shelves brimming with boxes. People scurried about, organizing and shuffling, moving boxes from one place to another.

"This is where all the journals are kept. When you finish one, you have to come back to this room to grab the next. Do you know how many volumes you have?"

Michael shook his head, still marveling at the expanse of the room, "Sixty-four years' worth."

Mary stared. "Are you kidding?"

"Driftveil?" a voice called from behind the desk. "Are you Driftveil?"

Michael hadn't even noticed the old woman at first. She was so small and ancient-looking, she was almost totally obscured by the desk.

"Yeah." He stepped forward nervously as she tapped her fingers on the module that sat on the desk.

"You've been assigned to J. Gregory's documents, and room six-twenty-two." Mary made a surprised sound behind him, but he didn't turn to look. "That room is a few blocks away. You'll want to get in the habit of hitching a ride or learning to drive a cart for when you need to get another journal. Your Archivist plate on your arm acts as your room key. Guards may enter your room at any time, so don't expect any privacy. You can eat in Cafeteria C, that's closest, but it's still a twenty-minute walk. You'll work it out." The old woman spoke quickly, and Michael tried desperately to absorb all this information. "We have our own Supply here, but you'll have to make requests three days in advance. Plan accordingly. That's room four-sixty-two. Don't try to leave the building without a military escort, or they will shoot you down. Medical is eight-oh-six if you get hurt. Also a three-day wait if it's not an emergency." A loud buzzer sounded throughout the room. The woman's eyes drifted to a spot behind Michael, and he turned to see an amber light flashing on the wall. "That means breakfast is in twenty minutes, so you'd best get going. Here's the first journal." She held out a pile of neatly folded cloth, topped with a worn book, and slid her eyes over to Mary. "Yours is already all set up in your room, dear." The two women shared a small, friendly smile, and then the old woman looked back to Michael and shook the bundle impatiently.

Michael's mouth hung open. He had never been a very good listener. "I . . . What?"

Mary grabbed the pile for him, sighing exaggeratedly. "I'll write it down for you," she assured him. "You'll be okay. Come on, let's go." She snatched a wax pencil from off the counter and stuck it behind one ear, then walked out of the room before Michael had a chance to form any of the questions that were swirling in his mind. Everything was happening at hyper speed, and Michael couldn't keep up.

What the hell is wrong with these people?

He was following Mary and her swinging braid again. She practically bounced down the hallways, a tiny ball of energy barreling through the few people that had begun leaving their rooms and shuffling through the halls. The other prisoners were slow and dejected-looking, clothed in grey robes and slippers. All of them had the same glassy expression on their face, and they appeared genderless, though Michael knew there must have been both men and women. Their skin was grey like old soup. A few looked greedily into the crate he carried as he hurried past. He clutched it more tightly to his chest.

Michael felt like they were all walking toward something terrible, each step echoing painfully in his mind like a hammer against a nail, but Mary seemed positively cheerful. She started humming, and it was so at odds with the depressed air that hung over everyone else that he wondered if he was imagining it. Michael looked around him at the grey people they were walking beside. If they heard the humming, they didn't show it. *I'm going to be part of this herd,* he thought with growing horror, *this slow moving mass of colorlessness. This is what they're going to turn me into. I'll be a member of the grey people.*

Oh, god.

Mary looked back at him and smiled. "Almost there. Man, I'm starving!" She bounced away even faster.

Michael decided right then and there that he needed to try to stay like her, even though he suspected she might be crazy. At least she hadn't lost her color.

The cafeteria was a bit livelier, though hardly cheery, with people sitting down in little clusters around old blue tables. Michael thought he even saw a few smiles, though they were small and fled quickly.

Mary stopped just inside the door and dug around in the pile of fabric she was holding for him. Triumphantly, she pulled out a little cloth bag and held it up. "These are your meal tokens, okay?" The small woman shoved the rest of the grey cloth, now unfolded and rumpled, into the crate he was holding, then placed the book reverently on top. "You need to hand over one of these tokens in order to eat. You'll get a new bag of tokens every time you turn in a journal. These bags don't have very many in them, so you can't drag your feet, yeah? And keep the bag safe so other people don't take your tokens away from you. They won't replace them if you didn't finish the journal."

Michael nodded solemnly and took the bag from her. It clinked as it switched hands, and Michael pulled out one of the tokens and examined it. It was a small worn circle about the size of his thumbnail, and it warmed quickly between his fingers. The edges were a copper color, but the rest of the token was a dirty silver, like the plate on his arm. He felt the two sides of it and inspected the embossing. It was too worn away to make out what it said, too many hands just like his having rubbed it between their fingers just like he was now. "What did it say?" he asked Mary, looking up from the small shape in his hand.

"Umm . . ." Mary walked over to stand beside him and craned her neck to look. She took the token from him, rotated it slightly, and then placed it back in his palm. "It's a face, see? Looking to the left."

"Oh." He didn't see it.

He followed Mary into the line and waited for his turn to get his food. Mary demonstrated how to slip the token into a small slot set into the wall. There was a soft clank as her token met the others that had been dropped into the hole before it, and then a door at her eye level slid open to reveal a beat-up metal tray. It was piled with steaming food, along with a single spoon that looked like it had been bent out of shape and back into shape far too many times. Michael's stomach growled loudly at the sight of the food, and he hurried to follow Mary's example.

They found an empty blue table and sat. None of the grey people sat down next to them. Michael began wolfing the food down before it cooled, and burned his tongue immediately. He didn't care. Mary watched him with mild interest as she scooped up a small pile of something that might have been mashed peas and blew on it carefully.

The food wasn't good. He thought the maybe-peas could use salt, and the soupy meat-and-egg mixture (was it supposed to be a chicken omelet? pork?) was like putting soap in his mouth, but for now, he was just happy to have anything in his stomach. They ate in silence, Michael finishing up well before Mary. He looked around him and saw for the first time the Minders standing around the room. Michael realized that they must be there to ensure that the prisoners didn't cause any problems, but they looked relaxed. A few even chatted with each other easily, guns holstered on their hips. There obviously hadn't been a disturbance in a while.

"You came off-batch." Mary's voice broke through his thoughts. She was scribbling on a cloth napkin with the wax pencil that had been behind her ear. "Usually the complexes hold people in the local cells for a few months and then bring them in in groups. They all read journals from Recorders that wrote for about the same amount of time, so they're all done within a few weeks of each other, and then they're released back to the complexes. But this group"—she nodded to the grey people around them—"they've all been here for at least six months. Some longer, of course, but most of them." She kept nodding, bobbing her head to music Michael couldn't hear, scribbling away all the while. "People get better the closer to Resurrection they get, not so boring and sad. Right now they still remember the old stuff. Give it another few months or so, though. Six isn't long enough."

"Resurrection?" He hadn't heard the word before.

"Yeah, when people go back to the complex with the Recorder's memories? That's what we call it here. The Bible and all that. It's a Resurrection for the Recorders." She snorted at her own joke, but Michael didn't know what she was talking about, and he was growing irritated with her for being so cavalier about it all.

"You know these are people, right? Real people?" he spat before he could stop himself. "Being forced to give themselves up. It's horrible."

"It's not so bad. In fact, it's better for you. You get rid of all the bad stuff inside you that made them want to send you here in the first place. And you get to further someone's legacy—someone that we know is good. It's a good system."

Michael decided then that he definitely did *not* want to try to be like Mary. He stared at his empty tray, seething. "They threw you in here, too," he said quietly. "You're not any better than these people. You broke the law, and you did it badly enough that they locked you away and want to chip away at what you are. I can't believe you think that it's okay that they're doing this to you."

She hummed in a way that let him know she didn't agree, and his anger notched a little higher. After a minute, she resumed talking. "But anyway, since you came off-batch, that means . . ." She stopped writing on the cloth and looked at him again, ducking her neck down so she could try to catch his eye. Michael looked at her despite himself. "Coleman wanted you for something special. She didn't want to wait. Now why would that be?" She peered at him for a moment more before sliding the napkin over to his side of the table.

There were markings on it that didn't look like letters. Michael had no idea what he was looking at.

"It's a map," Mary said, pushing it closer to him. "Look, this is the cafeteria we're in, here . . ." her finger tapped a big box-like shape near the center, "and then these are the corridors." Bitten nails trailed lines that arced away from a central room labeled CAGE. She tapped on it. "Where the journals are kept—we were just there." Her finger moved over to a spiky-looking symbol. "And this is your room: six-twenty-two. Marked with a star. See?"

Michael looked at the map for a long while, debating whether or not to accept the gift.

"It's so you don't get lost, and you know where everything is. I said I'd write it down for you." A flash of annoyance lit up behind her eyes. She obviously didn't like to have to explain herself.

Reluctantly, Michael snatched the napkin off the table and crushed it in his fist. He realized he was going to need it, and it would be stupid to not take advantage of every available resource.

As Mary pulled her arm away, Michael sat up and looked at her full-on. "Mary," he said evenly, with a calmness he didn't feel. "Where is your plate?"

For a moment, she looked back at him, confused, then glanced down at her tray. Michael watched as understanding dawned across her dark face. "Oh, yeah." She brought her arms back and showed him the bare skin. "They didn't 'throw' me in here, like you said. I'm a volunteer."

4

Michael stared at her. "Are you insane?" Why would someone *volunteer* to do this? His mind felt stuck, that one thought looping over and over in his mind until it started losing its weight.

Mary shrugged and stood up. "I think it's important, that's all." She started to walk away from him with her empty tray, and he heard another buzzer blat throughout the room. A red light on the wall started flashing, and the people around him immediately stood from their tables and grabbed their trays. Michael followed suit, trying to juggle the crate, his token pouch, and the empty tray, and he was back into the shuffle of grey quicker than he would have liked. Mary had disappeared. He dropped his tray with a loud clatter on the growing pile by the door, then bled out into the hallway, trying not to get lost.

He moved to the side, out of the flow of grey, to consult the . . . *What had she called it?* The map. He examined the small labeled halls, trying to remember the path she had traced for him to get to his room. Then he looked at the numbers on the doors around him. They were in the seven hundreds, and ascending. He needed to go the other way. Michael cursed, and attempted to turn around. The people around him grunted as he bumped into them with elbows and wooden corners, glaring at him with grey faces, and he apologized quickly. No one even acknowledged that he'd spoken.

On the map were scattered nine arcing halls, all connected by a mess of pass-throughs and shortcuts that made no sense to Michael, but at least Mary had marked off the most important rooms for him. His room, in the six hundred block, was marked with a "star." After several more minutes of studying the napkin he was reasonably confident that he had found his current location on the map, and he resumed walking.

The "map" was a great tool. He was annoyed that he needed it.

Michael was amazed at how many prisoners there were here. They choked the halls as he swam upstream to his assigned room. As he thought back, he could only recall a few dozen times that people from his complex had been sent here, in his entire lifetime. The fact that there seemed to be hundreds meant that there were many more complexes in this area than he had ever realized. That thought disturbed him for some reason he couldn't quite place.

The corridors became easier to navigate as more and more of the other prisoners found their own rooms and left the halls. Michael counted down the numbers, keeping one eye on the map in case he made a wrong turn.

Finally, he was there. He stared at the yellow numbers on the door for a very long time, trying to calm himself, before going in. He was shaking so hard, the tokens rattled within their cloth pouch. At last he steeled himself and stepped up to the threshold, holding out his right arm and trying not to look at the plate embedded in his flesh. He was startled when the door *whooshed* upward to let him enter.

Michael stepped inside and exhaled shakily.

Coleman was there, waiting for him.

She was sitting on a thin, bare mattress that was shoved in the corner, a Minder at attention by her side, his head gleaming in the light. When Michael entered, Coleman rose. She was dressed in blue again, and looked just as stern as she had the day before at the Law Building. "You kept me waiting," she snapped.

Michael crumpled the map in his fist so she couldn't see it. "I was lost."

She glared at him for a minute, sizing him up. Michael shifted from one foot to the other. The old woman didn't seem to like what she saw.

"Put your things on the floor and sit down there. I have work to do, so hurry up. Let's go."

Michael hastened to do as she said, then sat down in the chair she had gestured to. The chair was bolted to the ground and the right arm of it was a metal tube. Coleman looked pointedly at him, her face pinched and impatient, until he hesitantly slid his arm inside the tube. The metal immediately tightened around his forearm, and he felt electricity arcing across the plate. He smelled something peculiar, sniffed a few times before the pain started dully, and when he realized what it was he gagged: charred skin. The chair had burned him when it connected. Michael shuddered and hoped that wouldn't happen every time he sat down.

Coleman looked unconcerned. "Buchanan," she snapped, and the Minder moved to obey.

The man stepped up behind Michael and adjusted the headrest so that it rested flat against his neck. "Don't move."

The headrest pinched Michael's neck, right at the base of his skull, and he sighed in relief that it wasn't nearly as painful as the tube had been. Then something pierced the skin and he screamed.

Coleman swiveled a small standing tray over his lap and looked down at him. "Can you hear me, Michael?"

He was hissing from the pain, his jaw clenched and his eyes screwed shut. This pain was worse than the tagging had been. He tried to nod, but the thing in his neck made it impossible. The Minder smirked—slightly, just for a moment—at the colorful stream of curses that leapt from Michael's mouth. He clenched his fists tightly and glared at Coleman.

"He's restrained now," she said. "Buchanan, you may go back to your post."

Buchanan did a half-assed salute, waving his hand at Coleman, and left the room humming contentedly.

The woman turned back to Michael and began an obviously rehearsed speech, her high voice screeching in Michael's aching head. "You're to read each day until the chair releases you for meals. Dinner is the end of the day, and you are to sleep afterward in order to recover for the next day. Be sure you read out loud, and clearly, so the microphone"—she tapped a silver box that hung from the ceiling, six inches from his face—"can hear everything you're saying. Your job is to make sure that we have credible recordings for when these journals deteriorate." She walked quietly the three steps over to his crate, leaned down spryly and picked up the book he had been given from the small woman in front of the Cage. She laid it carefully on the tray.

"These journals are already quite fragile, especially the early ones. You *must* be careful with them. They are not to be removed from your room unless you are returning them to storage." Her eyes roamed over the worn green cover for several moments, her face calming. Michael could see where she might have been beautiful once, a long time ago, but then her pinched look came back and any semblance of beauty was gone.

"What am I looking for?" he asked quietly, drumming his fingers against the arms of the chair to distract himself from the pain still cocooning him.

She stilled and looked at him narrowly, contempt easily read on her pinched face. "You're here as a punishment, to preserve our culture, and to rehabilitate yourself. What makes you think you're *looking* for anything?"

Alarm prickled over Michael's scalp and he cleared his throat. "Someone just told me that I came at an unusual time, that's all.

Someone I met at breakfast. I thought there must have been something special you needed." The lie rolled easily off his tongue.

She leaned down till she was eye level with him, her brown eyes boring into his. "Mr. Driftveil, let's not beat around the bush. We both know why you're here. You may have been convicted of stealing a few shovels, but are you honestly so stupid to think we didn't know what you were really doing?"

Michael's face heated with shame and shock.

"You are not a good man, Michael. We've known that for a very long time, and now we are going to get rid of that nasty thieving habit of yours. You're not looking for anything other than a way to better yourself." She straightened. "Now. Read."

She stood back and waited for him to begin.

Michael's hand was shaking as he lifted the cover of the book. He cleared his throat.

"Day one. My name is Johnny. I'm eleven and a half years old. I want to go home."

5

My name is Johnny. I'm eleven and a half years old. I want to go home.

Dad told me to be good this morning, and said that I might not see him or Mom for a while. He didn't tell me why. Mom was crying. I tried to be brave but I cried too, like Sally Jacobs did the time she dropped her piece of birthday cake and there wasn't any left in third grade for my friend Sam's birthday. Only Sally cried forever, and I cried just a little. I didn't get to see Lucy before they took me. I asked the man operating the magnetruck to take me back home so I could say goodbye really quickly, but he didn't. He looked like a policeman, but he wasn't wearing a uniform, even though he still had a gun on his hip.

Dad's afraid of guns. He told me that once when I was a little kid a man came to his work with a gun, and he was very scared, and all he could think of was Mom and me. He told me that I should never play with guns because they are dangerous, and he doesn't want anything to happen to me. But he said this morning that the policeman was a good guy, so I could go with him as long as I promised to be good and do what I was told.

I tried to look out the window for the trip, because I love looking up at the different-colored buildings and the Reachee ships stretching way way up through the clouds when you fly through the city in the magnetruck. Most of the time when we go places we use the tunnels, so I don't get to see any Reachees at all except on the news, and I was hoping I'd get to see one with their long long arms and funny faces. We flew for a very long time though, and I started feeling funny and I think I slept for most of the way. A pretty woman shook me awake and smiled at me, and told me she was going to be my teacher while I was here. We must have left the city because the magnetruck had its wheels down when I got out of the cabin, so I know the pilot had to have taken me somewhere the magnetized tracks don't reach. I can't remember the last time I was in a vehicle with its wheels on the ground, so that made me a little nervous.

My other teacher at school, Ms. Greenborough, is not as pretty as this teacher. I think she said her name was Ms. Maggie. She's got long brown hair and blue eyes and was wearing pink glasses. She's younger than my mom, where Ms. Greenborough is probably a hundred years old, at least.

Ms. Maggie took me to my room, and the policeman that brought me here followed behind us with the stuff that Mom packed for me from home. The bag is very big, but I hope I'm not here long enough to wear all the clothes she packed for me. Especially since she packed me like twelve pairs of pants. That could last me six months, and I definitely don't want to be here that long.

Ms. Maggie showed me where the bathrooms are, and told me that I should probably stay in my new room unless an adult comes to get me. She doesn't want me to get lost. She showed me how to hold up my key to the door so it would open. She says only me and a few other adults have the key to my room, so I need to be very careful not to lose it. The little metal rectangle is on a chain so I can keep it around my neck. She gave me a little screen, and said it has some wordfiles for me to read, but she asked me to sit down at the desk and write as much as I can. I don't like writing with a pencil and paper, typing is much better, but I told her I would try. I asked her what I should write, and she told me to write everything.

Everything is a lot, I said, you'll have to give me more paper. She laughed and told me that I could have all the paper I wanted as long as I write really well, and detailed. So I'm going to be detailed right now.

My room is kind of boring. I can walk from one end to the other in fifteen steps on the long side, but the small side is only nine steps across. It's not painted, but there's a green rug on the floor, and a shelf on the wall where I can put the picture screen that Mom packed for me. There's one of all of us, Dad, Mom, me, and Lucy at my feet. And then there's another of just Lucy, one of the times we took her to the park and she has a tennis ball in her mouth. I wish Mom had loaded more pictures onto it, but she didn't.

Mom also packed one of my baby toys—a stuffed rabbit from when I was in preschool and didn't want to go anywhere without Mom, ever. I didn't unpack the rabbit, I'm too big for that now. I have to be brave.

Ms. Maggie said that tomorrow I'll get to meet some of the other kids in the program. She says that the other kids have senator parents too, like my dad. She also said that we were very lucky that our parents fought so hard to make sure we got in to the program. I asked her what the program was for, and she told me it was to make sure we always remember who we are and where we came from. I don't understand, but her smile was massive, almost like one of those fake smiles adults paste on so that you KNOW they're happy, and I didn't want to ask too many more questions and upset her. That happens a lot at school: I ask too many questions, and then Ms. Greenborough calls a meeting with my parents. My dad looks disappointed in those meetings. I wouldn't ask so many questions if they would explain it to me the first time.

I hope Ms. Maggie doesn't give out as much homework as Ms. Greenborough does.

My pencil is getting dull. I don't have a pencil sharpener with me, so I don't know what they expect me to do. Writing with a dull pencil sucks. It makes my handwriting really bad. If I were at home, Mom would make me rewrite this until it was neat, but I don't think she's going to see this paper so it will be our little secret, OK?

I don't think there are any windows in this building I'm in. The whole time we were walking inside when they were leading me to my room, I didn't see a single window. I don't know if I've ever been inside a building without windows. Maybe the aquarium? Unless the tanks count as windows. I guess they do.

There are a *lot* of people walking around the building though, and they all look really concerned and busy like something bad has happened. I don't know what it is. Maybe I'll ask Ms. Maggie tomorrow.

Someone just came into my room and said the lights would be going off in five minutes. I asked if he could wait, because I'm not tired yet and my mom lets me stay up until ten. He looked at me like *YEAH, RIGHT*. It was worth a shot anyway. He said that the lights in the entire bunker were going out at the same time, so everyone has to go to sleep.

Is that what this is? A bunker? Like from a long time ago in World War II? I read about that in Ms. Greenborough's class, and I think it's so cool!!! I can't wait to tell Mom.

Day 2

I went through half the day without realizing it was Saturday—and let me tell you, it got me really steamed. Apparently the people running this program don't know that weekends are for hologames and sleep. I got woken up by a soldier (?? I don't recognize these uniforms. Are they really soldiers? Was the policeman from yesterday a soldier? Is Ms. Maggie a soldier??), and I don't know what time it was but it felt EARLY. He turned his back while I changed my pajamas for real clothes, but he didn't leave the room like I asked him to. That was pretty annoying. It was like he didn't trust me that I knew how to dress myself.

When I was dressed, he told me that it was time to go to school, so I followed him through the halls. I'm glad he was there with me, because I would have gotten lost just like Ms. Maggie said. We walked for a long time before we got anywhere exciting. I think everyone else was still sleeping. I asked him what his name is and he said David. I made a joke that it should be Goliath, because he's so big. He smiled, but kept walking. David walks very quickly, and my legs are a lot shorter than his. I was almost jogging to keep up with him.

Eventually we got to a room marked CHILDREN, with some symbols next to it that I don't know. I didn't really like that because it makes us seem younger than we are. In a few months I'll be twelve, which is practically a teenager, so I think it should say YOUNG ADULTS instead, and then maybe the soldiers won't look at us like little kids.

Anyway, in the room it was set up like a classroom, only there were way more kids than at my class in my real school. Ms. Maggie was there, telling everyone to get into a big circle so we could introduce ourselves.

Not all of us are the same age, and Ms. Maggie says that's going to be an adjustment for all of us. There was a little kid there who looked like maybe seven, and he was crying the whole time. His name is Jeff, he told us in between crying. Ms. Maggie moved over to stand next to him in the circle and held his hand, which seemed to help a little bit.

Probably there are about ten kids in my grade. Elise, Becky, Johnson (that's his last name, but he wouldn't tell us his first name, he's kinda weird), two Jessicas, a Billy, and some others I don't remember. Then there are some little kids like Jeff, but mostly all the kids in the class are older. There's a big mean-looking kid whose name is Rock or something else stupid. His mustache looks like a big fuzzy caterpillar crawled up on his mouth and then a bird pecked it to death. I don't like him, he was making fun of Jeff. Ms. Maggie scolded him, which made his face go red and made a lot of us laugh. Then Ms. Maggie talked to all of us about having to cooperate with each other, because we're all very important to the project. She reminded us that our parents fought very hard for us to be here, so we need to make the most of it.

There's a group of three girls who seem kind of bratty, and they're already standing next to each other with their arms hooked together like they're best friends. I don't know how anyone could be best friends already, but they figured it out. They're a little older than me. During break I watched them go over to this girl named Angel. Angel's older than I am by a little more than a year, but it looks like more. I think the three girls asked her to be in their group too, but Angel shook her head no and the three girls got all huffy and walked away, connected like three cans of soda that haven't been taken out of the plastic rings yet. (Ms. Maggie told us that we should use similes and metaphors as often as we can, because that will help set the tone for when people after us read our journals. Did that help?)

Angel looks very sad, but I haven't seen her cry. She mostly sat by herself all day today, and she has green eyes.

I asked Ms. Maggie for a pencil sharpener, and a funny look came over her face. Like she hadn't thought to bring a sharpener. How can we have school without sharpeners? She gave me a pack of pens instead. They're all black, and they don't write very well. I think it would have been better if they had brought blue pens, but I guess black is easier to see on the paper. Can you read this all right? I hope so. It would suck to spend so much time writing and then have no one be able to read it.

I don't have much to write about anymore tonight. But all of the adults are telling us to write as much as possible. I'm trying to write everything down, but it's all getting stuck in my head at once and clogging my brain up.

My house is a light blue, and there are red flowers in the flower box on the second floor. Mexican sunflowers. I know that because my mom let me pick them out when we went to this big plant farm nursery thing when I was small. I liked them because I remembered that my mom had a hat with a red sunflower on it, so I figured that it was her favorite flower. Now I know that her favorite flower is lilies, but I don't think those would have looked as good in the flower boxes. The kitchen is big, but we don't cook in it much. My room has a lot of toys that I don't play with. I had some army men, which is how I know the soldiers aren't dressed in the right uniforms. These uniforms are a light blue, a little lighter than my house, and they have an eight-pointed star above the heart.

My bed at home had an orange and red quilt on it that my mom and grandma made together. I wish Mom would have packed that for me instead of so many clothes. The blanket on my mattress is really thick, and it gets really hot in this room.

There's a book in here that Ms. Maggie brought, it's called *Journey to the Center of the Earth*, and it takes place a couple of hundred years ago. I haven't gotten very far in it yet, but they're trying to solve a code written in runes. It seems pretty cool so far, but I hope we don't spend the whole book trying to figure out what it says.

Another soldier (not David) just told me lights out in five minutes. This time I didn't try to tell him that Mom lets me stay up late. I meant to ask him about the star, but I forgot.

Goodnight.

6

It took Michael several seconds to figure out where he was. The book was in front of him, sitting innocently enough on the tray. Johnny's handwriting had been extremely difficult to read at first, chicken scratch really, but Michael had . . . what? Stopped noticing it? That wasn't quite right. He stared at the book for a very long time before he noticed the amber light on the wall flicking *on, off, on, off.* There was a buzzer ringing loudly.

The chair had let him go. He frowned. That didn't seem right, he'd only been reading for a few minutes, but he wasn't about to volunteer to sit for another bout of this reading nonsense.

The moment Michael started to stand, the buzzer went silent. He was grateful for the quiet. His bones ached in a way that he'd never felt before, and his teeth chattered with cold. Hesitantly, he reached to the back of his neck and flinched when he touched the hole in his skin. It was wet. His fingers came back red.

The hunger hit him like a wave. He was ravenous.

Michael's body shook as he stumbled his way over to the crate he had set down minutes before. He rummaged through it and found the grey cloth Mary had shoved into it earlier. Pulling the cloth out and giving it a firm shake to untangle it, he was relieved to see that it was one of the robes the other prisoners had been wearing. He quickly pulled it on and wrapped his arms around his chest, jumping to get some warmth back into his blood.

Once, nearly a decade ago when he had just been moved out of his mother's house and they had both been assigned single huts, some sort of terrible beast had gotten through the fences around the livestock and massacred dozens of sheep. Michael had heard it in the night, the snarling and the crying of the flock. He had been too frightened to go out to the pen to fight off the animal, so he had cowered in his hut with his hands over his ears. He had felt so guilty when the men walked around to call people out to assist with the cleanup. He spent the better part of the morning carrying away the ruined flesh of the animals, half of them not even consumed, just butchered out of something's need to kill. The bodies had been cold and wrecked, near frozen in the night.

Michael now felt like one of those sheep.

There were small noises outside his room, a susurrus he couldn't quite believe he could hear. He walked up to the threshold and tried to brace himself for the rising of the door, but it still caught him by surprise. For a moment, he wondered if the noises he heard had been imagined. No one was speaking in the hallway, but there were dozens of people there. The grey people.

He listened closely, and realized what he was hearing. It was the shuffling of feet. They all traveled together as a pack, and as the hundreds of them walked, they made a sound that could only be described as misery. So this was what utter hopelessness sounded like. It echoed in his brain, and he couldn't ignore the power behind the noise now that he had heard it.

"Where are we going?" The words were out of his mouth before he could stop them, and he wanted them back immediately. Spoken to no one, they revealed a truth that he could no longer deny, but that he desperately wanted to:

Michael Driftveil was one of them.

Especially now, in his grey robe, feeling like a cold sheep. He fell in step with the crowd.

"Where are we going?" he asked again, touching the elbow of another Archivist (she might have been a woman, once) gently.

She looked at him with such sadness that he almost pulled back, went back to his room to sit down in the chair, went back to Johnny.

"Dinner," she said simply, but then looked startled, as if she hadn't meant to speak. After a stunned moment, the woman kept walking.

Michael stopped. The crowd of people simply flowed around him. Dinner? It was time for dinner already? He looked back, could still see the yellow numbers on his door. He hated them.

He had only read two days' worth of Johnny's stories. But no, that wasn't right either, because he hadn't just *read* them. He had *lived* them. He felt the tears on his mother's cheek as she kissed him goodbye; the fierce hug of his father just before he was loaded into a motorcart. Not like the motorcart Michael had ridden in the day before. This had cool air blasting out at him from little slats, and a voice making a sound sweeter than anything he had heard before, though Michael couldn't see the source of the voice, and the words weren't like any words he had ever spoken. And the view . . . the scene outside the windshield was unlike anything Michael had ever seen in his whole life. Had those been buildings? But they were so tall! They had towered over him, stacks of five and six and seven windows on top of one another. He knew what Ms. Maggie looked like, and that she smiled kindly at him. He saw the soldiers' sky blue uniforms, with the black star above the heart.

Michael began to scream.

The other Archivists shrank away from him as if he were diseased. They shuffled faster to escape him, and those that were behind him pressed against the walls as they passed, almost trampling each other to put as much distance between themselves and the terror that Michael had become.

A Minder was upon him in moments. It was the one from this morning—what was his name? Michael saw the man coming, the illum-strips in the ceiling glinting off of his shiny, sweating head as he barreled down the hallway, shoving other Archivists out of his way. There was another Minder trailing behind, his face worried and tight, but otherwise unspectacular. Michael tried to scramble out of the way, but there was nowhere to run.

The bald man grabbed him by the lapels of his robe and shook him, hard. Michael's world spun.

"No," Michael was crying. "No, no. This isn't right. No no no."

"Shut up!" the Minder hissed, his face angry and cruel, and a knee met Michael's stomach. As the wind left him, he fell to the floor, gasping, his cheek pressed into the rough grey Sonicrete, rubbing his skin raw. Black spots swam in front of his eyes, like the black, eight-pointed stars on the uniforms that he shouldn't recognize, but did.

The screams turned to whimpers.

Somewhere inside himself, something sneered at Michael. *Coward,* it chanted in one of the wrinkles of his brain, *Coward! Get off the floor and fight this! Get the hell out of here!* The voice hated him, and his weakness, and had no problem with letting Michael know it.

But he couldn't move, for Bald Head was on top of him, yanking his arm harshly behind his back at an awkward angle. Michael thought he could hear the man making a giggling noise, only it was vicious, coming straight out through the man's nose.

The other Minder, the plain one, was growling something angrily, but at Bald Head, not at Michael. Then he was pressing a needle into Michael's arm.

Michael struggled at first against the sharp pinching pain, but quickly grew still. What was one more needle stick? He had wounds all over his body at this point. After a moment, his blood ran cold again, and the hateful voice in his brain drew back and grew silent. He felt a distance slide over him. It was like dreaming, he thought, like he wasn't quite there, but he preferred it to the feeling he'd had in his bones when he'd finished reading. At least with this drug he knew that he was *Michael Goddamn Driftveil* and not some snot-nosed child.

Apparently satisfied that Michael was sedated enough, Bald Head pushed up and off of him, Michael groaning in protest at the pressure on his own elbow in the small of his back, his shoulder straining. The other one, the man who had drugged him, hoisted Michael up and brushed the dirt and dust off his chest, pocketing the capped needle in one of the Velcro pockets on his chest. Michael watched with mild interest.

"Y'carry drugs all th'time?" he asked, the words slurring and mingling as they left his lips. He felt drunk.

"Any time one of you needs it, sure." Plain Face patted his pocket, but then seemed to remember himself and straightened. "Proceed to the cafeteria immediately, Archivist." His voice had grown deeper, authoritative.

Bald Head snorted a laugh, clapped Plain Face on the shoulder roughly enough that the other man winced and tried to move away from the impact, then sauntered away from them, growling at any Archivists who were still foolish enough to be close by.

Michael shook his head. "Tokens . . . I left'm." He swiveled his head around to look back in the direction of his room.

Plain Face sighed tiredly, then nodded. He grabbed Michael's arm gently and pushed him back toward his room. Michael saw that the Minder was just a kid, really. Barely old enough to have his own hut. Just a kid.

The hallway tilted this way and that as they journeyed back down the hall, yellow numbers blurring in front of Michael's eyes, forming little more than a mess of lines. Michael thought he'd never make it, but the Minder kept a tight hold on his arm and dragged him along. When it became apparent that Michael had only a vague idea where he was going, Plain Face looked at the number sewn onto the grey robe's sleeve, then made a strangled noise in his throat.

"You're the new one?" His voice was high and nervous. Michael shrugged at him halfheartedly, focusing on not falling down.

When they reached his door, Michael reached for the doorknob before realizing there was none, the door having already risen up to allow him access. He tumbled inside the small room and headed straight for the mattress against the wall.

"Hey—wait. You can't, you have to go eat." Plain Face was trying to pull him back, but Michael was already halfway onto the hard surface. "Come on, this isn't allowed." The kid pulled harder. Michael squeezed his eyes shut and slept.

7

"You did *what?*"

"He . . . he was frightening the other Archivists, ma'am. I had to subdue him."

"So you drugged him. On his first goddamn night! Jennings, are you mentally deficient?"

"No, ma'am."

"'No, ma'am.' So tell me *how in the world* you could possibly have thought it was acceptable to take on a prisoner without calling for support? Why were you alone? *Why were you not at your assigned post?*"

"Ma'am, I was at my assigned post in Cafeteria C when I heard screaming. My first thought was for the wellbeing of the Archivists, ma'am. Buchanan responded first, and I followed."

"Funny, that's not what Buchanan told me. He said he had to come rescue you. Is Buchanan lying, Jennings?"

"He may be mistaken, ma'am."

"*Goddamn idiot.*"

"Ma'am?"

"That wasn't directed at you. All Minders in your sector were specifically instructed that a new Archivist was being delivered today, and that he was to be treated with extreme caution. Are you blind?"

"No, ma'am."

"Did this man *look* like the other prisoners in your sector?"

"No, ma'am."

"So you *were* aware that this was the Archivist you had been instructed about?"

"My first thought was eliminating the threat to the other prisoners, ma'am. After he was subdued I could see that he was new. It wasn't until I was bringing him back to his room and read his sleeve that I realized I was dealing with six-two-two."

"And because you drugged him—which, let me reiterate, was *entirely* and *hideously* stupid—he didn't eat."

"No, he didn't, ma'am."

"You had better make damn sure that he eats in the morning. Do you understand me? If he fails to eat again, you will be removed from this facility. You will be stripped of your pitiful rank. You *will not* be returned to your complex. Do you understand what I am telling you?"

"Yes, ma'am."

"Get the hell out of my office. Now."

8

Michael woke to that damn buzzer again. His head was pounding and his mouth was drier than it had ever felt, but the worst thing about waking up that morning was that there was a man staring at him.

"What are you doing in my room?" he asked groggily. The man stood incredibly straight, his eyes boring into Michael determinedly.

"Get up, Archivist. It's time for breakfast."

Michael was dazed, but he got up. He was fully dressed already—never mind that the clothes were a day old—and he counted that as a small victory for the morning. Reaching down into the crate on the cold Sonicrete floor, he grabbed his map and his token pouch, shoving them deep into the right pocket of his robe. Then he shrugged and stretched and popped his tired body, and dragged himself to the door, out into the hallway to merge with the grey swarm.

The Minder followed a step behind. The other Archivists didn't look up, but they shrank away, almost as if by instinct.

Michael kept glancing back at the man tailing him, trying to place his face. The night before flooded into his head, and he realized that this was the kid, the one who had brought him back to his room.

"You drugged me." It wasn't a question.

The Minder nodded. "Your behavior was unacceptable."

Michael bristled at the contempt in the other man's voice, but he let it go. His mind was too focused on food, on alleviating the terrible ache in his stomach.

The Minder followed him all the way through the line, nodded in satisfaction when Michael dropped the small metal token into the slot and took his tray. The smell was beautiful, even if the meal looked less than appetizing.

Just as he had the morning before, Michael sat himself down at the table closest to the end of the line and all but inhaled his food—some sort of peppery sausage with bland potatoes. Not that he tasted it much anyway.

The Minder turned to leave him, but Michael shot his hand out and caught a sleeve. The Minder's head whipped around to stare at him, his eyes wide in alarm.

"What's your name?" Michael asked.

The Minder paused, considering carefully. Michael could see the thoughts turning behind his green eyes. When Michael was younger, he'd had a friend with green eyes, but he hadn't seen green eyes in a long time. Then again, he hadn't seen any friends in a long time either.

"Cyrus," the Minder said after several moments.

Cyrus pulled away and walked over to stand over by the cafeteria wall, with the other Minders who stood watch.

Michael stared down at the empty tray in front of him, waiting for the buzzer that would tell him he could leave.

A metal tray full of food dropped down with a clatter onto the table beside him. Michael started, then raised his eyes to the tray's owner. Mary stood beside him, a question in her eyes. She looked embarrassed.

Michael shifted over on the bench to let her sit, too exhausted to maintain his anger at her from yesterday.

"Hey," she said by way of greeting.

Michael just nodded slowly, his gaze returning to his empty tray.

Mary scooped a single potato onto a bent spoon and brought it halfway to her mouth before stopping and glancing sidelong at him. Sighing, she put the spoon down. "I'm sorry for the way I spoke yesterday. It was entirely too insensitive. I know this is a punishment, and that it must seem terrible to you now."

Michael made no move to look at her or respond.

"But do you see how incredible this is? These people had to start over from scratch after they were almost totally obliterated. Johnny was eleven when he was put into the program—and he dedicated the rest of his life to making sure that the soul of our people wasn't completely lost. And with this tech we have now, we can understand exactly what he saw. Before too long, you'll be able to sense what he was *feeling* when he wrote this down. The chair and mics will pick up what you're reading and simulate the emotions for you. This technology is absolutely amazing."

"But I'll be killed in the process."

Mary sighed. "You'll be rehabilitated, Michael."

"I won't be *me*."

"No," she said quietly. "You'll be so much more than that."

They were quiet for several minutes as Mary slowly chewed her food.

A thought struck Michael. "How did you know that?"

"Know what?"

"That Johnny is eleven?"

Mary's mouth tightened and her dark brown eyes widened. "I wasn't supposed to say that."

"How, Mary?"

"We're not supposed to talk about what we read with each other."

He frowned at her and waited patiently.

Mary groaned and scrubbed her hands over her round face before answering him. "This time around I chose a Recorder who was in Johnny's class."

"Who?"

Mary shook her head *no* and refused to say.

"'This time around'? How many projects have you taken on? They let you choose?"

Mary nodded her head. "I can choose which Recorder's journals I want to read. I get a month-long break every three months, so the process doesn't stick to me as badly as it will with you. This one is the seventh person I've selected."

Michael didn't even pretend to understand her. "I think you're crazy."

"Yeah, I know." The buzzer sounded, signaling the end of breakfast. "It was nice to sit with you, Michael."

She stood and left with no further exchange between them.

A thought struck Michael, but he pushed it away. Thoughts like that wouldn't help him here.

9

Today I tried asking Ms. Maggie why everyone in the building looks so upset. The other kids in class quieted down to listen to her answer. We had been placed into small groups to talk to each other about what our lives were like back home.

I was paired up with Elise, who has a little brother named Oscar. Her baby brother didn't come here with her, and she misses him really bad. I guess he wasn't allowed to come since he doesn't know how to write yet. He's too small. I started to talk about how badly I missed Lucy, but I saw her face and knew that she didn't think that was the same thing. I think it should be, but Elise doesn't like dogs. I didn't want to give her a reason to dislike her, so I stopped talking about her altogether. But she had still upset me.

Elise has a bunch of dolls at home, and said that she wished she could have brought some with her. I told her that was stupid, and she started to cry. I shouldn't have said that to her, it was really mean. I saw Angel frowning at me from across the room.

Ms. Maggie came over almost immediately and asked what had happened. I didn't want to tell her, and Elise was crying too hard to say anything, but I knew Ms. Maggie wasn't going to drop it. When I told her that I'd said I thought Elise's dolls were stupid, I could feel my face getting hot.

Why would you say that to her? Ms. Maggie asked me. Her eyes were sad, and I knew that I had done that. My stomach hurt.

Because she doesn't like my dog, I said. Ms. Maggie shook her head a little before addressing the whole class.

She said that we all come from different houses, and different things are important to each of us. We need to be respectful of what other people find important, because we are all American and that's what it means to be American. And, she said, because we are all in the Conservation Program. We're all working together. She said this was something we would be working on for our entire time together, and she needs us to try our hardest.

When she was happy that everyone understood, she turned back to the two of us and asked us to keep talking. Everyone else went back to their partners.

I told Elise I was sorry. Apologizing makes me feel funny in my stomach. She had stopped crying while Ms. Maggie talked, but her nose was running and she was sniffling. Her eyes and face were bright red. I felt terrible.

Elise didn't say anything to me for a few minutes, so the three of us looked at each other silently. Ms. Maggie waited patiently. That's when I decided to ask her.

I said, Is something happening, Ms. Maggie? All the adults look upset all the time.

That's when the other kids got quiet. They had noticed too. Maybe they'd noticed it before they came here. My dad had the same look on his face for days before he sent me off. And then my mom did too, just the day before. They knew something and they didn't tell me. I think these other kids' parents probably looked the same way.

Ms. Maggie looked at us for a very long time. No one moved. Even that big stupid kid Rock was waiting for her answer.

No, Ms. Maggie said. No, nothing is wrong.

I know she lied to us today. I just don't know why.

Day 4

I'm carrying this with me everywhere. I don't want anyone to read it, not yet. I know you're reading this right now, but I don't know you. So that's OK.

Ms. Maggie did say today "that we need to be using quotation marks." I had forgotten about those. I asked her if I should go back and add them to the last few days since I hadn't remembered to use them and she told me "no." She said "try not to go back over what you've already written, because it might skewer the data." I don't know what she's talking about. But I did mention that, speaking of skewers, we should have a barbecue cookout to get to know each other better. That's what my parents always do. She laughed and asked why I had thought about that. I just told her that "I'm hungry." The food in this building isn't very good, but I don't know how you can screw up hot dogs and kabobs. Unless you burn them, but even a little crispy my dad will still eat them.

We went over a lot of rules today for writing our journals well. "You need to be as realistic as possible," Ms. Maggie said. "Make sure to vary sentence structure. Use STRONG words." She flexed her muscles for us, which made us laugh because she's kind of small. She doesn't look like she's strong enough to fold a piece of bread, she's so small.

"Use LOTS and LOTS of metaphors and similes so we know what you're thinking!"

I didn't tell her that she had already told that one to us. Neither did anyone else. I think we all like her a lot.

She also told us that we're going to start taking some math assessments so she can see where everyone is in their knowledge. Today was really easy, just simple addition and subtraction. Jeff needed Ms. Maggie's help, but I think he understood what he was supposed to do, he just wasn't as fast as everyone else. "Tomorrow will be all about multiplication," Ms. Maggie said, then "the day after will be division. I know some of you are probably going to get bored while I figure out what I need to be teaching. Just please try to be patient, OK? You can bring your journals with you every day and write, as long as you know the material backward and forward, and can pass the pre-tests I hand out in the morning."

"What about history, Ms. Maggie?"

The voice came from behind me. I twisted in my chair to see who had spoken.

Angel was sitting at her desk, her journal open in front of her. She was raising her hand, though she hadn't waited for Ms. Maggie to call on her, and her fingers were wrapped around her uncapped black pen.

"What about it, dear?"

"We're focusing on writing and math right now." Angel spoke patiently, but she didn't seem like she was used to having to explain herself. "That's cool. But when do we learn about history? Or music?"

I looked back to Ms. Maggie to see her chewing on her bottom lip. "Not right now, Angel. Sorry."

I frowned at Ms. Maggie. Why are we only learning two subjects? I looked back at Angel and could see that she was disappointed, looking down at her desk and fiddling with the pen. I don't like history that much, but it's obvious that Angel does. I feel bad for her.

After class today, David walked me back to my room. "Are you like my bodyguard?" I asked him.

He let out a deep laugh that shook his whole body and said, "Yeah, kid. Something like that."

I think that's really cool. I like David. Where Ms. Maggie is small, David is huge. He's taller than my dad, and probably taller than anyone I've ever seen. He has to duck in order to not hit his head on the metal columns that form the doorways in the building, and even when he's not ducking he has to kind of tuck his shoulders in to himself to fit in the hall next to me. His skin is brown like the cocoa powder mom cooks with at Christmas time, and I think he must have played football in college or something. I mean, this guy is BIG. I'll have to remember to ask him if he really did play, because that would be so cool.

Day 5

All we seem to do is write. Even when it's not in this journal, Ms. Maggie has us taking up tons of paper, doing assessment after assessment. All math and English. I'm bored.

I just want to go home, but nobody I ask knows when that might be. They don't know how long this program is supposed to last.

"It's like summer camp," one of the men in the cafeteria told me. His name is Mr. K. "It's fun!"

It's not though. I go to summer camp all the time, and we never do so much math. We do fun things, like swimming, and I told him so, and he just kind of smiled, like he knew what I meant but wasn't supposed to let me know he agreed. I don't like that they keep things from us.

"Don't you have daily journals in summer camp sometimes?"

I agreed with him, unhappily. I think I made a face at him that looked funny, because he started laughing. "Well there ya go! See? *Just* like summer camp!" He reminds me of my grandfather, only older. His hair's real white like winter, while Grandpa's hair is really not there. Grandpa's bad at lying like this guy, too.

I asked David what the black star meant today when he walked me back from lunch. He told me that he's in a special program, just like me, but this program deals with things in space.

"Like an astronaut?" I asked him, but he shook his head. "Not quite." "Like the Reachees?" He made a face at me just a little. "That's not a very nice name for them." I don't think it's so bad, but I said I'd try not to say it.

Then he said he'd give me just one hint. He told me that the star isn't really a star. I asked him what it was, and he just smiled at me. "It's a secret." I asked him if he would tell me if I guessed it right. David just laughed in that great big laugh that makes rooms shake, but he didn't answer me.

I guessed a flower, a bomb, a compass, an octopus? The sun?

"The sun *is* a star."

"Oh." I ran out of guesses pretty quick, which is annoying. But I think David and I are starting to be really good friends. I'll keep guessing and let you know when I figure it out.

The rest of the day was spent doing more math problems. I'm not as good at multiplication tables. I wish Ms. Maggie had more to teach us than just math though. Like I said, B.O.R.I.N.G.

At the end of the day (which must have been like sixteen hours long. There aren't any clocks in here, which means that they have us working way longer than they want us to know about. I wish Dad hadn't signed me up for this thing) Ms. Maggie lined us all up and told us to close our eyes. I heard some of the older kids complaining. They're bored too.

Jeff closed his eyes immediately. So did Angel and some of the other girls. For everyone else, Ms. Maggie had to say please a couple of times. It's not that I didn't want to listen to her, but I really wanted to see what the other kids would do. I feel kind of bad about it now, because she was getting upset that almost no one was paying attention to what she wanted them to do.

When everyone had closed their eyes and quieted down, she came around to each of us and pinned something to our shirts. I heard her say "Close your eyes, Rock!", and the big oaf grumbled and whined about how stupid this was.

After a few minutes, Ms. Maggie was talking about how important all of us are, and how grateful she is that all of us are helping the program. More grumbles.

"Open your eyes!" she said. She was very excited.

I looked down at my shirt and tried to read it upside down. It's a red ribbon, with that same black symbol (I saw Grandma sew something like it, is it a quilt square? What the heck is it supposed to be?) at the top. I had to lean down and read Jeff's because I'm not great at reading upside down or backward or anything. All down the ribbon it said:

R
E
C
O
R
D
E
R

"Seriously?" Rock said. I could feel my face getting hot, he was getting me so mad. "You made us close our eyes for a dumb ribbon? How about some ice cream or something *good?*"

Ms. Maggie's face got really sad, and she looked down at her feet. "Sorry, Rock, I don't have any ice cream."

"I hate it here, you're such a terrible teacher! All of us are bored, and you give us ribbons like we're ten. God." The other older kids laughed, one of the girls throwing her head back to show off her teeth like a horse eating corn on the cob through a picket fence. Another one had a face like a pole had hit it. I hated them.

I like the ribbons. I called Rock a big stupid monkey, and told him he was lucky Ms. Maggie was trying to teach him how to read. A different teacher would have given up the minute she heard his big dumb voice.

Boy, did his face get red QUICK. I was ready to knock his eyes out for being so mean to Ms. Maggie.

"What did you call me?" He stepped up and glared down at me, towering over me like some big tree, big fuzzy half-dead caterpillar on his face and all. I was madder than he was, and was ready to take him on.

But Ms. Maggie called out, "Rock, Johnny! Enough!" His red face kept on looking like he wanted to punch my lights out, but he stepped down. Just like he should have. I would have kicked out his yellow teeth. I hate him.

Ms. Maggie told me that she needed me to stay after class, and that everyone else was done for the day, so they should find their escorts and head back to their rooms. "Don't forget your homework for tomorrow." (More math problems.)

I could see stupid Rock's smirk out of the corner of my eye as I looked at Ms. Maggie unhappily. My stomach was twisting inside me. I didn't want to be in trouble with her again, not so soon.

Ms. Maggie walked over to her desk and sat down while I stood at the other side of the room, humiliated. I didn't want the other kids to see me embarrassed, so I stood up very straight and tall like Dad's always telling me to do. That helped a little, at least until everyone had collected their things and filed out of the room, whispering to each other and pretending I couldn't hear them talking about me.

When everyone was gone, I felt myself start slouching, and shoved my hands in my jeans pockets. I wasn't going to apologize for what I'd said, because all of it's true.

"You can't start fights like that, John."

"Johnny," I muttered. I don't like the name John. It sounds like a boring old man.

"Johnny. Sorry." She sighed and put her head in her hands. I heard her sniff a little bit, and knew she was crying. I felt terrible. I hadn't meant to make her cry.

"I miss my mom, too, Johnny. And my dad. Just like you guys do."

I blinked at her. I hadn't thought about her having parents, though I guess all adults do. "Write them a letter," I suggested. "Or have them come to visit?"

She nodded in her hands, just a little. I would have missed it if I hadn't been looking for it.

"You're not a bad teacher, Ms. Maggie," I said. I was hoping that was what she was upset about, and not the mean (TRUE) things I had said to Rock.

She looked up at me, her eyes all red. Some of that black makeup crap girls put around their eyes was smeared on her face.

"Really?" she said. "I've never done it before."

I winced. Being a new teacher must suck. "You sure?" I tried to make her feel better. "I thought you must have been a teacher forever, you're so good at it."

I knew she didn't believe me, but she smiled a little anyway.

"Promise me you won't start any fights with the other kids."

I nodded at her.

"Promise? I mean REALLY promise?"

I sighed. "Yes, Ms. Maggie, I promise not to start any fights. With the other kids or with stupid Rock."

She gave me a look like I shouldn't have said that, but she didn't tell me I was wrong.

"Thank you, Johnny." Then she said quietly, "You can go find David now. Remember your homework."

I left, glad she wasn't angry with me again. I hope she writes that letter. She doesn't need to be sad.

10

The first several weeks were much of the same for Michael. Wake from a fitful sleep full of images—things he couldn't name, people he didn't know—to the godawful buzzer, trudge to breakfast, inhale the alternately tasteless or over-salted food, shuffle back to his room. Stare at the chair for a few moments.

That part was the worst for him: knowing that he was going to sit down, and that his plate would char him, and that the terrible spike would be jammed into his neck and it would *hurt*. But every day, without fail, he'd sit down and try not to thrash too badly. If he delayed his reading for any considerable length of time, he'd run out of tokens, and he wouldn't be able to eat. And considering the only thing he was fully conscious for anymore was eating, he wasn't liable to give that up too easily. So to hang on to that one little freedom, he forced himself to sit in the chair, and he tried to fall into the trance the chair put him into as quickly as he could, to escape the pain.

It was a bit like being lifted away from himself. Not quite falling asleep. On some plane, far away, he knew he was reading words on a page, scrawled by a kid less than half his age more than a hundred years ago. The handwriting was challenging, and sometimes Michael glossed over the words without really thinking or worrying about their meaning. Still, words that he had never heard or seen before came easily to his lips. After a time he discovered that if he thought about it enough the sense of a word would float into his mind. Each time he pulled that little trick, though, the effort left his head ringing, so he avoided searching for definitions if he could help it. After his spell of reading Michael would awake to the grating alarm, and melt into the grey crowd to head to dinner. Sometimes Mary would sit with him; most times he would sit alone.

As the days passed, Michael's memories seemed to grow fuzzy and slide out of focus. Sometimes they faded away entirely, replaced by the memories of his Recorder. One morning over a bland breakfast, back when he first started reading, Michael had been recalling a rather vivid meal that he'd had with his mother and grandmother. He could taste the little bits of beef that his grandmother had been able to afford to add into the stew, along with the rich carrots and thick, thick broth that slid down his throat and made him feel incredibly warm inside. Michael had been very small in this memory. But the more he thought about that delicious food, the less taste it seemed to hold in his mouth. And after several minutes, he couldn't remember if his mother had been there too, or if it was just his grandmother and him. Then he couldn't remember if it had been beef stew at all. Maybe he had been eating a cut of chicken, roasted over the fire till it was slightly overcooked, or had he been eating rice and beans? It slipped away from him like it had been only a dream, and he had panicked. It was one of his favorite memories, and just by trying to remember it, it was being dismantled before him.

Chicken, he had decided after a moment. It had definitely been chicken. And Michael had smirked, content with his little victory over the tech of the Archives. They wanted to reprogram him, but he had stopped it. Later when he went to visit that memory again, staring at a particularly sorry dinner of overly soft steamed carrots and rice, placed on top of a brick of a biscuit, Michael was surprised to find that his young self had been seated across from his grandfather at that meal. He almost cried. He'd never known his grandfather, but that was the only solid indication that this was no longer *his* memory. It otherwise felt perfect. It had been inserted seamlessly into his brain, and he hated Coleman and her Archivist program for having done this to him.

Johnny's life was almost as dull as Michael's. Wake up, breakfast, class, lunch, class, a few hours of writing time, and then bed. Every. Single. Day.

It was a dreadful way to spend a childhood, and Michael could feel Johnny's growing unrest with each journal entry. By the time Michael had worked through nearly six months of journals, Johnny was pulling his hair out with boredom and trying to find ways to get in trouble. Most days, unease sat hard and cold in Michael's stomach as he waited for the moment when Johnny would be caught and chastised by an adult. But that moment didn't come.

Johnny liked stealing from the kitchen. His descriptions of food sometimes made Michael want to weep. Back then, it seemed that almost every meal they ate had meat in it, served in ridiculous quantities, and the thought made Michael's mouth water. He couldn't even begin to imagine how they had sustained all that carnivorous behavior. Johnny talked about the cafeteria being stocked with an amazing array of food in those first months; cookies and small cakes were among his favorite things to pilfer. One of his favorite games was offering to help prepare the meal for the day, then seeing how many things he could get into his pockets before the head cook, Mr. K—a grandfatherly fellow, but still not one to be pushed—chased him out of the kitchens. So far, his largest bounty had been three peanut butter cookies (stashed in his back left pocket), a small loaf of bread (slipped under his shirt and held close to his body), an orange (tucked in the crook of an elbow with arms folded), and a small slice of apple pie that he had carefully wrapped in a napkin and slid into his front pocket. Unfortunately, the pie had been so mutilated by the time Johnny was done that he almost immediately threw it away, and his pocket was sticky and unusable for weeks until he felt like bringing it down to the laundry.

To Michael, apple pie was something that was reserved for celebrations: births, weddings, a first assignment. The thought of Johnny throwing a piece away had made Michael cringe, and his stomach had rumbled all throughout his next dinner of bland soup and mealy potato dumplings. He thought he would probably never taste apple pie again—certainly not as a felon. Johnny had described it well, but Michael could only still get a faint ghost of a taste of it on his tongue. He wanted more.

A few months in, Johnny started writing things Michael couldn't read in the margins of his journals. No matter how hard Michael stared at the markings, they didn't make letters that he recognized. The lines almost danced across the page with each other. It was as aggravating as it was interesting. Each time he turned in a journal without deciphering those scribbles, Michael felt defeated. But his meal tokens would be running low, or empty, and he would have no choice but to keep going.

A few times he had tried to mention the markings to Mary at meals. She always gave him a look, and refused to speak to him about it. At one point, she had actually put her hands over her ears and sang loudly so she wouldn't hear him. Michael had resorted to shaking the tiny woman to get her to stop.

He didn't understand why the Archivists weren't meant to share what they read with each other. If it was for the preservation of culture—it was, wasn't it?—then why wouldn't they collaborate and discuss what they had read?

"We *can't*," Mary told him for what seemed like the fiftieth time, sighing loudly as if she couldn't believe how dense he insisted on being. And no further explanation was provided.

As Michael felt more and more drained each day, he noticed that the other Archivists were growing more talkative and less depressed. They chatted with each other at mealtimes, and occasionally even in the halls. It was still a dampened sort of chatter, spoken in low whispers as eyes darted around to check that Minders weren't around to listen, but it was better than the dull, stupid silence Michael had been surrounded with before. Michael ached to ask them what they were learning about, to get any sort of information about what had happened before the Loss—other than how delicious the food had been. Unfortunately, just like Mary, every other Archivist Michael approached refused to talk about the before. It was a rule that they all understood, but for the life of him, Michael couldn't figure out why it was so important.

One morning, after Michael had spent the night dreaming of a particularly beautiful and painful entry about Johnny's favorite day of the year—a holiday called Thanksgiving, which seemed to Michael like a self-indulgent excuse to eat mountains of decadent food for hours and hours—a tray of beige carrots and a rather soupy-looking portion of grits clattered down onto the table beside him.

Feeling rather sour after the night of hungry torture, Michael grunted, expecting Mary to sit down beside him. Instead a hand was thrust in front of his face, and Michael looked up sharply, startled.

"Ho, friend!" A man was standing beside Michael with a large, somewhat frightening grin on his face. Michael knew from the tattered grey robe draped across his frail shoulders that he was a fellow Archivist. The man was ancient, with large unruly eyebrows that seemed to jump from his face with his mad smile. His hair was just as untamed, a wild mane of salt-and-pepper curls that looked like it hadn't seen a hairbrush the entire time he'd been at the Archives. He had a pair of spectacles perched on his nose, but one lens was cracked and spider-webbed while the other was missing entirely. He spoke in a way that Michael had never heard before, some deformity with his tongue or teeth causing the words to come out thick and slightly garbled. Michael stared.

"My name is Thomas, my friend. You would be liking some company? I will sit here with you?"

Michael's mouth was hanging open, he knew, but he couldn't force himself to close his jaw. No Archivist had ever approached him before, and now this one—the only one to ever so much as acknowledge him—seemed positively insane. An image came to Michael quickly before fleeing just as swiftly. *Mad scientist*, Johnny's voice whispered to him in a small corner of his brain. But what the hell was that?

Then Mary appeared on his other side, laughing.

Michael looked up at her face, dumbstruck. She collapsed into another fit of giggles at the sight of his confused frown. *Oh god, they're all crazy. Everyone's lost it but me*, Michael thought in dull horror.

"He's Resurrected! What fun!" Mary cried, wiping tears from her eyes.

Michael looked back to the man, who was still waiting expectantly for Michael's permission to sit, and tried to voice his approval. The words didn't come out.

"Sit, sit," Mary insisted, plopping herself down at the table. "Tell us about yourself, please!" Her smile was bigger than Michael had ever seen, and her eyes were huge and round, seeming to take up her whole face in her excitement.

Thomas smiled happily and sat, grinning at her. "Thanking you very much. They call me Thomas. I'm a foreign consult for your great country, very happy for being here, yes." He shook her hand heartily, stretching across Michael's breakfast.

Michael shook his head, at a loss. Thomas stressed odd syllables in his speech, and Michael was having a hard time understanding the man. Mary looked more than fascinated.

"So you'll be going back soon, then?" she asked him, her eyes glowing with delight.

"Ahhh," Thomas sighed heavily. "If only I knew the motherland was still in one piece, I would head back. But they fear it may have been destroyed with the great exploding holes. There's been no word for weeks."

Michael sat up and tried very hard to decipher the man's words, hungry for the information.

"Oh, lovely, you're *Russian*!" Mary beamed. "I wondered what that sounded like." She looked love-struck.

"He's what?" Michael asked her, turning in his chair. Mary waved a hand at him dismissively and leaned heavily on the tabletop to see Thomas better.

"What is your country like, Thomas?" she whispered, smiling.

"Oh, beauty, it is the most wonderful thing in the world. But her winters!" Thomas exaggerated a shiver and made a *brrr* noise with his lips, shaking his head back and forth rapidly. "Her winters are not for the weak!" He let out a booming laugh that made Michael wince, then dug in to his food like a man starving.

Mary was positively giddy. "I love when this happens," she remarked to Michael, bouncing up and down in her seat. "Most people that get Resurrected are still pretty boring, but they did have a few ambassadors and visiting dignitaries that got caught in the bunkers when the Loss hit that weren't quite as white-bread dull as everyone else." She dug her elbow into his side and waggled her eyebrows at him.

Michael shook his head at her, frowning. "What's wrong with his mouth?"

Her smile grew. "It's an accent. It's because he didn't grow up speaking English."

Michael wrinkled his nose. "What's English?"

This earned a snort from Mary. "That's what you're speaking now, crazy head. We didn't start calling it Republican until after the Loss."

Michael *hmmm*ed and turned back to Thomas. "Who were you before you started reading?"

Mary frowned at him and muttered a low warning, but Michael pretended not to hear her or see her out of the corner of his eye.

There was a brief flash of distress behind Thomas's eyes, but then the old man laughed heartily. "Ahaha, a good joke that is! Very funny, I like it. I understand. Only through education do we find ourselves, eh?" He slapped his knee and shoved a spoonful of carrots into his mouth, laughing throughout.

"No." Michael didn't like that the man was laughing at him. "You know what I mean. I meant before you were sent here. What complex did you come from? Who's your family? Which job were you assigned? How old are you?"

With each little question, Michael could see Thomas's smile grow more and more dim. He didn't want to stop his barrage of questions—he was very much interested to know what Thomas remembered of his life before becoming an Archivist—but Mary slammed her fist down on the table.

"What?" Michael asked her, irritated. Her face was a mask of thinly veiled disgust.

"Why are you being so cruel to him?" she asked quietly.

Michael was about to protest, but then swiveled his head to look back at the old man. Thomas's eyes were pooled with tears. Michael felt ashamed, and resorted to pushing the off-color carrots around on his beat-up tray.

Mary reached across him and placed her hand on Thomas's old wrinkled hand, then smiled gently. "So, Thomas." The effect her cheerful voice had on the man was instantaneous, and he grinned at her with missing teeth. "What brought you to America?"

The old man launched off into a grand tale of espionage and something called a space program until the buzzer signaled the end of breakfast. Michael was too sullen to listen to his story.

11

Day 185

It's Angel's birthday in a couple of days. She told me today, and I feel bad knowing she won't be with her family. I was expecting to be home before now, but I think we're going home soon anyway. I heard some of the adults talking about it when they didn't know any of us were around. They said that nothing's happened in six months, so they think it's over. I wasn't entirely sure what they were talking about, and I couldn't ask them since I was supposed to be in my room, not walking around without David.

I like David, but I think he's supposed to be watching me to make sure I don't get into any trouble—which means that I'm supposed to be in my room whenever I'm not in school or eating in the cafeteria or with him. A lot of the time I can't find him when I want to go somewhere, so I just leave. It's not a problem, not really. I've gotten the hang of the building, so I don't get lost as much as I used to.

I'm not technically breaking any rules—Ms. Maggie never said I *couldn't* leave, just that I shouldn't—but I still try to be careful.

Anyway, the two adults were just talking in the hallway, so I wasn't really spying on them. Anyone could have heard. But there was a man and a woman, talking very quietly. They weren't dressed in the soldiers' uniforms, they were dressed like scientists, in white lab coats, and both of them had glasses on.

"Sweethill (I think that's what the guy said, but I'm not sure) said in the meeting this morning that there hasn't been a single event in six months. He thinks it's over." He didn't look happy.

"That's fantastic!" the woman said. Her hair was blond and very curly, and looked like it hadn't been brushed in a while. Maybe she forgot to pack one. I could have gone back to my room and given her my hairbrush, I don't use it, but I didn't want to miss what they were saying. "So it's over? We'll go home soon? We can stop all this."

He didn't smile. "Yeah, I guess. If they decide the threat is over . . ."

They started walking away from me, and I didn't want to follow them in case they saw me. I held still in the hall for a few moments, and that's when I decided that I wanted to go see Angel. To see if she knew what they were talking about. She's really smart, so if anyone knows what's going on, it's her.

The boys' rooms are in a different hall than the girls' rooms, and all the boys were told never to go into the girls' rooms ever. So we don't kiss or something, I don't know. But just this one time I ignored that rule, and when I knocked on Angel's door and she opened it, I asked her if I could come in. I didn't want anyone else hearing what I was going to ask her.

She looked confused, but said "Sure," and let me in anyway. She didn't seem too worried that we were breaking the rules.

Angel's room is way cleaner than mine. I could even see her floor. Looking around, I think I started to realize just how gross I am. She doesn't have any stolen food lying around or anything. All of her dirty clothes are in the hamper. All her CLEAN clothes look like they've been put away. I was astounded.

Her journal was open on her desk, and she hurried over and shut it quickly as soon as she saw my eyes land on it. Her face turned bright red, even though I promised I was too far away to read any of it. Girls are weird.

She had some playing cards laid out on the floor.

"Solitaire?" I asked her. She nodded and moved to sit on the floor in front of the cards, folding her legs carefully underneath her. "I never learned how to play that. I really only play hologames." I felt lame, knowing that I had interrupted her day. I hate when people keep me from playing hologames, it drives me crazy because I get so bored.

"I'm not really any good at hologames. My dad taught me to play Solitaire, but I'm still sucky at it," she said, her face not as red now. "Sometime I could teach you, but I want to get better at it first. Do you know how to play War?"

I told her I did, but it's only because there's a hologame version of it on my module at home. It's kind of a boring game, but she starts dealing the cards out—half for me, half for her—and I didn't want to tell her not to. I guess I figured if she wanted to play a game with me, then I wouldn't seem quite so lame for being there.

She's really good at War, which is kind of surprising since I always thought the game came down to how the cards are dealt the first time. But her hands are very quick, which means that I have to pay very close attention or I miss something, and then she takes all my cards.

Before long, the first game was over and I was staring at her in shock. She grinned at me.

"Again?" she asked, and I found myself nodding before I really thought about it.

She dealt the cards. Within minutes, she had won again.

I sighed and flopped backward onto the floor, and Angel laughed at me. I started laughing, too. I don't know what happened, but soon we were almost crying from laughing so hard. We rolled around on the floor clutching our stomachs. I hadn't been so happy in forever.

When we caught our breath, Angel asked me, "Did you need something from me?"

I nodded at her, but I felt dumb, and it was really hard for me to get my question out. She waited for me, just kind of smiling like she already understood why this was so hard for me. I don't think I even knew why it was so difficult, it just was. I was afraid of knowing, I guess.

"Is something happening?"

She didn't pretend to not know what I was talking about. She just dropped her smile and started looking very sad.

"Someone's been attacking people." That's all she started out with. I waited for her to continue, but it took a few moments. She was picking at the edge of the rug we were sitting on with her fingernails. "Making them disappear."

I frowned at her. "Like magic?" I asked, but she shook her head.

"I don't think so." She looked really unhappy, and I think she would have cried if I wasn't there. But then, if I wasn't there, I wouldn't be asking her, so she wouldn't need to be crying anyway. "My dad told me that it's making whole cities go away, like they never existed. There's big black holes in the ground where cities used to be, and no one can remember them, or anyone that lived there, or what the cities used to be called . . ." she shook her head, and I felt bad for asking her about this. "You ever heard of Toke-yo?"

I told her I hadn't. "That's what I'm talking about." She said. "It's a big city in Japan. Or it was."

I didn't believe her, and I still don't. "How come YOU can remember it then?" I asked her. My voice didn't sound very friendly just then, and it must have startled her because she looked up at me real fast. I should have apologized, but I was just teasing her, so I didn't.

"I DON'T," she said. She looked at me upset, and I put my hands on my hips to show her that I wasn't buying it. "I'm not lying," she insisted. "My dad told me. And we have an almanac in our living room to look at, which is why I know that Toke-yo USED to be a city and now it's not."

I frowned at her some more. "How do you know it's not there anymore? What happened to the people that lived there?"

She shrugged and stood up, scooping up the pile of cards she had won from me in the last round and fixing them so that they were all laid flat and stacked neatly against each other. She didn't have the box to put them in, only a plastic bag, which meant that as soon as she put the cards in, they slid out of the order she had put them in and looked all messy again. She looked at the bag all annoyed before tossing it on her bed.

"Why isn't it everywhere on the news, then?" I asked. "If someone is trying to start a war, it should be everywhere."

"And how are we supposed to care about something that we can't remember?" she said. "No one knows about it anymore, it never existed. Putting it on the news would be a waste." She was busy arranging things on her desk and bookshelf. Ms. Maggie must have brought her a few books just like I had in my room. I recognized the big quote book that I've been reading every once in a while. "We're here because they think D.C. is going to be hit, too."

I stood up too, hurting a little bit because my leg had fallen asleep under me. "Well . . . if that's true, then I guess we're going home soon. I heard some of the grownups talking about how nothing has happened in six months, so they think it's safe. If the only reason we're here is because they wanted to keep us safe" (I don't believe that, it sounds too crazy) "then we can go home if there's no more danger." Something about what I said didn't seem quite right, but I couldn't really figure out why. Her eyes lit up though. She asked me if I thought they'd let us go home tomorrow.

"I don't know," I said. "Why?"

She grinned at me. "Wednesday's my birthday."

At the time, I was very happy for her. But after that, when I went back to my room and waited for Ms. Maggie or David or someone to come by and tell me that it was time to go home, no one came. And I'm starting to think that we're not going home tomorrow at all.

I shouldn't have gotten so excited. But I was this afternoon, so now, with just a few minutes until lights out, I'm really disappointed.

It's not possible for a whole city to just disappear, right? I can't believe what Angel told me, even if she didn't think she was lying. You can think you're telling the truth, but you can still be wrong. I think Angel's wrong. If we don't get to go home tomorrow morning, I think I'll try to steal a cupcake for her. Maybe that would make her feel better?

Day 186

Today I woke up looking forward to heading to the kitchen as soon as I could. It was hoping that there was a slice of cake or a cupcake or something like that for me to take, and my whole plan was to find a candle and give whatever I could find to Angel so that her birthday tomorrow wouldn't be so sad. I felt terrible that she was spending her birthday away from her family, and I didn't want her to go the whole day without a birthday cake. What good is a birthday if there's no birthday cake, right?

I know that as I slipped out of my room—it was still very early, probably an hour or so before David would come to wake me up for class—I was thinking about all the birthday parties my parents have thrown for me. One time we went to the zoo, and my mom had someone bring in a cake that was striped like a zebra. The inside was striped, too, and she was so proud of it. The person who had made it did a really good job, even though Dad said it was a little dry. I didn't mind.

When I made it to the kitchen, there was no cake waiting on a cooling rack. No cupcakes. No pies. I stood there, staring at the bare countertops with my hands in my pockets, my throat closing up from the bitter taste I suddenly found in my mouth. There wasn't anything for Angel here. I started getting angry, although I don't know who I was angry at. There was almost *always* something that the cook had made from the night before, or for the night to come, stored under a plastic dome on one of the counters. Yesterday it had been a big pan of pecan pie. All I could think was that I wished I hadn't eaten the plateful I had stolen. If I had saved even a bit of it, I could have given *that* to Angel and her birthday wouldn't be ruined. I was furious, and incredibly sad.

Last night after dinner, we had all been given a little powdered doughnut. Where were the leftovers from that? I figured that even if that had been the only thing left out, I could have still put a candle in it. But there was *nothing*.

As I was frowning at the empty kitchen, Mr. K, the chef, crept up behind me. I was so steamed, I didn't even hear him coming.

"Aha!" he yelled, grabbing my shoulders. He had caught me trying to steal again. I yelled at him. I don't know what I yelled, but whatever it was made his eyes widen and he frowned at me.

"What's wrong with you, Johnny?" He wasn't quite scolding me. He definitely wasn't happy, but I think he realized that I was only yelling because I was upset. That seemed to make him not want to scream at me.

"I wanted to get a cake or something for a friend, and there's nothing here!" I shouldn't have been yelling at him still. Mr. K didn't look impressed, and I was thinking that he didn't believe me.

I stamped my foot. I knew I was throwing a fit for no good reason. Someone in my family used to tell me that I was far too old to be throwing temper tantrums, and in that moment I heard their voice in my head. I wish I could remember if that had been my mom or dad or grandmother or what. I don't know.

"Why does your friend need a cake?" he asked me, and I started to feel very silly. My face was hot.

"It's her birthday tomorrow, and we're not going home, so her mom can't make her a cake. I wanted to bring her one," I snapped at him. I should really go talk to him about how bratty I was being. He ended up being really helpful and nice.

When Mr. K heard about Angel's birthday, his face seemed to relax, and then his eyes crinkled in the corners. He was smiling, kind of. Well, he was smiling as much as he ever smiles at me, in any case. I know I'm not his favorite since I keep stealing from him, and he knows I steal. I don't know why he's never told anyone else how much I steal, though. I would probably be in a whole lot more trouble all the time if he had.

"I moved all the leftovers from the counter last night because I didn't want you to take them, Johnny. It's not fair for everyone else if you take all of the dessert. But, considering, let's make your friend a good cake for her birthday. Sound good?"

I stared at him for a while, thinking that he was probably just joking with me or being mean. But when he kept almost-smiling at me, I asked him, "Why?"

"Because birthdays are special!" was all he said, and then he started working his way around the kitchen. He was almost all the way to the ginormous refrigerator when he looked at me sideways. "You should be in your room, shouldn't you?"

I scuffed the floor with my shoe, pretending not to have heard him. Mr. K sighed and then walked back over to me, crouching down. I don't like when adults do that because it makes me feel small, but I let it slide since he was offering to help me with the birthday cake. "Who's your escort, Johnny? When he goes to your room to wake you up and you're not there, he's going to be very worried."

I told him it was David, the big one, not the skinny one that has pimples all over his face. He laughed briefly, and then walked over to the call panel on the wall. He pressed the blue button and waited for the other side to pick up. The panel buzzed until they did.

"Hello?"

"Hey, Cheryl? I've got one of the kids with me down in the kitchens. He snuck in here this morning," he shot me a look, and I pretended to kick dirt across the floor again, "and now he's going to help me prep lunch. Could you let his escort know that he's not in his room?"

"Sure, Kerry. Who is it?"

I frowned, and probably wrinkled my nose judging by the look he gave me. I didn't like that his name was Kerry: it sounds like a girl's name, but whatever. I just think Mr. K sounds better.

"David." His eyes crinkled again. "The big one, not the scrawny one."

I heard Cheryl laugh at the other end of the panel, her voice all tinny and weird-sounding through the speaker, "Will do, Kerry. Want me to let Maggie know too?"

"Sure." Mr. K hit the red button on the panel to end the call without saying goodbye or thank you. Mr. K is kind of rude, although he's not particularly mean. He's just got crappy manners. I remember thinking that my mom would have been horrified.

"All right, my assistants are going to be in here to start making breakfast soon, so we need to hurry if we want to get a good spot in the oven. The left side is kind of touchy."

I didn't really know what he was talking about, but he didn't stop to explain either. Mr. K went to the rack in the corner and threw an apron at me. It was way too big. When I put it on, it reached a little bit past my knees. I'm shorter than I should be, I know, but even still it was a long apron.

"We get food deliveries every week, you know that?" he said to me, over at the oven setting the temperature. "Every Monday. So you're lucky that I've got a whole box of fresh eggs, otherwise I wouldn't be doing this. If it was any later on in the week, you'd have to think of something else."

I asked him, "How many people are in this building?"

Mr. K raised his shoulders in something that could have passed for a shrug. "Two thousand, give or take a few hundred, maybe? There are three other sections beside this one, and I've got to worry about feeding a little bit over three hundred people in this section. This section is the only one with kids"—Mr. K shook his head, and just for a moment he looked very tired— "which is why we make dessert almost every night. All of your parents insisted on it." He snorted. I thought that was a very weird thing for him to say, since I've never eaten as many sweets in my life as I have here. I had a hard time imagining my parents demanding that I be allowed to eat cake after every dinner.

He started grabbing ingredients from the pantry and ordering them on one end of the counter. "You pay attention now. I'm going to teach you how to make a yellow cake, and I don't want you to forget it. You should write it down in your journal when you get back to your room tonight." It's been several hours since he told me that, so I hope I'm remembering it all right.

I told him that my mom had already taught me how to make a cake. Mr. K told me that I was going to learn again anyway. I was kind of annoyed.

"Cake flour—two cups," he told me, pointing to the bag. "Baking powder, stick of butter, cup of sugar, three eggs, vanilla, and three quarters of a cup of milk. Study the ingredients, please."

Mr. K is not a very good teacher, I thought. He's kind of short with his instructions. I stepped up to the counter, which rested at my elbows, and looked at the ingredients carefully. I nodded at him to let him know I knew exactly what I needed.

"OK." Mr. K was trying not to smile again. "Now go over to the hallway and wait for me to call you back."

I frowned at him, but went out into the hallway. People were starting to wake up and walk around. A few kitchen assistants walked past me and into the kitchen, looking at me strangely. After a couple of minutes, Mr. K stuck his head out of the kitchen and asked me to come back in. The counter was all cleared.

"What did you do? You're not done already, are you?" I thought that maybe he was ridiculously fast at making cake, so I looked at the oven to see if he had already put it in. There was nothing in the oven.

"You studied the ingredients, right? Get them out for me."

"Oh." I heard some of the assistants start to laugh, because they knew exactly why Mr. K had asked me to get the stuff back out. They knew, and then I realized, too, that I hadn't really studied the ingredients enough. My face heated up again. Mr. K waited, his eyes crinkling.

I sighed and walked over to the pantry to grab the flour. There were three different types of flour bags on the shelf, each hand-labeled FLOUR, but in different colors. I had no idea which one was right. I grabbed the green one, knowing that I was most probably going to be wrong, and then set about grabbing the baking powder and the vanilla. I walked back to the counter and put my ingredients down, and Mr. K was laughing at me, so I knew I had already screwed it up. I got a little bit angry with him again, but I pushed it down and went to the oversized fridge. I pulled out three eggs and a stick of butter, and then, having tucked my eggs and butter into my elbow, tried to pour three quarters of a cup of milk into the measuring cup I was holding. Two eggs tumbled out of my arm and splatted onto the floor. I heard Mr. K sigh, but tried not to look at him. I was embarrassed. I started looking around for a mop, but Mr. K told me to leave it. He asked Ana, one of his assistants who had been chopping a stack of veggies for breakfast, to please mop it up. She frowned at him, and I immediately felt worse.

"Ignore her, Johnny. You've got a job to do!" He sounded very cheerful. If this guy likes anything, it's cooking. And baking, too, I guess. I saw Ana stick her tongue out at him when he wasn't looking, and then shoot a small smile over at me. That made me feel a little better, even though her eyes didn't crinkle like Mr. K's do. I grabbed two more eggs from the kitchen.

After setting up all my ingredients on the counter, Mr. K asked, "Are you missing anything?" I looked at the pile, frowning, then decided he was only asking to trip me up.

"I probably have the wrong flour," I offered. He asked me if there was anything else, and I shook my head no.

"You're right about the flour—you want the one with the red label, that's the cake flour. And you want how much?"

"Two cups," I said quickly, knowing that part easily.

Mr. K nodded at me. "Right. You're missing salt, though. And you grabbed baking powder instead of baking soda. Your cake won't be very tasty with what you've got here, I'm afraid."

I shoved my hands into my pockets and rolled my foot so that I was stepping on the side of my shoe. "Sorry, Mr. K." I felt dumb.

"That's okay, Johnny. This is why I'm teaching you." He reached over me to start putting the ingredients back. "You don't have to go back out into the hall, but close your eyes for me. We're going to do it again."

I did as he told me. When he tapped me on the shoulder, I opened my eyes and raced to the pantry to gather the right ingredients this time around, then to the fridge, sidestepping around Ana, who was just finishing with the mop.

So I finally had the right ingredients for the cake. Mr. K told me that he would teach me how to make the icing another time, because he didn't want me to get too confused and he already had some buttercream made up in the fridge. He also said that the butter and eggs had to come to room temperature before we could start making the batter, so he set me to work next to Ana to help her chop the vegetables.

Ana told me we'd be having omelets for breakfast, and three hundred people can go through a lot of vegetables. I made a face at her, and she laughed. Another assistant, a grumpy-looking woman with frizzy grey hair held back by a net—she *looked* like a lunch lady, and a mean one at that—glared at us.

"We're running out of time. Help or don't, but please don't distract Ana," she grouched at us, then turned back to whisking a ridiculous number of eggs. Ana stuck out her tongue at her, too. I tried not to laugh. I decided then that I wanted to work with Ana if I came back to the kitchens to work later on.

So once I chopped just about a million vegetables, most of which I will never eat in my life ever, Mr. K let me know that it was time to make the cake batter.

He showed me how to add all of the dry ingredients together and whisk them up so that they're all distributed evenly, and then how to use the huge stand mixer that's nested on one of the side counters to cream the butter and the sugar together. He helped me beat in the eggs, carefully, and the vanilla, and then slowly add the dry mixture and milk, alternating them and adding just the littlest bits at a time so that the batter doesn't get all lumpy and gross. It took forever, but Mr. K didn't seem to mind.

"When did you start cooking?" I asked him.

"Probably when I was a few years younger than you. My grandfather taught me. It's a family tradition, I suppose." I thought he looked a little sad.

"Did you teach your grandson?"

If he hadn't looked sad before, he certainly did then. "Yes, I've been teaching him. He's six." He cleared his throat. "He lives with my daughter in D.C. Or did. They should have left by now." He shook his head quickly. I didn't want to ask any more questions that would make him look that sad ever again.

"OK!" he chirped. "Time for the cake to go into the pan."

He spread a little butter all the way around two circular pans, and made me pour half of the batter into each one. I started to overfill one, but Mr. K stopped me quickly before I had a chance to ruin it. If you overfill it, he told me, they might not cook evenly.

And then he told me to slide them into the right side of the big oven, which I did. He set a timer for twenty minutes, and I saw that the oven was set at three-fifty. For those twenty minutes, I watched Ana and the grumpy lunch lady cooking omelets on the giant cooktop, then immediately transferring them into another oven to keep them warm. I tried to imagine ever wanting to cook so many omelets for people. I decided then that that wasn't something I wanted to do, not ever. They didn't look like they were having very much fun.

Mr. K took the cakes out of the oven when the timer went off. They were beautiful, all golden and yummy-looking, although the smell of them mixed with the cooking eggs wasn't very good. He told me we had to wait to let the cakes cool for a few minutes before we put them on the cooling rack to cool all the way, and then we could frost it. I already knew that part, but I let him tell me anyway.

When he finally flipped the cakes over onto the wire rack, I held my breath. I really did want the cake to be perfect, and I was very very very relieved when I saw that the cake hadn't stuck to the pans any. Now we had to wait some more. I didn't realize how long baking a cake took, and I said so to Mr. K. He looked at me sternly and said, "That's why I don't like when you steal from my kitchen." I looked away from him, embarrassed again.

"Sorry," I muttered, and he nodded to let me know that had been the right thing to say.

"Forgiven, as long as you don't do it again."

I couldn't promise. I didn't tell him that, but I know I can't.

The next hour was spent peeling potatoes for lunch. I didn't like it, but I was too nervous to leave the cake out on the rack unattended and go to class. I convinced Mr. K that I had already read ahead in our math book, so I didn't really need to be in the lesson today anyway.

Thinking back, we didn't even eat those potatoes for lunch. I think he was trying to give me the boring work so that I would leave and get out of the way. Oh well.

After peeling a million potatoes, Mr. K let me know that it was time to frost the cake. He had buttercream (it was blue, but I think yellow would have been better) sitting out on the counter, and he showed me how to use this thing that looks like a knife but isn't sharp to spread it around the cake. But that's only after the two layers were put together with frosting in between to have them stick to each other.

Mr. K even showed me how to do this little twisting thing with the icing knife so that the icing comes up in little mountains all around the edge of the cake. I tried to do it, but it looked terrible, so I scraped it off and asked him to do it so I wouldn't give Angel an ugly cake.

His eyes crinkled, and he said OK. I don't know why he thought that was funny, because I was being completely serious. When we were done frosting the cake, Mr. K put it on a little cart and went back to the pantry to find a candle. Wait, that was after the cake was put on a serving dish. We put it on a big white plate before we started frosting it.

The candle wasn't a birthday candle, it was like a table candle, and it looked like it had been used a couple of times. White wax already dripped down the sides and the wick was charred black. Mr. K grunted an apology at me before handing it over, but I didn't mind too much. Candles are candles. It would have been nice if there were birthday candles, but the bunker doesn't really strike me as a place that would take birthdays seriously enough to have party supplies, so I wasn't too surprised.

Day 187

Angel wasn't wrong. We aren't going home anymore.

12

Michael frowned at the page he was reading for a very long time. That was the end of the fourth journal, and it seemed like a weird place to end. He wanted to know more. Why had Johnny written that, only to stop? The next several pages—the last ten or so—were filled with ink, but no words. The odd stopping point hadn't been because the child had run out of space; it was like Johnny had just decided he didn't want to write any more. Instead, he'd drawn loops on the page, over and over and over, and then had gone back over those loops with more loops until the white of the page underneath couldn't be seen.

Michael ran his fingers over the paper, feeling the indentations that Johnny's pen had made so long ago. The ink was all black. While the other pages in the journals felt brittle, like they could crumble apart under his fingertips if he wasn't careful, these last few pages had been strengthened by the ink spread across them. These pages would last long after the others had decayed fully.

Michael's chest felt tight.

He cleared his throat and spoke very clearly into the microphone: "End of Journal."

The chair released him, *shink,* and Michael stood and stretched his arms above his head as far as he could. His shoulders screamed at him, aching from weeks of sitting stooped over the journals. The spike that went into his neck didn't allow him to sit up straight, which was another reason he felt smaller by the day. His body was caving in on itself.

Happily, he realized that he didn't feel as if he was starving. Which meant that he probably had more than enough time to make it down to the cage before dinner. He was always afraid that he would end a journal near when a buzzer would go off, and he would lose time to eat.

He took a few moments to just sit on the edge of his bed and breathe deeply, relishing this small moment of freedom. He felt weak and useless, and a deep depression settled over him, just as it always did when he finished reading.

He needed to get moving, he knew. Sighing, Michael rose from the bed and shuffled into his slippers. His toes felt frozen, and he was too afraid to look down to see what color they were. He was sure they wouldn't be pretty.

Oddly, his grey robe and slippers had become something of a comfort to Michael in the weeks he'd been in the Archives. It was easy for him to think of them as a uniform, something that he wore while he was working, and an outfit that he would never wear once he finished his shift. And now that the other Archivists were starting to show some personality—rather than just being indistinguishable members of a dull, colorless army—he found it easier to think of them as his co-workers, no different than the people beside him on the farms had been. The people who worked the fields all wore wide-brimmed green hats to keep the sun off their face, but those hats also served to mark them as part of a group. There was a sense of camaraderie that came with the green hats, even if Michael didn't know many of those folks, outside of the ones that worked in his section.

The halls were empty as he walked, leisurely, toward the Cage. He didn't need his map anymore, but every few minutes he would pat the pocket of his robe to be sure that it was still there. He couldn't help but think of it as a talisman; he was worried that if he didn't have it on him, something bad would happen. It was completely irrational, he knew, but he couldn't bring himself to leave his room without it.

As he walked, he took pleasure in keeping his mind as empty as he could, often just focusing on his footsteps on the smooth concrete. He was tired of having so many thoughts inside his head. Even when he slept, the nightmares kept his mind from really being calm. The quiet of the empty hallways was lovely.

When he reached room 0001, Michael sighed, knowing his walk had come to an end. The ancient woman behind the big wooden desk—Michael really should ask her name one of these days, but not today, he didn't want to ask today—was bundled up in a silver coat, a hat pulled down over her ears, and a scarf wrapped up to her nose. She looked miserable.

"Cold?" Michael asked, trying for a pleasant tone and failing. His voice was scratchy and gruff, his abused throat sore from spending nearly every waking moment speaking. *Occupational hazard*, he thought dully.

The woman glared at him. "You Archivists aren't reading quickly enough." Her tiny voice was muffled by the thick scarf covering her mouth. "The whole building's getting colder and colder."

Michael frowned at the woman, not understanding what the Archivists reading any faster had to do with the temperature. *She's crazy*, he decided, shaking his head.

It was interesting, however, to realize that the coldness in his bones wasn't entirely from reading. He'd always just assumed that his constant shivering was from sitting stock-still for hours on end. Michael had never suspected that the building itself was part of the problem.

Giving up on words, he held the journal out in front of him silently so she could grab it. The woman's hand snaked out from her coat sleeve, her skin papery and translucent. She grumbled incoherently as she took the journal from him, then proceeded back into the cage. Michael drummed his frozen fingers against the desk, trying to clear his head one more time before the woman came back.

It took him a few minutes to push everything out of his head, and as soon as he succeeded, the woman was right back in front of him, thrusting a new journal and a stack of tokens under his nose. Michael sighed, disappointed, but took the new book from her dutifully. He mumbled a quick "thanks" as he scooped the new tokens into the little cloth bag he had brought with him. The woman didn't acknowledge him, just busied herself with bundling back up in the oversized heavy coat, burrowing down into the fabric. Michael shook his head and started walking back to his room.

He walked slowly, cautiously. He was too nervous to zone out now that he had a fresh stack of tokens in his pocket. Mary's words of warning came back to him. He had yet to have someone try to take his meal tokens, but he didn't want to give them the opportunity, either.

Back in his room, Michael thought about sitting back down in the chair. His arm burned and his neck ached. He weighed his tokens in his hand and contemplated how badly he wanted to find out what happened next to Johnny.

He decided that he didn't need to know all of that immediately. After all, Johnny's words weren't going to go anywhere. Savoring the little thrill he got from this small act of rebellion, Michael placed the journal onto the little rolling desk and then went and lay down in his bed.

His mattress was dreadfully hard, and his blanket was so worn and threadbare that it really offered no extra warmth, but Michael was smiling as he drifted off to sleep. It was the first time in ages that he didn't dream of things he didn't recognize. Instead, Michael Driftveil dreamt of a flowerpot by the window.

13

The office is cold, and in general she likes it that way. It keeps her alert. Most days she can ignore the spread of gooseflesh across her arms and the clamminess of her palms as she goes through the logs for that day, sitting stiff in the used-to-be padded chair she's inherited. Other days, bad days, like today, her bones creak and her head feels like it's splitting in half, and she can't stop shivering. She's freezing, even though she's still wearing that god-awful blue uniform jacket, the one that scratches her thin, papery skin on the back of her neck and is too tight in the shoulders and smells like rot because it was pulled out of a damp closet and shoved at her like a joke. *Here, you take this one, girlie,* and the laughing that came afterward. Even the pet name was an insult—those bastards just wanted to let her know that they knew exactly how old she was getting, how time kept slipping away from her and soon she'd be on the west hill rotting just like this jacket had been in that damn closet. Her hair used to be brown, didn't it? A rich, warm color that had so often fallen into her eyes. Sometimes on purpose, to appear cute and slightly mousy to endear herself that boy—what had his name been when they were together?—until one day she was noticing it start to get a little dull, and then a little pale, and then a lot grey and there were lines on her face and her eyes seemed cloudy and she couldn't hear for shit anymore and hell, when had she gotten so old?

And somehow during all those years she had grown lonely, too. How did that happen?

So that's why she's sitting in the cold office, turning to ice, and trying to find the answer to the Republic's pest problem. She sits in the hard chair and looks at the monitors in front of her, the modules cycling through all of the readings from today. When she came up with the idea to use the Archives to find the answer, they had laughed so hard and told her to go ahead and try. And now she's been at it for ten years, which just makes the higher-ups laugh harder at her. But she knows the answer is in here somewhere. And it's getting closer.

She lines herself up in front of the microphone and clears her throat, trying to figure out what words to search for today. Often, it seems like she's getting nowhere, that the scale is too great, that she'll never be able to search for the right thing to make sense of all the jumbled journals people have written. Sighing, she straightens up and speaks: "Weapon."

It's never yielded good results before, but she doesn't know why. It seems like that word would lead her where she needs to go, every time.

The module whirrs for a moment, the thin screens—physical ones, all of them, the frames around them black and scratched and an inch wide because the Republic is unwilling to dump any more into this project and give her good holoscreens, those bastards— throwing up fuzzy lines and static as they try to make sense of what the modules are telling them to do. How old is this technology? Two hundred years? Older even than her. She laughs bitterly at herself.

Finally the module comes up with the hits, and she looks at the screen for a long time before sighing and hitting return. There's a batch getting ready to be released in the next few weeks, and only twenty of the Archivists have spoken about weapons today. Another group, useless. None of their Recorders knew anything about the weapon at all. Most of the hits were just people reminiscing about weapon collections back home (there are two of these, which is interesting because it means that the Recorders weren't from the affected cities, but it's not interesting enough to keep her attention for long), or the Old Star Soldiers writing about how many times they cleaned their guns to stave off the boredom. She's frustrated.

There is one though . . . Her eyes flick up to the corner of the monitor and she notes the room number. It's the volunteer's room. She frowns before pressing return a few times. Mary isn't supposed to have any relevant projects, because she *likes* Mary. She looks at the center screen, the Recorder bio off to the left of the desk as she scrolls through what Mary has read today. After a few moments, she flicks her eyes over to the bio screen in confusion, hitting the down arrow impatiently a few times. Ten years of this machine and she still isn't entirely used to not having touch control. Ridiculous.

The Recorder was just a kid when she started, and not one of the important ones either. She frowns again. This kid wasn't one of the ones to go out and investigate—in fact, the kid ended up having a kid of her own and then . . . oh.

She looks at the name again. Oh.

Damn.

She purses her thin lips, sucking on her teeth for a minute before bringing her wristcom up to her mouth. "I need the volunteer in here now, please. Who's closest to her room?" Her voice sounds scratchy and weak again, so she clears her throat and listens to the com crackling before one of the Minders answers her in a flood of static.

"Buchanan in. I'll get her."

She closes her eyes in agitation. Of course Buchanan is closest. He's probably running through the halls to make sure he gets to her first. She speaks into the com again. "No, Buchanan, someone else."

More static. "Too late, I'm here." His voice is smug, and she rolls her eyes. In all honesty, she should probably take him off detail and send him home. He's too aggressive, and he causes the most problems with the Archivists. His hands wander. But he's one of the only Minders who will willingly help her with the information quarantine. That's reason enough to keep him, and she knows it. And he knows she knows it. Ass.

A few minutes go by and she studies her hands. Such old, thin, blue hands. They disgust her. *She* disgusts her.

The door flies open without the courtesy of Buchanan buzzing in to let her know he's arrived. That annoys her more than it should. He's looking way too self-satisfied, while Mary looks harassed and angry. The Minder guides the young girl—*her* hands are beautiful, even stained with old ink—into the room, his hand much lower than is acceptable. Both women, however uncomfortable, say nothing to him about it. She should, and she wants to, but she doesn't want it getting back to the highers that she stood up to him. She's not technically a Minder, and even if strictly speaking she has authority over this man, the men in charge of *her* won't appreciate it.

"Buchanan, go back to your post," she snaps, harsher than she should.

His hand lingers, and Mary's eyes narrow as he pats her. Poor Mary's spine and shoulders are so stiff that she could be used to hammer the tower out front back together. He leers at the back of Mary's head before shooting off a half-assed salute and sauntering from the room. The moment the door lowers shut behind him, rushing to meet the floor and enclose the two women in the cold room together, Mary sags forward and her lip trembles.

"Mary, did he hurt you?" She can't do anything about it if he did, but she asks anyway. She likes to think that her voice sounds gentle in these moments, but she knows she just sounds like a dozen spoons being hurled against the concrete, clattering, high and dissonant.

Mary shakes her head no, her dark braid swinging down by her waist behind her back, and she shoves her hands—such young hands—up into her armpits. "It's cold in here."

She nods, and then motions for Mary to sit in the chair beside her own, hitting the punch buttons on the monitors so that the screens go dark and Mary can't see what she's been trying to find. She smiles, she hopes warmly. "I was just noticing who you picked out for your go-around this time. Are you liking her so far?"

Mary's eyebrows arch, and she smiles, pleased that Coleman is taking an interest. "Oh, yes," she breathes. "She's such an interesting woman. She was one of the kids, and she knew a little bit of what was happening because her father told her. She didn't live in D.C., so it's really quite fortunate she made it into the program at all. She could have been lost to the virus if they hadn't admitted her." Mary has the grace to look embarrassed. "I'm sorry, ma'am, you probably knew all that."

She waves Mary's concern aside easily. "Oh, that's fine, dear." *Dear.* She sounds like a grandmother. *Oh, don't worry about it, darling. Don't fret, sweetheart.* She tries not to cringe, but if she fails, Mary doesn't seem to notice. "How far have you gotten?"

Mary's smile falters a little bit.

That far, then.

"The research team left the bunker a few months ago. She's almost due."

She looks at the girl for a long while then, not saying anything, trying to remember exactly how old Mary is. Sometimes she seems much older than she could possibly be, her face lined with wrinkles that aren't her own, the memories of battles she hasn't fought behind her eyes. Sometimes she acts like a child, her eyes round and sparkling and taking everything in. Right now Mary just looks sad— and that doesn't lend itself to any one age.

Thirty-five, she decides. No, twenty-seven. No, forty. No, she thinks, no it's none of those, those are all wrong. It's twenty. She has no idea if she's even close, so she stops worrying about it and speaks again. "You're becoming friends with one of the other Archivists. People have noticed."

Something flashes behind Mary's eyes before it's carefully hidden away again. That's not good at all. "Oh," Mary says, "really? That's odd. I didn't think I had been." Her voice is neutral enough.

"I worry about you, Mary, you know that." Mary's uncomfortable now. Just because she isn't a prisoner doesn't mean they're friends. She's overstepped her bounds.

"Y-yeah." Mary's voice is unsure, but she plays along anyway. Mary's a smart girl. She knows.

"I don't want you to get mixed up with the wrong person. The other Archivists are dangerous, Mary." She feels like she's scolding a child, and tries to make her voice gentler, more pleasant. "There's an Archivist whose name is . . . oh, what was it?" She makes a great show of spinning away in her chair and digging for a file on another desk. The file is cold and damp, and the ink has run on the recycled pages, and the report is on something completely irrelevant, a new shipment of journals from one of the other bunkers that is just now being excavated, but Mary doesn't need to know that. She rifles through it uninterestedly for just a moment or two before setting it down out of the way.

"Driftveil? Michael Driftveil? This says here that he was on the motorcart you came back with the time before last." She notices that Mary's eyes linger on the file for several seconds too long before slowly dragging themselves away to meet hers. "That boy is dangerous." Now she sounds just like her mother did. She can feel her face twisting up in distaste before she has time to stop it. Oh well.

Mary pretends only mild interest. "Oh, right. I know him, a little. He didn't know where to go, so I showed him the Cage. And he doesn't like eating alone, so I sit with him sometimes, to be polite."

She sighs heavily, dramatically, and leans forward in her chair, resting her elbows on her knees and ignoring how her uniform coat stretches uncomfortably taut across her old shoulders. "Oh, Mary,

Mary . . ." Her fingers become steepled in front of her and she studies them. "You're so young. I remember being that young—I understand." She tries to look as sympathetic as possible. Mary's dark eyes are wary and tired. "But you must realize that every other Archivist is here for a reason, and that reason is because they are the worst criminals the Republic has. You don't really know anything about what he's done, dear." Her voice sounds disgusting, even to her, but she's trying.

Mary chews her lip for a moment before speaking. "He said he only stole something."

She lets out an airy little snort, intended to give the girl the impression her remark was funny, and hopes it worked. "Oh Mary, he didn't. Is that really what he told you?" She lets that hang between them for a minute, Mary now gazing down at her shoes. The girl looks like a child now, properly chastised. Good.

She sighs again. "I just want to make sure you're safe. You'll stay away from him?"

The nod from the young girl is almost imperceptible, but it's enough. She reaches out an old, papery hand and pats Mary on the shoulder, trying to be as friendly as possible. She has no idea if it's working—she was never very good at friends, and especially not other women.

"Well, I'll let you get back to the girl then. And please, understand that if that project stops holding interest for you, let me know and I'll have you pick a new Recorder. Do we have a deal?" It would be so much better if Mary would just abandon this set and move on to something less important.

That tiny little nod again, and Mary is out the door.

She leans back in her chair and relaxes, just a small bit. After a thought, she raises her wristcom back to her mouth. "I'm going to need full surveillance on the volunteer until further notice. Please respond."

The old speaker crackles. She's already anticipated the voice that speaks up to volunteer, and she's ready to deny him: "No, Buchanan, I'm going to need another officer. We've got some contamination pending and I'll need you for cleanup."

The grumbled assent that statics and scratches its way through the com only annoys her more.

14

I don't really know how to describe what happened last week. All of us have been wandering around, not really sure what we're supposed to do. We haven't had class. My brain feels muggy, like I've been asleep for weeks. The whole building has been very quiet.

Mr. K and the kitchen staff are having a really hard time with it all. I know that, because everyone has pretty much eaten the same thing all week: every meal has been chicken soup, and the broth keeps getting thinner and thinner like he just keeps filling the pot with water when the broth gets low. I should go talk to him. He told me last week that I needed to write down how to make the cake, almost as if he knew what was going to happen. I guess it's a good thing he taught me again instead of just making it for me, because otherwise I might have forgotten after all this crap happened.

I asked Ms. Maggie what we should do yesterday. She told me to keep writing. Her face was all red, so I know she was crying. A lot of people have been crying.

I don't understand how I'm supposed to keep writing after all of this, but I'll try. I can't write about anything from before, but I'll try to explain what's happened since then. I haven't written in days, so I have to make up for it. I'll be writing about anything interesting that happened, because we're supposed to write at least five pages a day, so I really have a lot of pages that I'm supposed to make up. Even the interesting stuff is probably kind of boring. Sorry.

Did it happen on Wednesday, is that right? I think so, but we don't really use days of the week, just day numbers. We've all restarted our counts, and now it's officially been one week since it happened. I want to scream.

It had to have been Wednesday because that was Angel's birthday. That makes sense. I remember that part.

Mr. K had told me to meet him after lunch in the kitchen before going back to class, so we could get the cake ready. He'd already told Ms. Maggie what was happening, and he told me that she was happy I was looking out for my classmate. When it was time to go I tried to make sure that Angel didn't see me sneaking off, because I didn't want her to suspect anything.

Mr. K had everything ready already when I walked back there, so we waited a few minutes so that everyone could get settled in class before we walked in. Finally, with the long candle on the cake on the plate on the cart, Mr. K and I wheeled down the hallway toward the classroom.

I was excited, and I couldn't wait to see the look on Angel's face when she realized that she was going to get to have a birthday party after all. We met a few people in the hallway, most of them the soldiers with the black patches above their hearts (I still haven't found out what that shape is supposed to be, and David won't tell me), but all of them looked relaxed, nobody rushing around with binders or books in their hands, none of their faces frowning. I remember thinking that everyone must have heard the news, that we were all going to go home soon because whatever it was that was worrying everyone was done. Whether it was the attacks like Angel said, or something else I didn't know about yet, the threat was gone and no one was worried anymore. And then I passed under an air vent, the cool air blasting down on us at an angle, and I could smell the birthday cake we had made, and I stopped wondering about anything else except how happy I was to have rescued Angel's birthday. The fact that the cake smelled amazing and I couldn't wait to taste it didn't hurt.

We entered into the back of the classroom, as quietly as possible. No one even looked back at us, and Mr. K hit the button on the wall to leave the door open so that the sound of it closing wouldn't tip anyone off. I wanted Angel to know the cake was for her, so I didn't want any of the other kids in class to see it before she did. I was really nervous that one of the three bratty girls would see it and immediately start squealing and jumping around and cutting into it. I would have had to have decked them.

Ms. Maggie was up at the board, writing a complicated-looking algebra problem with her finger, the computer underneath the screen already reading her handwriting and calculating the answer. They were going over the homework from the night before (which I hadn't done, not that it matters a whole lot now). A little yellow star blinked next to the equal sign, letting everyone know that it had come up with the solution, and it would show us if we just tapped the star once. The computer was very eager to tell everyone the answer, but Ms. Maggie always waits for one of us to raise our hand and explain the answer we came up with before she taps the star. If we wait too long, the computer gets impatient and kind of shakes the star a little bit, blinking just the tiniest bit faster, as if to remind us that it's still there, and it knows exactly what we want to know. I try very hard to work out the answers before the star does its little seizure dance—I've got tally marks in the front of my school notebook for all the times I've done it. The page is half full of little marks.

I spotted Angel near the middle of the class, writing very diligently in her own notebook. Only she wasn't writing math. I'm not sure exactly what she was doing, but she definitely wasn't paying attention to Ms. Maggie and the dancing star. Her nose was buried so far into her book that it's a wonder she didn't stab one of her green eyes out with her pen.

Ms. Maggie definitely saw Mr. K and I walk in, but she didn't let any of the other kids know. She just stood at the front of the room, eyes roaming the class as she waited for someone to raise their hand. The star on the board gave an impatient little shake.

When no one raised their hand, Ms. Maggie half-smiled. She must have realized that this was the perfect opportunity, because suddenly her half-smile turned into a full-on grin. "Angel?"

Behind me, Mr. K pulled a matchbook out of his pocket and got ready over the candle. Angel was so busy with her writing that she didn't even look up at Ms. Maggie.

"Aaaaangel!" Ms. Maggie sang, her eyes smiling, but her hands on her hips, pretending to be unhappy. Angel's head snapped up so fast she might have broken her neck. Her eyes were as big as I've ever seen them, and she was obviously thinking that she had just gotten caught doing . . . whatever that was.

"Yes, Ms. Maggie?" she said, her voice all shaky. I felt a little bad that she figured she was in trouble, but mostly I just tried really hard not to laugh and spoil the surprise. I loved Ms. Maggie right then for playing along.

"Would you like to let the class know the answer you came up with?"

If I had ever seen anyone's face red from embarrassment, it was never half as red as Angel got just then. I could see it creeping up her neck onto her ears, and she looked positively miserable. "I-I-I . . . I don't . . . um." Poor Angel stuttered really bad, her hands working to cover up her journal so that no one around her could see what she'd been doing. All eyes were trained on her; no one even thought to take a look at us, standing in the doorway, delicious birthday cake in hand.

I shot Mr. K a look, like *Whoops, that wasn't supposed to happen*, and he just looked at me with his crinkled eyes. He thought this was funny, just like Ms. Maggie did. She was pretending not to notice how embarrassed Angel was, which was probably a little terrible, but it was for a good cause. She chirped happily, "Why don't you come up here and show us your work?" Ms. Maggie beamed at the class, very pleased with herself. I saw out of the corner of my eye Mr. K giving her a thumbs-up.

Angel scrubbed at her face with her hands before sighing and standing up, her chair scraping against the concrete floor, *screeeeeech*. She really didn't want to go up to the board. I could see her staring directly at the screen, her brain working furiously to try and figure out the math problem before she got up there.

Once she was up at the board, she looked right at it for several more moments. She didn't know the answer, and worse than that, she didn't know where to begin. Some giggles started up around the classroom, and I saw her shoulders hunch a bit. That's when I figured that it was time, because I didn't want her to stay embarrassed for too long. This was a pretty mean prank that we had decided to pull on her.

I turned to Mr. K, then looked pointedly at the light switch. He grinned at me—really grinned—and nodded. Just as I waved my hand over the switch to turn the lights out, Mr. K struck the match and lit the candle. One girl screamed, probably one of the Jennifers, and then everyone whirled around to see who had turned the lights out. Including Angel.

As soon as Angel had turned completely, Ms. Maggie started singing:

"Happy birthday to you . . ."

Mr. K and I joined in with her. "Happy birthday to you . . .."

Some of the kids started singing too, a little bit behind and not really sure who they were singing for.

"Happy BIRTHDAY dear Aaaaaaaangel . . ." Angel's name was sung loud and long by Ms. Maggie, Mr. K and I, giving the other kids time to catch up.

"Haaaaaappy birthday to youuuuuuu!"

Everyone clapped, and Angel ran over to blow out her candle. She was grinning right at me, I remember that very plainly. Then she squeezed her eyes shut and made a wish, her lips moving in the yellow light from the tiny flame. Wish accomplished, Angel leaned down and let out a heavy, short breath to extinguish the fire, and right as she blew the candle out Mr. K flicked the lights on again. Everyone clapped some more.

This part coming up next is what I have such a hard time thinking about, which is why it's going to be very hard to describe it to you. Those last few moments—where Angel was smiling at me and making a wish on her candle—are the last moments I can remember before everything gets fuzzy. I feel like what happened next turned me into someone else, even though I'm still me. I don't really know how to tell you.

There was a big shake, I know that much. Everything seemed to slow down for a few seconds, and everyone in the room looked up in confusion, although I was looking right at Angel. At that point she still had a huge grin on her face. I like to think that she was so excited about the cake that she just didn't realize that something was happening.

Ms. Maggie knew something was happening though. I could see her at the front of the room, just over Angel's shoulder. She shouted something that sounded a lot like "No!" but could have been something else entirely, before all the sound was sucked out of the room.

I worried for a few seconds that I had gone deaf, and the lights flickered and died in a bright flash. Several seconds behind the flash—definitely delayed although I couldn't tell you how—there was a loud *pop!* Like someone slamming an empty cup onto a tabletop. That's when everyone started screaming again.

The room still shook around us, and, you're going to think I'm silly, but my first thought was of the birthday cake. I reached out to try and steady the cart and plate that it was on, before I really stopped to think about how scary the shaking was. It reminded me of when you throw a bit of water on a hot pan and watch the little drops dance around and evaporate, sizzling in an angry sort of way, except this was every second growing more scary. I know it had to have been an earthquake, but it was so much worse than how I've ever seen and heard earthquakes described. I worried about the earth rolling underneath and around us, crushing us in a pile of dirt and concrete and steel bars. There was nowhere for us to really go— I think we all figured out months ago that we're all underground. Everyone was glued to their seats. I felt like I was being shaken apart.

This whole mess took about fifteen seconds, or maybe even less, I'm not sure. I know it wasn't very much longer than that, as I think back on it now. But at the time, it felt like the world was ending, and it just kept going, on and on and on.

Then, seconds after everything had stopped, the sound hit us. This was not the pop of lights going out. It was not the clatter of tipping chairs and fallen schoolbooks and rattling bones. This was something much worse—something completely awful. I can't think of a way to describe it to you, as I've never heard anything like it before, and I hope I'll never have to hear it again.

The sound was sadness. It was a roar of such volume that my eyes watered and I clutched my hands over my ears, abandoning the cake. Angel shrieked, and somehow that sound was better than the other sound that we were all hearing. I wanted to bring her closer, have her scream directly into my ear so that I wouldn't have to listen to the terrible rumble of the earthquake. I felt like I was being drained away, and that feeling was worse than anything else—more terrible than the nameless noise, and a million times more horrible than the darkness and shuddering dirt that shifted around our concrete prison. I thought I was going to die, tears and snot and fear choking me and making it so I couldn't breathe. That's not a pretty description, so I'm sorry if you're squeamish, but that's how it was.

Just as suddenly as it started, everything stilled around us. The lights kicked back on, and of course by now I know that that was from the backup generators, which had been gathering power from a whole bunch of solar panels up top. The fact that they're still working means that the world hasn't ended, it's just been—misplaced? The sun still rises in the morning, anyway.

I can't believe I thought this . . . but in that moment, as the lights fizzled on, I wished the bunker really had collapsed down around us. It was better than the feeling I had in the pit of my stomach, a hurting that I knew I wasn't going to be able to get rid of. Not any time soon. I still feel it.

Ms. Maggie was sobbing, looking so terrible that I had to turn my head and not look at her anymore. Mr. K was paler than I had ever seen him, and his hand was clutching the necklace he had pulled out of his pocket, his mouth moving slowly, silently. He had tears in his eyes, like the rest of us.

Angel had fallen to the floor. I was too shaken up to help her stand. Little Jeff had dived under his desk, and clung to the legs of his chair. Even stupid Rock had his big hands thrown over his face in terror.

As I looked at the other kids, almost all of them looking shocked, and every one of them with tears on their faces, it began to dawn on me. We were all looking at each other with the same confusion and loss on our faces: we knew that something had been taken away from us. We didn't know what it was, or at least I didn't. I just knew that moments before I had felt so much *more* than I did right then. I was missing parts of me. But that was ridiculous, because I couldn't seem to recall any part of me that I couldn't pin down. As far as I could tell, I was completely unharmed, but I knew that I wasn't. I have no idea how to describe this feeling to you, and I'm sorry. I know that because you're reading this, I'm meant to be illustrating my life for you, and I'm doing a very bad job right now. But there was nothing, as much as I searched for it, anything, that I could find that was wrong with me. I just knew I wasn't *right*.

Everyone else was dealing with the same problem—I could see it in their faces.

With the earthquake over, the only two still crying were the adults. It took a very long time for them to pull themselves together, and Mr. K was the one who managed it first. He tucked his necklace back into his pocket and walked up to Ms. Maggie, looking as calm as he had before the quake. He grabbed her shoulders and hugged her, squeezing her so tightly I thought she might pop. She was screaming into his shoulder—all of us could hear it. Some of the girls started to cry again, just from listening to Ms. Maggie cry.

I don't know what made me think of this then, but that's when I realized that Ms. Maggie was young. Very very young. When she told me that she'd never been a teacher before, I didn't really pay attention. But watching her cry and listening to her melt down in front of all of us, I could see that she isn't even a grownup. She's older than all of us, yeah. But how much older? Because just then, she looked like she might not even be out of high school. She's a kid just like we are, and she had known what was coming. When she told me that she missed her parents too . . . it's because she was put into the program just like us. Her parents sent her here. And I think, just by being the oldest, she got stuck with being the teacher. Which is why the older kids treat her so bad—they're not going to listen to somebody just a few years older than they are.

That train of thought is what helped me realize what had happened. I knew in my bones that my parents had sent me here. We've all talked about it in the breaks between lessons, how our parents sent us here, how much they told us before we went. I knew all that.

But what I didn't know—I realized just then—was who my parents were.

15

Michael's heart hurt when he came to, jolting into the present as the chair released him and the buzzer screamed in his ear. He felt absolutely miserable. Sniffing, he reached up to wipe his nose on his sleeve—and felt the tears on his cheeks. He hadn't even known that he was crying.

He supposed, hollowly, that his experiences with his memories being replaced made him more fortunate than Johnny. Sure, Michael had to endure the knowledge that his memories were not his own, and it sickened him daily. But even as terrible as that knowledge was, Michael knew that he would rather have the slow slipping feeling of something being not quite right than to having everything ripped away from him at once. He could feel Johnny's desperation, his depression at losing his family—and at not being able to recall a thing about them. The panic had surrounded the poor kid as he scribbled the words down, his handwriting even worse than usual. Though Johnny never mentioned it in the journal, Michael knew that the increased illegibility of the boy's chicken scratch was because Johnny had been absolutely shaking with grief as he wrote. Michael had no business knowing that, but somehow he did. He could feel it in his bones.

This feeling, this incomparable loss that Johnny was feeling right now—*No, it's not right now,* Michael had to remind himself forcefully; *it's almost a whole goddamn century ago*—was Michael's first experience with the chair recreating something for him that hadn't been expressly written down. It frightened him. And he had no idea what to do about it. As Michael shrugged his robe and slippers on, gasping at how thin and frail his hands had become, he decided to ask Mary about it if she was at dinner tonight. *Maybe I'm just imagining it*, he thought, rubbing harshly on his arms to try and warm up. He hoped he was imagining it.

Michael didn't even attempt to identify whatever was on his tray that he was supposed to eat for dinner. He just ate it mechanically, chewing only as much as was needed to swallow it down, trying not to breathe in while it was in his mouth. The smell was awful.

Thomas plopped himself down next to Michael at their usual table and voiced his hearty approval for the meal before digging in. *Maybe it's something Russian*, Michael thought blandly as he stared at the purple blob on his plate. He didn't want to eat something like this ever again. Thomas apparently didn't agree though, as he couldn't stop complimenting it. Michael watched, shaking his head in disgust, as Thomas cleaned his plate, tossed it onto the pile by the door, and then fished another token out of his cloth pouch to get a second helping.

Michael couldn't watch Thomas eat it again, so he turned away and looked for Mary.

She wasn't sitting with them, and from the looks of it, she wasn't planning on sitting with them either. Michael tamped down the spike of jealousy he felt as he watched her talking with a Minder that was leaning against the wall, tipping her head back to laugh at something he had said. The Minder's flash of white teeth as he grinned at her made Michael clench his hand around his bent spoon. He felt ridiculous, staring across a crowded room at a woman, acting like . . . well, like Johnny, actually. This is what Johnny did when Angel didn't sit next to him. Michael shuddered in distaste, and forced himself to peel his eyes away from the two adults by the wall.

Thomas was reaching the end of his second tray, and smacked his lips happily. He reached for his cloth pouch in the pocket of his robe again, but Michael shot out a hand and held on to the other man's wrist.

Startled, Thomas looked at Michael with confused eyes. "My friend?" His grey frizzy mane was hanging down into his eyes.

Michael shook his head at the Russian. "Don't, Thomas. You shouldn't use your tokens on this. You need to save them for tomorrow and the days to come." As odd as Thomas was, Michael didn't want to see the man starve himself in the next few weeks because he'd used too many food tokens too early. Unwittingly, Michael had started to think of Thomas as a friend, and he had no desire to watch a friend waste away any more than he already had.

Thomas looked mournfully at his empty plate, and Michael saw a flash of the sad man underneath. Thomas's depression from the days reading seemed to double; he looked absolutely heartbroken. Michael slapped the old man on the back a few times, then pushed his own tray over to him. Michael hadn't quite been able to stomach all of the purple whatever-it-was. Thomas's eyes lit up at the sight of the paltry offering, and Michael felt even worse for the man.

"Oh, many thanks, my friend Michael!" Thomas laughed, a deep belly laugh that was suited for a much larger man, and devoured the food that Michael hadn't been able to stand.

"No problem, my friend," Michael said quietly, slapping Thomas on the back again before closing his eyes. He wanted to clear his mind again. But he couldn't, and when the buzzer rang for them to go back to their rooms, his eyes popped open, and he looked immediately over to where Mary was, with that Minder. He ground his teeth together when he saw her take the man's hand and lead him from the room, practically skipping with glee. The Minder had a very happy look on his face.

Michael grimaced at the two of them and scraped his chair across the floor as he pushed back to leave. He was in a poor mood, and wanted very much to go to sleep.

16

We're done with math and English for a while, Ms. Maggie said. We're getting back into doing lessons regularly, and she also said that we're going to be writing more than we have been. She passed out textbooks for the first time, and they look brand new, so that's always exciting. It's nice to have something that hasn't been all scratched up and doodled in by someone else. It's a world history textbook, and it's got a map of the country on it with all sixty-three states and the years they were founded. I was staring at it because I thought there had been less—whatever happened must have taken that from me too. I don't understand how it works.

There's a soldier in the classroom with us now. When Jenn asked what was going on, he said he was only there to protect us. I don't know what he's protecting us from. We've already lost anything we had before.

Ms. Maggie introduced him after that, because everyone was staring at him. "Everyone, this is Mr. Grenley," she said. I thought soldiers were supposed to have their rank in front of their names, like titles, but then again our escorts are soldiers too, and we only call them by their first names. I don't know why we call them by their first names and we have to call this one by his last one. It makes me like him a little less, because it's like he's too stuffy to be friendly.

He's grumpy-looking, too, with really dark eyes and tan wrinkly skin that makes him look like a deflated football. His mouth is frowning all the time. He's got a gun on his hip, and he doesn't hide it under his shirt like everyone else does.

I'm actually a little scared of him.

Mr. Grenley came up to the front of the room to stand beside Ms. Maggie, and when he did it made Ms. Maggie look so ridiculously small. He might even be more giant than David. "Listen here, kids," (this didn't make me dislike him any less—I wish they wouldn't call us kids) "from here on out, each of you is going to need to write down exactly what you learned in class each day, and your thoughts on the subject matter." When he talks it sounds like barking. "You're going to turn in your journals every night before bed, and they will be reviewed for accuracy."

Everyone started talking all at once, angry, because Ms. Maggie told us before that these journals were only for us, and people like you who are going to come after us. This new rule sounds a whole lot like our journals are going to be graded.

One of the Jessicas shot her hand up immediately, and he pointed to her, asking her to stand up so he could hear the question. "Everyone else, shut your mouth."

Ms. Maggie looked uncomfortable.

Jessica with the black hair stood up, biting her lip, and said, "Who's going to read the journals? Is it you?"

"Speak up!" he barked at her. I was starting to hate him at this point. She said it perfectly loud the first time. If he can't hear well, that's not her fault, and he didn't have to yell at her.

She repeated her question, a little louder, but her voice was way shakier. He made her repeat it two more times before he was happy, and by then she looked like she was going to cry. After she sat down, Ms. Maggie crossed slowly over to her and laid a hand on her shoulder to calm her down.

"Oh, don't coddle them," Mr. Grenley complained.

Ms. Maggie drew herself up, looking angry. "You will NOT tell me how to treat my students unless it's endangering them, *sir*." They stared at each other for a long moment, both of them looking furious. I don't know why Ms. Maggie is letting him in the classroom at all—it seems like she likes him about as much as the rest of us do.

Finally one of them backed down . . . I don't know which one of them it was, because it looked like both of them relaxed at the same time. They still didn't look happy, but Ms. Maggie went back to comforting Jessica and Mr. Grenley went back to barking.

"For the time being, Ms. Maggie will review your journals. If there are any problems, such as if Ms. Maggie finds that you are not being diligent with what you students are supposed to be writing, the task will fall to me. When that happens, you will write your daily journals under my supervision after class each day."

My pen snapped in my hand, the ink bleeding out and making my hand black and sticky. Everyone turned to stare at me. I could feel my face getting hot, and started to wipe my hand on my jeans. Ms. Maggie just about dove across the aisle to catch my hand, "No no no, don't do that, you'll ruin them and we can't get any more." I stared at her, and I'm telling you now that I almost started crying. I don't even know why.

"Let's go to the restroom, right now," she said, and I nodded quickly. "Everyone behave for Mr. Grenley. I'll be right back."

The bathroom isn't too far from the class, so it was a short walk. Ms. Maggie waited outside while I washed my hands, and while I was in there I stared at the mirror really hard. I've gotten pretty fat being here, eating cake and cookies and crap food every day. But today I looked only tired. I guess I hadn't eaten very much.

When I was done I went outside, and Ms. Maggie was leaning against the wall, looking at her yellow high heels. I realized, standing next to her, that I've grown since coming here. I used to look up at her a little bit, but now, even with her wearing heels, we're about the same height.

"You OK?" I asked her, not wanting to let her stay upset if I could help it.

"Yeah. I'm great, Johnny." She didn't look up for a minute, so we both just stood in the hallway. I kicked at a rock that wasn't really there, pretended that it made it all the way down the long curving hall until I couldn't see it anymore, and then pretended that it went even further.

"I know," I started, kicking at another imaginary rock, and Ms. Maggie finally looked up, "I know you're not old enough to be a real teacher."

She blinked at me, silent, admitting nothing.

"I figure you were picked to be in the program just like the rest of us were. Only you probably already graduated high school, so they couldn't really put you in a classroom, and they didn't have any teachers available, so . . ."

She smiled a little. "You've got a good imagination, kiddo. I bet you'd write some pretty good stories." I shrugged.

I needed to ask her. "Did you lose your parents too?" I always thought it was weird when people said they lost someone when they died. That never seemed like the right word to use before. It's the right word now. We've lost the people from before, and we don't know where they went to in our minds. I'm pretty sure they died, from what Angel told me before, but they're not just dead, they're lost, too.

"I lost my mother, and someone else too . . . my fiancé, I think."

I frowned at her. "That sucks. I'm sorry." I felt really bad for her, and looked down at her hand. The ring that was there before was gone. She'd taken it off. Poor Ms. Maggie.

"Your dad?" I asked her.

She didn't answer me, but I watched as her eyes trailed back down the hall to the classroom.

"Huh. Maggie Grenley." She looked at me, startled, and I would've laughed if it hadn't been so sad. "That's kind of a cool name. Like a fairy tale character."

"How did you . . .?"

I grinned at her as big as I could. "I'm brilliant. Didn't I tell you?"

She did laugh at me then. "Oh, of course. I knew that." She shook her head at me, still laughing. "You're a funny kid."

"That, too."

I waited for her to finish laughing before I asked my next question, unsure if she would even answer it, but before I could get the words out she grew very serious and grabbed my shoulders so I would know just how serious this was.

"You need to keep that a secret, Johnny. No one is supposed to know that. You may not tell anyone. Do you understand me? Do you promise?"

I said, very steadily, "Did you want to come here, or did you want to stay? I saw you when it happened—you knew what was going on." I tried not to sound angry, but I think I might have. (Ms. Maggie, I'm not angry with you for knowing about it.)

She got quiet and sad-looking, then said, "Come on, let's go back to everyone else." She started walking down the hall.

I felt like crap, but I didn't follow her. "I promise!" I called out. "I wasn't going to tell anyone." And I wasn't. I just wanted her to answer the question I had.

She sighed and turned back to me. "Johnny . . ." She shook her head and put her hands on her hips. I don't think she was mad at me, but she was mad at something. "No one asked me."

I think maybe that's worse than asking not to be put here and having it happen anyway. My stomach hurt and I kicked at another imaginary rock—and missed.

"Now," Ms. Maggie said, back to normal and all smiley, "come on."

I followed her back to class and sat down. Mr. Grenley was at the board, talking about some war that had happened. I'd already missed most of the lecture, so I didn't pay too much attention. Ms. Maggie sat down at her desk and looked at her hands, ignoring Mr. Grenley.

17

The buzzer wasn't going off, but Michael was awake. He knew he hadn't been reading, not for several minutes. What looked up at him from the page had startled him out of the rhythm he always lost himself in when reading, knocking him out of the trance that the chair constantly forced him into, and he had sat for a very long time looking at this . . . thing. He had been searching his brain for a word that would describe it.

Lines of ink from Johnny's pen had bent and curved around the page, with no regard for the light, parallel lines across the paper that Johnny usually anchored his writing to. The swirls of ink didn't form letters, so Michael hadn't been able to read a lick of it. His brain ran in circles thinking of what it could be. Sweat broke out over his body as he began to panic, the thought of this alien thing more frightening than it should have been.

All of a sudden, as if Michael had breached the surface of a cold, deep lake, two words entered into his consciousness and he gasped, snatching them so they wouldn't flit away. The words cleared the mess of anxiety that had taken root in his mind, calming him almost immediately.

Drawing. His brain told him the first word, though he didn't know a definition for it. It must be one of Johnny's words, Michael decided. He must have read it and immediately glossed over it, not caring for the meaning. *Cathedral* was the other word. That held no more meaning for him than the first, but at last he had a name for this thing.

He spoke the words clearly, if haltingly, into the mic that hung before his face, and was disappointed when nothing happened. He had expected a deeper understanding would flood his mind, as if the words were a magic spell that would grant him enlightenment. There was none of that. He sighed.

The buzzer went off, and the chair released him with a *shink*, the tube loosening and the spike withdrawing from his spine. Time for dinner.

He eased his body out of the chair, groaning, and grabbed his tokens from off the bed. He was feeling more and more depressed by the day. When he tried to recall his mother, he saw only Johnny's. This was something that greatly disturbed him, but he pushed it out of his mind every time a thought such as this came up.

They came up often.

If he thought of nothing at all from before he came here, he would be better off. For now, he thought only of dinner.

The small pouch that held his tokens felt light. He peered inside, was dismayed to find that there were only six small silver rounds within. He only had three days to memorize the *cathedral*. He didn't want to forget what a beautiful thing it was. He wondered how Johnny had done it.

The cafeteria was loud already by the time he'd gathered himself enough to make it out to the hallway, keeping his eyes trained on his threadbare slippers. The other Archivists, in their sea of worn, cold grey, moved a little more quickly than they had the day before, eager to get food in their bellies, and he stumbled a little trying to match their pace. He could hear the clatter of people eating and talking bouncing down the curved concrete hall toward him, hardly muffled by the bodies that stood between him and Cafeteria C.

A loud peal of laughter bubbled up somewhere behind him like a gunshot, and Michael jumped, startled. He swung his head around to find the source, and as he did so, he noted in surprise that that quite a few of the Archivists had color on their faces, their eyes bright and aware. He stopped in his tracks, his mouth hanging open. They looked *human*.

"Excuse me!" an Archivist—a woman—sang brightly beside him, giving him a dazzling smile. Her brown hair, while slightly dull and tinged with white, was brushed neatly and pulled into a style that made her look terribly young, too young for her face. "So sorry, but could I get by you, please?"

"Your mouth!" he cried at her, staring at the deep purple on her lips, wondering what could have bruised her so badly.

She giggled and touched her hand to her lips. "Oh, do you like it?" She grinned again, flashing broken, grey teeth. "I had to make it myself, but the shade is *just* like a lipstick I have back home called 'Perfectly Plum.' Isn't it beautiful?"

She shot him a look that made his stomach clench uncomfortably, and he shrank back a bit before she skipped off toward the cafeteria. Michael felt sick. He always felt sick lately.

He found himself in line for his tray of food, dropping a token into the slot, taking his tray, and sitting down at a nearby empty table. He didn't want to eat, couldn't feel the hunger in his stomach, so he just sat with his eyes closed, listening to the people talk excitedly all around him while dread settled deep inside his chest.

At some point Mary sat beside him, but he didn't even notice until she put her hand over his own.

"Michael?" she asked gently, concern thick in her voice. "Mikey Moose, are you okay?"

He looked at her, his face wrinkling. "What did you just call me?" That nickname sounded strange coming from her mouth, but it felt familiar, too. He couldn't remember.

She blinked at him. "Michael?"

"You said something else."

"No, I didn't."

He glared at her.

Mary looked back at him, her head tilted to the side, eyes worried. "Are you okay?"

For a minute he said nothing. Then he sighed and scrubbed his hands over his face. He was so tired.

"What's a cathedral?"

Mary frowned at the table. "Um . . . It's a big church. Right? I think that's right."

He nodded. That sounded right. Once she said it, he knew exactly what it was. How could he have not known?

"And lipstick? Drawing?"

"Lipstick is paint that goes on your mouth. Drawing is . . . Why?"

"I know the word, but Johnny didn't write down what it was."

Mary looked uncomfortable. "We're not supposed to talk about the journals too much. If he didn't write it, you probably shouldn't know."

"But you told me the other two," he pointed out, agitation slipping into his voice.

"I shouldn't have. We can't talk about it." She shut her mouth and didn't say any more.

"Fine." But it wasn't. Michael put his pounding head down on the table and wished he could go back to his room, his tray of food uneaten. The little cloth pouch felt light in his hand. He was already mourning the missing, wasted token.

18

When Christopher Columbus sailed across the ocean to try to find a different land right before 1500, he ran into a country that wasn't a country yet, America. There were people there already, but they lived in the dirt and were sickly and didn't have enough food to eat. (Mr. Grenley said here that people who live in the dirt shouldn't, and that people who live in buildings should do everything they can to help them and get them living in buildings because that's how people are supposed to live.) Columbus came with a lot of food and medicine, and tried to save the Indians by making them healthier. The Indians used up so much food and medicine that when other ships started coming across the ocean from Europe years and years later, there was nothing for the pilgrims to eat. The pilgrims were so generous that they almost starved, but the Indians felt bad so they brought food that they had grown to share so that the people of Europe could continue to help them. This is where we get Thanksgiving: the Indians were so thankful that the pilgrims were so willing to help them, so the Indians decided to help the pilgrims, too (this was over a hundred years later).

After Thanksgiving happened, a lot of colonies started popping up all over the place on the east coast, and more and more people came over from Europe. These people didn't have medicine like we do today and they got very sick very often.

Many people died from not having the medicine, and because they all lived so closely together, the Indians started dying too. The colonists tried to get the Indians to move away, to the west, away from the colonies so they wouldn't get sick. But the Indians got angry, and a lot of them refused to leave. They tried to fight the colonists, who were only trying to help them, and the colonists had to fight back or be killed. Eventually, after many many years, the colonists were able to keep the Indians back, and they moved into the west. The colonists had won.

19

Michael dropped his last silver token into the meal slot reluctantly, and felt a piece of himself go down the hole with it. The journal in his pocket felt like lead. He wanted the token back, to give him another few hours with the drawings within the pages, but it was too late, and now there was a tray of steaming grey stew in front of him.

The food felt like ash in his mouth.

Neither Thomas nor Mary came to sit with him, but Michael could see Mary off to the side of the cafeteria, flirting with another Minder, and it only served to darken his mood.

Without him realizing it, he had finished his dinner and the buzzer was going off again with a screech. He walked woodenly to the Cage and surrendered the journal. He gave up the cathedral.

As he walked back to his room, Michael Driftveil cried.

_{Part} Two

The Sickness

20

He wanted to see the cathedral again so badly. There were more drawings in the later journals, but only a few, and none of them as detailed or as beautiful. Johnny called them doodles. Mr. Grenley had said he didn't approve of the drawings, that he wanted the kids to focus on recalling the lessons and recording them, and to do that Johnny had to pay attention to the lectures, not spend hours copying pictures out of the textbook. The loss of the drawing saddened Michael, and he carried that feeling around with him in his bones in the days that followed.

Finally he couldn't stand it anymore, and he did something he hadn't dared to do since he'd arrived. After he woke and ate (hurriedly, without seeking out either Mary or Thomas), Michael rushed to the Cage. He was so eager that he hailed down a Minder passing on a motorcart and asked for a ride on the back. Happily the Minder wasn't Buchanan, as he would undoubtedly have tried to ruin Michael's morning. After a few minutes, far shorter a time than Michael could have hoped, they reached the Cage and Michael hopped off the cart. The small woman behind the desk was surprised to see him.

"It's only been a few days," she said curiously. "Are you really finished already?"

He was surprised that she recognized him, as he knew that she must attend to all the other Archivists as well. But then again, everyone in this place seemed to recognize him.

"No, no, I'm . . ." His voice was rough. He was reminded of the Voice that had helped to sentence him, months ago, and the terrible, hoarse sound that had come from her abused vocal chords. And then, like smoke dissipating, she was gone, and Michael couldn't remember what he had been thinking about. He gritted his teeth in agitation, feeling the muscles in his neck tense.

The woman arched tiny, over-plucked eyebrow at him. Her big, shiny, silver coat made her look like she was wrapped in tinfoil—something Johnny used, Michael guessed, since he couldn't recall what the material was used for.

"I just wanted to see one of the journals I turned in a few days ago, please." He tried to be as polite as possible, but he still sounded like he was growling.

The woman frowned at him and tilted her head to the side. "Why? We can't do that."

He had to think fast. "I remembered a section that I skipped the other day. I started reading it, but the handwriting was bad, and I skipped it and moved on and now I want to try to give it another go. Could have been important stuff in there." He wasn't as good at lying as he had been back before they caught him. His voice shook—what was left of it anyway.

Her frown only deepened. *"You must never do that again!"*

Michael shrank back from her suddenly shrill, too-loud voice. He was apologizing to her almost immediately, tripping over his tongue. He bit it and he cringed.

She slammed her tiny fist on the enormous desk and shook her head, glaring at the wall behind Michael.

"I'm so sorry," he repeated, eyes wide. "I want to fix it."

"I'll have to call the director." She started moving away.

"What?" *Coleman!* "No, no, don't call her. Please, just let me have the journal back and I'll read the section and she doesn't have to know about it at all. I can fix it."

"You can't, though." She shook her head sadly, muttering to herself as she moved back toward the wire cage. "I can't believe that happened. The chairs are supposed to keep that from happening! They can't wake up without reading everything. They promised me, damn it . . ." Michael couldn't hear the rest of whatever it was she was muttering under her breath.

The woman reached through one of the spaces between the thick metal bars and picked up a black band—like some sort of utilitarian bracelet—off a small table on the other side. The librarian that was sorting journals at the table shook her head disapprovingly at him, her dishwater hair barely moving with the subtlety of the motion.

The tiny woman in the tinfoil coat brought the small band up to her mouth. "Director, can I have a channel?"

It's a wristcom, Michael realized with dread. *An old one.* He hadn't recognized it, it was so much bulkier than the com-patches most of the Republic's military used. Any second now, Coleman would come on and he would be screwed. He fought to keep his breakfast down, and considered running away, back to his room.

There was chatter on the line. Michael could barely hear it across the five-foot chasm that separated them now.

'Channel four, Librarian.'

Coleman's voice was high and cruel, and Michael closed his eyes.

After fiddling with the wristcom a bit to get it to the right channel, the librarian spoke again. "Are you there, Director? This is Jacqueline."

There was less static on the line now. Coleman's voice was crisper, and that that much more terrifying for it. "*I'm here. What's the problem?*"

"I've got an Archivist reporting he skipped a section in a journal."

Michael looked at the woman miserably, begging her with his eyes to take pity on him and put the com down.

"*Do we still have the journal?*" Coleman's voice was deadly calm.

"No, ma'am. It was taken to be burned last week."

Michael Driftveil vomited, the meager amount of nourishment he had managed to consume spilling onto the concrete floor. He didn't even realize he had done it; the librarian's words were still bouncing around in his head.

Jacqueline, her face full of crags and wrinkles and age, glared at him and wrinkled her nose in disgust. "Filthy Archivist," she sniffed. It was the first time she had really shown any unpleasantness toward him, and Michael felt shame wash over him, quickly chased off by horror.

It's gone? He didn't want to believe it. *They burned it? The cathedral is gone?* He felt like weeping.

"*How did he skip it? How is that possible?*"

The woman glowered at him harder, but he didn't care. "He says the handwriting was too bad." Her voice was like venom.

A moment of silence, and then Coleman's voice came through cautiously. "*Which Recorder wrote it?*"

"J. Gregory."

There was a long, long silence on the line now. Michael sat on the floor, right beside his puddle of sick, too shell-shocked to care. He put his head in his hands and waited for Coleman to decide his punishment.

Still nothing from Coleman.

After a minute, Jacqueline shook the little band impatiently, holding it up to her ear. "Director?" She shook it a little more. "Are you there, Director?"

Michael hoped the com had cut out before Coleman had heard that it had been his screw-up. Maybe he could leave now and nothing would happen to him. Maybe . . .

The little speaker in the wristcom popped and crackled, and he groaned.

"Thank you. I've sent a Minder to collect the Archivist. He should arrive shortly. I'm disconnecting the channel." There was a loud click as the connection was cut.

Less than a minute later he heard heavy footsteps behind him. He knew who it was before he turned around.

"Archivist, stand!" The command was barked at him and he was hauled to his feet, the Minder having less difficulty than if he were lifting a child's doll. The hand's iron grip cut painfully into Michael's arm.

Michael looked up wearily into Buchanan's cold eyes. The Minder was leering at him, his crooked teeth mere inches from Michael's face. The smell was horrendous.

"Heard you got into some trouble. Isn't that too bad. We'll have to make sure this doesn't happen again." He grinned.

Michael wrenched his arm away from the stronger man, and regretted it immediately.

The sadist blinked stupidly for a moment, then his eyes got impossibly angry and he grabbed his prisoner again. He dragged Michael out of the room and shoved him roughly into the wall as soon as they were clear of the doorway.

Michael's head bounced against the hard concrete wall, but he refused to cry out at the sharp pain that burst in front of his eyes. The Minder was looking for that, and Michael wasn't going to give it to him easily.

Grinning madly, Buchanan clutched at Michael's neck, pinning him to the wall.

The cathedral is gone. They burned it. How could they burn it?

Buchanan took his gun off his hip and flashed it at Michael, smiling as if it were a loved one. He pressed the barrel to the center of Michael's head.

Michael felt fear roil through him, but forced himself not to flinch, to keep his eyes steady and trained right on the Minder's.

"I could say you ran from me." The monster pinning him sneered, happily and cruelly all at the same terrible time. "No one would question it. Not really."

"Except that they'd be able to tell that you had me up against the wall, what with my whole brain being splattered on it and everything." *I can't believe those bastards burnt something so beautiful. Those monsters.*

The Minder scowled. "Like they'd really care about an Archivist being shot against a wall." He laughed.

"Coleman would care," Michael said quietly. He saw something new flash briefly in Buchanan's eyes. "Hasn't she told you how important I am?" He was bluffing, but from the brute's face he could see he wasn't incorrect. "She needs me alive, you idiot."

Buchanan took the gun from Michael's face and struck him hard with it, across the jaw. Michael would have fallen to the ground if he hadn't still been pinned to the wall. His ears rung.

"You're not *that* important, you prick," Buchanan growled at him, shaking him a little before bringing his knee up to collide with Michael's groin.

Michael groaned and his knees buckled. He started to choke from the rough hand constricting his airway, the only thing keeping him upright. Dark spots popped and swam in front of his eyes, trying to obstruct his view of Buchanan's elated face—the face of a child playing his favorite game—and Michael brought his skeletal hands up to try to claw the man's face off. His nails were jagged and dirty, and with meek satisfaction he heard Buchanan let out a high whine of pain, then a roar.

The hand around his throat released him, and he fell, down, down, to crumple on the cold floor. The Minder was kicking him, cruel boots colliding over and over again with Michael's legs, his ribs, his face.

God, how do I keep them from burning the rest?

Michael threw his arms over his head and neck, tried to curl up tight, tighter still so Buchanan would have a harder time killing him. He tried not to make any noise, but he didn't know if he was succeeding. He couldn't hear himself over his assailant's grunts and guttural curses, or over the sick thud of those shining boots hitting his bones.

21

Today the soldiers went outside the bunker to try to see what was out there. David went with them. Mr. Grenley had us line up in the hallway to watch them go past, even though Ms. Maggie didn't want us to look.

The hallways are very wide, but the soldiers were wearing so much gear that they kind of waddled like penguins or something and we had to squish ourselves way back against the wall so they wouldn't hit us. (I pointed out to a couple of the other kids that they looked like penguins, but only a few knew what I was talking about. Why didn't everyone forget the same things?)

Anyway, I could tell which one was David just because of how much bigger he was than anyone else. Seriously, I could climb on that guy like a jungle gym, he's eight feet tall. With the mask pulled over his face and tubes running out of it like snakes and into the backpack he was wearing, he looked like he could have been an alien. All of them had gloves up to their elbows and thick heavy boots and suits with grey and blue fabric (that black shape still above their hearts) that covered up every inch of skin they had. All of them, big shiny aliens with big bug-eyed goggles, sounding like air-conditioning units. I waved to David when I saw him, but he shook his head at me. Only his head was so weighed down he couldn't move it very fast, so it was more like a gradual turn from side to side. The other kids looked scared of the soldiers, but I wasn't.

When they had all made it through the hall, everyone was looking down the way they had gone, toward the outside, but I turned back and looked as Ms. Maggie. She was wringing her hands together and she looked afraid—not of the soldiers, of something else. (Ms. Maggie, are you OK? Nothing can get to us in here, and you don't need to be scared of anything out there.)

We made it back to the classroom, but Mr. Grenley and Miss Maggie didn't start up a lesson right away—they were talking quietly to each other—so we started shoving our desks into little groups to guess what the soldiers were going to find outside.

Little Jeff said that nothing is going to be different, that the soldiers are going to come back and all of this worry will be over nothing, and they'll tell us to go home. Natalie asked him, "Where is home, Jeffy?" and he got really sad and looked like he was going to cry, and got up to go write in his journal by himself. I glared at Natalie and told her that was really mean. She stuck her tongue out at me, but I saw her face and I know she felt bad. Angel didn't say anything.

Eventually Natalie got tired of us being boring and moved away to go talk to the Jessicas. She's not really in their little group, but she tries to be. I'm not in a group with anyone, except maybe Angel.

"You OK?" I asked her. I almost reached out to hold her hand, but she would have thought I liked her so I didn't. I drummed my hands on my knees waiting for her to answer, and I had to wait a long time because she had to think so long about what to say.

"I can't really feel sad, can I?" she said, but she still looked sad. "You all lost your families. I didn't, not yet."

I stared at her for a while, not really getting what she was telling me. "What do you mean?" That's when I realized that I hadn't even tried to talk to her about it yet. We haven't been talking much at all the last couple days, actually.

"I still remember my dad, so that means—" She shook her head for a while. "That means he wasn't in the city when it got hit, you know?"

"How do you know that?" I'm jealous of her, and a little angry, though it's hard for me to be angry at her because she looks so sad all the time. I want to remember my home and my parents. I've got a picture of a dog that my photo screen is stuck on, and I'm scared to reset it because even though I don't know the dog, I'm worried that it'll glitch out on me and it won't come back on. I don't know what other photos are on there—maybe ones of my parents—but I don't want to chance losing the dog.

Miss Maggie told us to strike through the remaining pages in the journals we'd been writing in before it happened. I didn't care too much when she told us, because I was still feeling weird and loopy and sad, but I didn't think to go back through any of the journals to try to remember anything before she collected them all and told us they would be kept safe. I don't know the dog's name, or my parents' names, but I would have written those down. Right? And Angel remembers her dad and I'm jealous.

"That's how it works. Watch, when the soldiers come back all they'll say is that there's a big hole in the ground with nobody in it. And no one outside will be able to remember what was there before, but it was some kind of city with lots of people, and nobody remembers them, either."

"That doesn't mean your dad wasn't there. What if you just think you remember him?" What if she's making it up?

"I remember him," she snapped at me, and I felt my face get hot. "His name is Peter. He's got brown hair but green eyes like me, and he yelled at me one time for dropping a full glass of orange juice and having it spill all over the floor because he told me to only fill it up halfway or I'd waste it. And he wasn't in that city because I remember him and he's not dead. So I can't be sad." But she started crying anyway.

"No lecture today," Miss Maggie said. "We're taking you guys back to your rooms. Boys with Mr. Grenley, girls with me."

And Angel shoved off from her desk angrily, still crying but trying very hard not to, and I went with Mr. Grenley to go back to my room. On the way back I asked him what the soldiers had found when the other attacks had happened on the other cities. He looked at me, and I was worried that he was angry. Especially when he had the other boys go to their rooms first, while I waited out at the end of the hallway. I started fidgeting while I waited, but he came back and crouched down so I didn't have to look up at him. When he did that, I could see that he really did look like Miss Maggie a little bit, and at my level he's not so scary. He asked me who told me about other cities. I know he can pull my old journals out and read them if he wants to, so I didn't try to lie. I told him that Angel's dad told her, and she told me. I don't want Angel to get in trouble, so I said that too.

"She won't be in trouble," he said, and I hope she won't be, because it was supposed to be a secret that she told me.

I asked him again what they found in the other countries that were attacked, but he just shook his head.

"There aren't any other countries now, John. Just us."

I asked him what he meant, because I can still remember the names of other places, like Mexico behind Longwall, so I know they still have to be there. But he told me that Longwall doesn't exist anymore either, so I shouldn't write about it. He said, "All that exists anymore is us." And he asked me if I understood.

I'm trying to understand, but I don't. I just want to know what happened outside.

Day 16

There was a war that happened in our country because some people from outside the country wanted to keep selling us slaves, and also because they weren't happy with how nice we were treating the people they sold to us. Mr. Grenley said that bad people sold their neighbors and family members over to us as workers. We paid for them, because if we didn't we were afraid that the sellers would sell them to another country, someone who wouldn't be as kind to them as we could be, and then we gave the workers food and water and places to sleep, and we made sure that these people could be with other people who had been sold to us, so they wouldn't be lonely.

But the sellers wanted us to be meaner to the workers, wanted us to call them slaves and hurt them. Mr. Grenley said they were very mad at us for making the workers think they were normal people. I watched Ms. Maggie's face while Mr. Grenley was explaining, and she looked sick and unhappy. The sellers sound like really terrible people, and it makes me sad that they could want to make other people feel that way. They came over to our country and invaded, and took the South, and we starting calling the sellers the Confederacy. The workers tried to run away from the Confederacy into the northern part of our country, but the Confederacy hunted them down and tried to drag them back to hurt them.

This was when we put our foot down, and we told the strangers that they had to leave our country and stop selling anyone, no matter what they were called, workers or slaves. The Confederacy got mad and started killing us, but we fought back hard, and eventually President Abraham Lincoln told everyone the Emancipation Proclamation, which let the workers join the Northern Army to fight against the southern invaders.

The Civility War lasted for four years, and lots of people died, but eventually we won and were able to drive out the invaders, and no one was a slave anymore, although the president was assassinated and that made everyone very sad for a long time. Mr. Grenley made a very big point about how lucky we are that we come from a country of such kind and gracious people, even back hundreds of years. He said that any other country would have taken advantage of the workers and would have abused them, but luckily they had been a part of a country that had fought to protect them.

The whole day was on the Civility War. There's a lot more stuff in the textbook about it, but we're not being tested so if I need to remember something I'll just go back and read it again.

At the end of the day Angel was frowning at her textbook though. I walked over to her, unsure if she was still mad at me, and waited for her to look up before saying anything, just in case she wanted to tell me to buzz off.

She asked me after a minute if I remembered learning any of the Civility War stuff in school. Her nose was all crinkled up. I told her I didn't really remember much of anything from school. "That's not because of the attack, though. I've always been like that, ha ha." I tried to make her laugh, but she didn't find it funny. Girls suck.

She told me, "I remember pieces . . . I used to go to school in a place called Savannah . . ."

I knew Savannah—that's in Georgia. I haven't thought about other places besides the bunker in such a long time, it's crazy.

"This textbook is *stupid*." She slammed the cover of it down and crossed her arms. I asked her what she meant and she put her head down in her hands.

"Johnny,"—she sounded annoyed—"that's not how it happened. That's not even what the war was *called*." She shook her head and made a noise with her throat like a frog being squished. Normally I would have been impressed, but coming from her it was just gross.

"Then what really happened?" I asked her. She can really be a know-it-all sometimes, even when she's wrong.

She frowned at me, and couldn't say. I crossed my arms and grinned at her, declared myself the winner of our little battle.

"You are such an *ass*," she snapped, then looked embarrassed for saying a curse word.

Jenn heard her. "Ooooooooooooo." She sounded like a monkey. "I'm gonna teeeeeeelllll."

"Shut up, Jennifer. Or I'll tell Mr. Grenley that you told me he was a fart bag." She didn't really say anything like that, but Jennifer's face still got really white before she scuttled off to another group.

Angel looked back to me and smiled, just a little. "I'm telling you, Johnny," she looked at me dead-on with her green eyes and my mouth got dry, "everything they're teaching us is wrong." She got her stuff together and left to go back to her room.

She sounds like a crazy person.

Day 17

The soldiers are back. They got back in late last night while we were all sleeping, and this morning after breakfast we were told that there wasn't going to be a lesson in class today. Instead, Mr. Grenley said he was going to tell us what they found outside.

"The only reason," he began. He sounded very serious, but not mean like usual. And he looked a little pale. "The only reason I am telling you all this is because I believe you are adult enough to understand it. If anyone doesn't think they want to know, let me know now. OK?" He looked at Jeffy, who just turned eight last month. Jeffy looked real tough, letting Mr. Grenley know he could handle it, but his lip shook a little and Ms. Maggie went to go sit next to him and hold his hand, just in case.

Mr. Grenley nodded. "Now," he said, "you all know that the soldiers left two days ago. They were going out to see what they would find out there."

We all nodded at him.

"What the soldiers had to report was that . . . it appears that we were attacked. Before the attack, there was a city outside which, according to our maps, was named Washington, D.C." (I remember reading ahead about that city in our textbook, but I didn't say anything because I didn't want to interrupt Mr. Grenley.) "This was the city that most of you used to live in."

I didn't like the way he said that, because he made it seem right away like we weren't ever going back. He doesn't know that yet. We could go back, someday, once it's safe.

"When the city was attacked, this bunker became the safest place to be. We're going to send out patrols in the coming weeks to locate survivors and bring them back here, to be kept safe with the rest of you."

"Why can't we remember?" Jenn asked. She's always the one with the first question.

"We're still trying to discover that." Mr. Grenley looked uncomfortable.

"Who attacked us? Are we going to go kill them?" Rock this time. He looked very angry.

"We don't know."

"When do we get to leave?" Angel asked. I looked at her, and she glanced my way at the same time. I wanted to tell her I was sorry, that she was right and I shouldn't have teased her, but I didn't.

Mr. Grenley looked flustered, and Ms. Maggie stepped up to the front.

"Kids," she said, "the soldiers are reporting that there are . . . things out there that are making it unsafe for us to go out. We're monitoring outside with cameras, and as soon as they're gone we'll make a plan—"

"THEY?" Jeffy said, squeaking. "You said things, but now you're talking about people? They're still there?" The kid's sharp.

"Not people, Jeffy," Angel said. "She's talking about monsters."

"Angel!" Ms. Maggie hollered, but she didn't say anything else. I kept waiting for Ms. Maggie to say that Angel was wrong, but she never did.

Everyone started chattering again, scared. I don't know how Angel knew that it was monsters, and I didn't ask. I just looked at her, and she looked right back at me. Maybe her escort told her.

Mr. Grenley and Ms. Maggie were talking quietly again to each other, I think trying to figure out what they were going to do. After a minute or two Mr. Grenley said that the day was over. I was happy, because I figured that we'd all just be able to get together and talk about what was happening without the adults listening to us, but they took us straight to our rooms and told us we couldn't speak to each other. They even delivered dinner to our rooms, so I've just been sitting in my room by myself for hours.

I don't know what's really happening, but I don't like it.

22

The buzzer was screaming at him again. How he hated it. His stomach clenched and gurgled, needing its host to feed it. Michael ignored the pain and stood from the chair carefully, shaking life back into his charred arm and rolling his head to ease the tension in his shoulders.

He wanted to eat and, shivering, he let himself think for a moment of the rice that might be in the cafeteria, or the meat he could buy with a token, pale and flavorless but nourishing and better than anything he'd had in a week. He'd decided, after the beating, that if he could hold out, keep himself from using his tokens until he absolutely needed to, he'd at least be able to buy a little more time before the journals had to be taken back to the Cage. Back to be *burned*. Michael shuddered.

He'd managed to convince Thomas, bless the man, to let him take the trays from the table to the pile by the door. There generally weren't any Minders looking that way, so he was able to hold the trays close to his face and inhale the scent of Thomas's food. Sometimes there would be a grain of rice, or a shred of a piece of pasta, and Michael would savor it, caressing the tiny morsel of food with his tongue and teeth until it was obliterated.

His stomach cold and hard like a stone, Michael lugged himself toward the cafeteria. The metal tray he had smuggled out of the cafeteria three days ago sat under his too-big shirt and robe, pressing hard on the thin skin that covered the sharp points of his hips. He'd discovered that not a single one of the Minders questioned him if he just held the tray on the table as if he'd already eaten.

He crossed through the line as quickly as he could, holding his breath to keep from smelling the food coming through the window. He was acutely aware of the little pouch in his pocket, with the lone, singular token inside, taunting him with its potential to grant him caloric bliss. He wanted to spend it. *Needed* to spend it, needed to eat. He shimmied the empty tray out from under his shirt and held it close to him, hunched over it so that no Minder would notice it didn't have any food on it. And then, depressed, he crossed the room and sat down at an empty table, hating himself.

Before long the Russian came to sit beside him, the man that had once been so slight and withered now starting to gain some weight. Michael was shrinking while everyone around him grew, and he felt anger flash inside him. He held the drawing of a lake in his mind and forced himself to relax.

Michael watched Thomas intently as he sopped up a brown, thin portion of soup with half a heel of hard, grey bread. There were carrots and mushrooms in the stew, which Thomas mushed into his tray with the crust of the bread until they were unrecognizable. The Russian complained loudly about the blandness of the broth, nudging his tablemate and looking for affirmation, but Michael didn't hear it. He just sat there, staring, clutching at his own empty tray, the light from the illum-strips glinting off the bare surface.

Despite his complaints, Thomas ate everything on his plate. Michael was starting to hate him, too.

When Michael offered to clear Thomas's tray, Thomas grinned at him, thanked him, and pushed it across the table with a scraping noise. Thomas either didn't notice or didn't care that he hadn't seen Michael eat in days.

Michael placed his pilfered tray underneath Thomas's and walked slowly to the door. When he was certain that no Minder was eyeing him, he hid the dish under his shirt again, shivering when it touched his skin.

When he reached the pile, he noticed with manic delight that there were a few drops of soup broth left in a corner of the recessed square at the top of Thomas's tray. Shaking in anticipation, he pressed his mouth to the metal and let the liquid touch his tongue. It was better than he could have imagined, and he kept that thought with him when the broth was gone, disappeared into his mouth, and he had to put the tray down to be cleaned.

23

People are starting to get sick. Not the kids in my class, but everyone else. We can see it happening, which is really scary.

I noticed it in David first. I looked at him a couple of days ago and he just looked *smaller*. He's a giant, like ten feet tall, but these last few days he's been just kind of hunched over and small. Normal sized. He doesn't look like he takes up nearly as much space as he used to, and he's started to forget things. Today he forgot to come get me for class, and I had to walk to class by myself so I wouldn't be late.

I'm worried that Mr. K has it too, because he won't let me come in the kitchen anymore to help cook. I miss it.

Our journals haven't been collected in two weeks, although Mr. Grenley is still as mean as ever. Now he trails off when he's talking though, and he gets this look on his face like he's lost and has no clue where he is.

I'm scared. The whole class is.

24

The weeks of hanging on to the journals until he couldn't take the hunger anymore had robbed Michael's body of the lean muscles he'd built up over his years of working on the farms. He had shrunk, he knew, folding in on himself and wasting away from the extreme self-imposed rationing. He could feel it. But still he tore himself away from the cafeteria, away from the smells and promise of nourishment, clutching at his empty stomach.

After dinner one night Michael stood in the bathroom he shared with the other forty-eight Archivists in the lower 600s, trying to convince himself that he had enough energy to make it back to his cell. Before him was a cracked mirror that was cloudy and speckled with black, but he focused on the weak stream of water that trickled from the dull faucet as he scrubbed. He tried not to look at himself whenever he had to wash his hands. He knew that since his hands were grey and lifeless, the rest of him must be even worse. He felt like a ghost.

Michael remembered being scared silly by ghost stories swapped between him and his friends before the lights went out in the bunker, all the boys clustered in groups in the hall, trying not to make too much noise in case one of the Minder escorts came and told them to go back to their rooms. Jeff had told him that his aunt's home in Louisiana was haunted and that when he was visiting her he'd wake up to find his shoelaces tied together every night, so he'd started putting one shoe downstairs and one shoe upstairs so that the ghost couldn't tie them to each other. Jeff claimed that the ghost had gotten so angry that one night it pulled little Jeffy off his bed and down onto the floor and his hand landed on a toy truck, leaving a big scar on his palm. He'd shown off his scar, shaped like a little checkmark, as proof. None of the boys, not even Michael, had dared question that.

Michael remembered that vividly, even though little Jeffy was probably an old man or dead by the time Michael was born. He knew it wasn't real. Michael tried to remember if he thought ghosts were real. *I don't believe in them,* he decided. *I know ghosts don't exist. Don't I?* Johnny's thoughts were taking up too much room in his brain, and it was becoming harder and harder to keep Michael's thoughts and Johnny's thoughts separate. Every day he felt himself slipping more.

I'm disappearing. Michael stared at his hands—his grey, cold hands, dirty no matter how much he scrubbed at them—and he wondered what his face looked like. He stood at the sink for several minutes more than he was allowed, expecting a Minder to barge in and yank him out of the bathroom, to hurt him and make him go back to his room so he would read more journals. A few more minutes, and still no one came.

He chanced a small peek at the glass.

And Michael Driftveil began to vomit into the sink.

25

The last few days, people have been disappearing.

I didn't think about it too much until one of the Jessicas pointed out that there are a lot fewer adults in the hallways than there used to be. She hasn't even seen her escort in two days.

I asked Ms. Maggie if there are a lot of people in the clinic, from being so sick. She told me that all the sick people have been moved to another sector, which is why the older kids are running the kitchen now. I hadn't even realized Mr. K was gone.

Ms. Maggie almost started crying, which is how I know she's lying. Something is very wrong.

We didn't have a lesson today because Mr. Grenley didn't even show up. Ms. Maggie just told us to read ahead in the textbook, but I wanted to trace pictures instead, which is why like the last ten pages are all filled up. I'm getting better at drawing, and it takes up more pages than just writing, which makes it easier. Hope you're okay with that.

I sat next to Angel and she told me that her escort is gone, too. I asked her, "What do you think is wrong with them? Where did they go?"

She looked at her journal for a minute, thinking, then said, "I think they're just too sad to come out."

I didn't say it, but I agree with her.

David came to get me at the end of the day, but then he saw how sad Ms. Maggie looked and asked if I could make my way back on my own. I said I could, but I really wanted to ask him how he was doing, and I was a little upset with him. Hopefully he'll let me ask tomorrow.

Day 94

Ms. Maggie and David are gone.

I found them, hugging each other, when I walked to class yesterday. I was the first one there.

I went to go get some adults for help, but I couldn't find any. So I ended up having to go get some of the older boys out of their rooms instead. Stephen, Jordan, and Chris. I didn't talk to them much.

I couldn't tell them what was wrong, so I had to show them. Then they were apologizing to me and telling me how sorry they were that they didn't get there first. They said that they've been trying to keep us younger kids from seeing. I helped them move the bodies to the garbage chute. I tossed the gun in, too, before the boys could tell me not to.

Stephen leaned down and asked me if I was OK. I told him I wished we could have buried them.

Day 98

I think the last of the adults are gone. They left us here, so we're alone now. There are forty-two of us. Stephen and Chris locked up the classroom so that no one will go in there anymore, but eventually we're going to have to figure out a way to clean it.

26

I'm going to die. I can't do this anymore. Michael shut his eyes against the buzzing from the wall, the screaming noise that dictated his life. He wanted to go back to being Johnny, to a place where he wasn't hungry all the time, a place where he could look in a mirror and not see the harsh indentations of skin stretched taut over the spaces between ribs.

He had the same nightmare when he slept now, over and over, and he wondered if it was driving him insane.

In the dream, he was Johnny—fat, healthy Johnny—eating cakes and cookies and pudding so sweet it would stick to his face and hands, and he was happy. He played with Lucy in the yard, the dog's fur so soft against his laughing face, surrounded by towering buildings and vehicles without wheels or tires, and his mother called out to him from the porch of the blue house. He could never see her face, but he knew as he ran to her that she was afraid. She would pick him up and bury his face in her hair—sometimes it was red and sometimes it was blond—and tell him not to look. And then the whole world would begin to shake.

Even though he would always close his eyes, he could still see the dark pinpoint opening up in the middle of the city, starting small and then growing, pushing everything in its way out farther and farther until everything was pushed too much and it was all crushed into nothing. The pushing caused hills to form around the pit, deep indentations in the earth like ripples in a pond. And he looked at the depressions, and he realized he wasn't a little boy but a man grown, and his mother was gone, and the hills, oh the hills were his ribs and he was so thin, and his name wasn't Johnny and he was alone and starving and he always woke up screaming.

He'd had that dream more than he could count now, and he was sick of it.

Michael stared at the journal that rested on the little tray in front of him. Pages and pages of this one were filled with drawings, now that there was no Mr. Grenley to yell at Johnny to stop. There was no anyone to tell Johnny he was doing anything wrong. The kids were alone.

Michael looked at the date of the drawing—Day 387, when had that happened?—that he'd passed a few entries ago. It was a girl, smiling, but not at him. Her eyes were fixed on something off-page. The likeness wasn't perfect, but Michael still felt such a strong sense of familiarity. He shook his head, trying to remember that *he* didn't know this girl, Johnny had. It was titled *Angel*, of course. Everything was Angel for Johnny. The kid had it bad.

Michael held the journal in his hands, rubbing the old leather on the cover with his fingers. How many journals had been bought for the program? The government had been prepared, at least for the most part. There were close to two thousand Recorders in the bunker, Mr. K had told Johnny, so all of those had to have enough journals waiting for them, empty, waiting to be filled. And this wasn't even the only bunker. Michael had a memory—his? Johnny's?—of being told that the government from before had facilities set up all over the country for funneling important people into. Those bunkers all had to have been stocked up, too.

Michael tried to guess how many journals Johnny had filled up in his time as Recorder. A hundred and fifty? Two hundred? Had that many been set aside for each person? Were there warehouses somewhere full of empty journals, waiting to be needed? The thought made him sad.

Or maybe the government had known that people wouldn't be writing for years and years, but only for a mere handful of months. Had they known about the sickness that would consume those who couldn't adapt? That thought made him even sadder.

Michael was on journal number fifteen. He felt his shoulders sag. He might spend the rest of his life here, the way things were going. He wasn't going to last much longer if he didn't start eating more.

A thought entered his mind, and once it was there he couldn't get rid of it. He chewed on his thin cheek, rolling the thought over and over in his brain, trying to see if there was another way. Michael didn't think he'd be able to survive the beating that Coleman would prescribe if they caught him.

He licked his lips, which were suddenly dry, and ran his thumb over the corners of the pages, bending them back slightly before letting them go so that they would fall back in line with their brothers, one by one. Johnny had used to make flipbooks in class, so that when he dragged his thumb over a corner, a picture would move across the pages, dancing. Michael's favorite was an early one Johnny had made on scrap paper, of a little black bird that leapt off the ground to circle a tall building before landing on a windowsill. Michael wished he could have seen that one, but all he had was a memory. It had probably already been burned before he was even born.

Michael squared his shoulders and sucked in a breath, flipping to the page where Angel's face looked out at the world. His fingers were shaking. Slowly, so slowly he wondered if he was even moving at all, he took the top of the page between his thumb and forefinger, close to the spine, and held it there. The paper felt too fragile when held like that, and it sent a round of sickness rushing through his gut.

Before he could change his mind, Michael exhaled quickly and began to pull down.

The sound that came from the journal made him cringe, and he worried that a Minder would hear from outside and come in and shoot him, so he tried to rip faster. That was a mistake. He tore out the page, but it didn't rip cleanly, and the bottom left corner of the drawing stayed bound to the rest of the journal. Michael cried out before clamping his mouth shut hard. He stared at that displaced corner and felt as if the wind had been knocked from his lungs. He tried to tell himself that it was just part of an empty spot on the page, that it didn't matter, but he knew it did anyway. *Carefully, Driftveil!* he scolded himself.

He held the page up to his face and stared. It was too light in his hands, but Angel was smiling happily still. Michael smiled back at her, then put her down on the little tray and began thumbing through the journal again, almost feverishly.

This time the ripping sound was exhilarating, and he took his time with it. The extracting from the binding went far better than he could have hoped, and now he was staring at a sketch of David, giant David taking up the whole page with his wide shoulders and sad smile. It wasn't titled, and didn't have as much detail as the drawing of Angel—Johnny had been starting to forget what David had looked like—but Michael knew it was him just the same.

Michael removed four more pages: a statue sitting cross-legged with a hand held up (titled *False Prophet*), a long wall stretching off into the horizon like a snake, a man yelling and standing on a podium in front of a backdrop of stars (*Leader*), and a sort of vehicle, all sleek lines and sharp angles, low to the ground where all four wheels rested. These were copied out of that textbook Johnny had, Michael knew. He held the sheaf of drawings together, his heart racing, and shut the old journal, praying it wasn't obvious that there were now several pages missing. If he stared at the top or bottom of the book, right by the glue on the spine, he could see little gaps where he had torn the drawings out. He hoped the librarian wouldn't notice.

Where to put the pages now? He hadn't thought of that at all. The smile slipped from his face. Slowly, Michael hobbled back over to his bed and crouched down. Johnny had seen this in a movie once, Michael thought, where a prisoner had needed to hide contraband and they had shoved it into the mattress. And Michael used to do it with his tickets in his hut, but his tickets had never been as important or as forbidden as the drawings were. He worried that sleeping on them every night would damage them.

Michael picked at a seam on the corner of the mattress, near the wall, just barely wide enough to get his hand through. The stuffing was damp, and he hoped the old ink wouldn't run as he slid the pages in, trying hard not to crumple them. He kept waiting for the door to fly open and to be caught, but no one came in, and soon he was covering the corner with the mat he had been given to use as a pillow, and making the bed with the thin grey blanket.

He tried to forget that in Johnny's movies the contraband was always found by a random room sweep.

27

He'd seen Mary around—in the cafeteria, and brief glimpses in the halls on the way to pick up more journals (she always looked away from him quickly, and he tried not to show his hurt feelings)—but it had been a very long time since they had eaten together. So when she sat down a seat away from him, he stared at her, surprised.

"Hi, stranger," he said dryly, before returning to his plate of food. It was gone in moments, disappearing too quickly into his mouth before he had really even looked at what it was. He stared at the empty tray mournfully, but his stomach was quiet, so he didn't go back for more.

Mary was eating more slowly, looking around the room as she chewed. "Where's Thomas?" she asked quietly, never looking at Michael. It was like she didn't want to appear to be sitting with him at all.

Michael blinked, and looked up at her.

"Don't," she warned, and he looked back down at his grey hands resting on the table, gripping the tray.

"I haven't seen him in a while." And he hadn't. Michael hadn't even realized that Thomas wasn't eating with him anymore—he'd been too preoccupied with his sudden income of meal tokens to notice. "Did he get released?" Michael was happy for him and jealous all at once.

"I . . . thought he had more journals left." Something crossed over Mary's face—he could see it out of the corner of his eye. "He must have been sent home, yeah." But she sounded sad, and Michael frowned at his hands.

"What's wrong, Mary?"

She shook her head, so he left it alone, still frowning.

When the buzzer went off he offered to clear her tray, out of habit. Mary looked up at him in surprise before pushing it toward him and rushing out of the cafeteria. Michael looked after her curiously.

The other Archivists started filing out of the cafeteria, chattering all the while. There seemed to be fewer of them now, which meant that people must really be finishing their sentences and heading home. He shook his head as he dropped the trays, one of the very last to leave. He'd be the last one to be released, too, out of every Archivist currently reading. They'd all be gone soon, and he'd stay behind for years. He shuddered.

Just before he left the room, a low laugh reached his ears from up ahead, and he stopped, listening. He knew who that laugh belonged to, and he didn't feel like getting his ribs kicked in today.

"Stop, that's awful," a different voice groaned, and Michael's muscles tensed. He wanted to run.

Buchanan only laughed harder, and Michael pressed himself into the wall, his skin crawling.

"Oh, man," Buchanan guffawed, "his face when he realized he wasn't going home! When he saw my gun!" More giggles.

"That's sick, man. It's not his fault he was contaminated. You're fucked up."

"*Not his fault?* Are you shittin' me? Of course it was his fault! He's the one who landed his ass in this place to begin with. He got sentenced just like every other piece of shit here, his Recorder just knew a little bit more than the others. You shouldn't be surprised— the Russians always know some bullshit they shouldn't."

Russian? Michael clenched his fists at his sides, his dirty, jagged fingernails cutting into his palms, and he held his breath. Suddenly he could hear the blood in his ears.

"And that thing he did with his voice—Christ, it sounded like he had rocks in his mouth."

Buchanan's voice was vicious as he began chuckling again, and Michael's dinner began to roil in his stomach. He didn't want to understand what they were saying, wished he could forget he'd heard it.

"He wasn't sentenced to *die,* Buch, Jesus. Just to read. Just to be Resurrected. *Fuck."* Michael heard the man walking away, boots clicking on the concrete.

"Yeah? Saying shit like that is why the old lady never puts you on decontamination. I'll just keep at it, keep all the fun to myself!" Buchanan shouted at the other man as he walked away.

Michael closed his eyes, thinking of the small man who used to eat with him. When had he seen him last? How many days? Three? Four? And now he was gone.

"What the *fuck* are you still doing in here?"

Michael's eyes flew open, and he found the Minder's face inches from his own, at first deathly white but then turning red in anger.

Michael's blood went cold. *He knows I heard him.* He looked around for help. There was none.

"Hey! I asked you a question, goddamnit!" Buchanan wound his hand back, ready to cuff Michael's jaw. The bastard always went straight for pain.

Michael thought fast. He flinched and cried out. "Wait! Where's Mom?"

Buchanan's fist was already in motion, but surprise drained all the power from his swing. Even so, when the fist connected with Michael's jaw, it was hard enough to make his ears ring.

"What?"

Michael was woozy from the blow, but he stayed standing. "Do . . . Do you know where my mom is?" He tried to make his voice as small as possible, tried to make himself cry. It was easier than he would have liked to admit, but he was hoping it was going to save his life, and within seconds he had snot and tears running down into his mouth, his shoulders shaking as he wailed.

"The fuck? How old are you, asshole?"

"Tw-twelve. Where's my mom?" He kept crying, hugging himself and bouncing around on his feet. Johnny never acted like this, but the idiot standing in front of him didn't know that.

"Aw, hell." Buchanan's shoulders sagged. "Stop crying, will ya? Jesus."

Michael still hated the man, but it was interesting to note that the Minder didn't seem to want to beat a child—not even a child in a man's body. Michael hadn't pegged him for the gentle type, but he was glad his bluff seemed to be working.

Buchanan looked uneasy, and he raised his wrist to his mouth. "Can I get some help in Cafeteria C? Some guy just Resurrected right after dinner. It's . . ." He peered closer, his eyes widening when he recognized Michael through all the snot. "Fuck, it's six-twenty-two. I need help ASAP, he's looking for his mommy." Buchanan sneered at Michael, his lip curling in disgust.

"*I'm on my way*," came a crackling voice from the Minder's wrist, and Michael stared at him, letting big tears roll down his face, breaths shuddering through his body.

Buchanan looked like he might be sick, and he leaned his body out the doorway to see how far away help was. He scowled at Michael, and then a thought crossed his face.

"Hey, kid," he said, his face still uneasy but his eyes glittering with something dark, "what do you know about the weapon, huh? You know anything about that yet? Where it is? You can tell me, and I'll take you to your mom."

Michael's blood ran cold. *He's feeling me out.* He let a big sniff buy him a few seconds more. The Minder wrinkled his nose at the sound. *That's what they want to know.*

Michael shook his head, keeping his eyes wide. "Huh? Weapon? Like my BB gun?" He didn't know what that was, but it sounded right. Must have read it a while ago.

"*No*, not like your stupid BB gun, like a big-fucking-hole-in-the-ground weapon, you idiot." Buchanan shook his head angrily. "Look, when you hear something about it, why don't you come find me? All right?" He tried to sound pleasant, but just couldn't quite get his voice to cooperate.

Yeah, I'll hop right on that, Michael thought. He stared down at his shoes, worried that if he looked at Buchanan any more the man would notice how much hate was behind his eyes. This was the man who'd drugged him on his first night. This was the man who'd beat him half to death for saying he skipped a section of a journal. This was the man who'd shot his friend, and the man who'd made it very clear that he wouldn't hesitate to do the same to Michael.

"Buch?" Another familiar voice from the hallway. "You still need help?"

Michael glanced up. It was Cyrus, looking at him with worry in his eyes. Michael quickly dropped his gaze back down.

"Yeah." Buchanan stepped back and started to walk away. "Could you take this baby back to his room? I don't want to deal with his snot everywhere. He's trying to find his mom." Michael just barely heard him mutter under his breath, "I can't decontaminate a fucking kid. Jesus."

Michael began to shake. There was no longer any more need for acting. The scared tears in his eyes were now real as well.

"Hey?" Cyrus leaned down to meet his eyes, "You okay, kid? What's your name?"

"Johnny," Michael whispered, shuddering.

Cyrus didn't say anything or make any move to go. After a minute, Michael glanced up.

"No." Cyrus sighed. "You know that's not your name. Your name's Michael. Isn't it?" Cyrus waited.

He knows I'm lying. "I'm Johnny. Do you know where my mom is?"

Cyrus's eyes grew colder. "No. But come on, we'll go back to your room."

It was easier than Michael expected to keep the tears coming as they started back to his cell, but still the walk seemed much longer than normal. He knew how ridiculous he must have looked to Cyrus, even more so because he could tell the Minder knew the whole act was a lie, but he still couldn't seem to make himself stop sniffling and blubbering like a child. He was humiliated. He was mourning his friend. And he was scared.

They spent the walk in silence, save for the sounds that came from Michael without belonging to him. Maybe he *was* Resurrecting and just didn't know it, and that's why he couldn't stop crying. The thought made him sob harder, and he wrapped his arms around his middle to comfort himself.

He thought of Johnny, and how scared and angry he felt all the time, and how he hadn't cried since he'd been sent away from home. And then he thought of Lily, who almost seemed like a dream now, so far away and hazy, and her small face when she got scared. How her green eyes, her grandmother's eyes, lit up when he brought her a present. He had once saved up luxury tickets for six months to buy her a little toy for her birthday, despite Jonah's warnings that he shouldn't. And she had loved it, which had angered Jonah and thus made it a greater success, but he couldn't remember what the toy had been now. So he cried for the loss of that memory, and then he wept for the impending loss of the other memories he still had, and then he wailed for the memories he'd never get to have.

By the time the door to cell 622 finally slid upward, he was mercifully all cried out, and only little shaking gasps escaped from him here or there. He felt better for having cried. It felt like that sadness had been pent up inside him for an eternity.

But before he could retreat into his room, the Minder caught the sleeve of his robe. Michael looked at him questioningly, his face still wet.

"I thought," Cyrus said, looking hurt, "you knew I'm not like Buchanan. You didn't have to lie to me. I wouldn't have hit you."

Michael said nothing. He didn't want to admit to the lie, so he just looked.

"I'm Mary's friend," Cyrus continued. He said it like that should explain everything. "She told me you stole something. That she thought it was a mistake you were sent here. Is that true?" He waited for an answer.

Michael studied the Minder. Cyrus was still just a kid. The Archives would have been his first assignment after moving from his family's home. *What a horrible place to be assigned.*

"I—" His voice was rough and he had to clear his throat. "I wasn't supposed to be sent here." *I was supposed to be killed.* "But I don't think it was a mistake. I think it was a choice someone made." He'd been kicking the thought around in his head for a while, but it was the first time he'd said it out loud. The sound of the confession startled him.

Cyrus drew in a deep breath. He looked uncomfortable. "If that's true," he fidgeted with the gun on his hip, and Michael winced, "then you were sent here for something important. Mary and I talked about that, too."

Michael was suddenly jealous of all the time Cyrus seemed to have been spending with Mary, but he pushed the feeling down and out of the way. The kid was trying to say something significant, however slowly it was coming out of his mouth.

"Archivists who read important things don't get to go home,"
Cyrus said, his lips pressed into a thin line. "I know you must have
heard us in the hallway. You won't go home. You'll go see
Buchanan, and you *won't go home.*"

Cyrus couldn't bring himself to say any more, which was fine
with Michael, because his ears were ringing anyway. Cyrus had just
flat-out confirmed what Michael had been fearing for the last half
hour or so: Coleman was going to have him killed.

Cyrus nodded at him, his eyes sad. Then he turned and left, and
Michael was alone.

28

Michael took the map out of his pocket, where it had been nestled with the drawing's he'd carefully removed from his mattress, the blood rushing in his ears. It was after lights-out, but there was a small sliver of a golden beam spilling in under the crack between the door and the floor. He slipped from his hard mattress and onto the cool grey—Johnny knew it was "concrete," so Michael knew it too—and lay on the ground, taking great care to keep his right arm, the plated one, as far away from the door as possible. He didn't want the door flying open when he wasn't ready.

He could see his room on the map, the star Mary had drawn for him in the lower 600s. He traced the curve of the hall with his finger, trying to orient himself, and then followed the path he could take to get to Mary.

Come see me if you need any help, she had said as she'd tapped on the square she'd added to the drawing.

Michael smiled grimly. He certainly needed her help now. If she didn't help him escape, he was going to disappear; too many pieces of him had already been chipped away and sculpted into somebody else. And Coleman would use him, and then Buchanan would finally do what he'd been promising since Michael's first day. He tried not to imagine how it would feel when the bullet tore through his head.

Michael shrank back from the door as a shadow crossed the light. Heavy footsteps. Not an Archivist, then—one of the Minders looking for people outside their rooms past curfew. He held his breath until the footsteps faded.

Closing his eyes against the dark, he wondered if he had gone insane. They were going to shoot him as soon as they saw him. What was the point of escaping the execution Coleman had planned for him if he was going to be shot anyway for his attempt?

For many long minutes he hesitated, just lying on the cold floor, his heart hammering in his chest as he weighed his options. The fingers of his left hand roamed across the rough cloth of his map, and he could feel the wax of the crayon Mary had used to make it for him. How had she known how to do that? To make a diagram to lay out the hallways for him? He'd never seen anyone do something like that before, and she had just sat down and done it without a second thought. He started wondering, chewing on his tongue: could he draw like that? Johnny could, so shouldn't he be able to now? Mary had to have learned it from one of her previous projects.

As soon as I get out of here, Michael promised himself with a dark feeling in his soul, *I'm going to sit down with a piece of paper and waste it. I'm going to see if I can draw.* The notion was mouth-watering. He wanted to be able to create something as beautiful as the cathedral.

His thoughts were interrupted by more footsteps, this time heading in the opposite direction. Michael held his breath and counted in his head, only daring to breathe again when the footsteps were gone. He leaned his head on his left arm, keeping the Archivist plate behind him still, and focused on the numbers running through his mind. He tried to count as steadily he could, and hoped that his nervousness wouldn't speed him up and give him an inaccurate estimate.

Two hundred and ten seconds later—he hoped that was right— the heavy footsteps and dark shadows crossed his little shred of light again. He tried to do the math in his head. That meant that it had taken the Minder three and a half minutes to make the circuit from his door to the end of the hall and back. Which gave Michael a minute and forty five seconds during which the Minder was facing away from his door. But could Michael even make it out of his room without the Minder hearing? He didn't know.

Michael felt like he was going to be sick again. *Coward!* shouted his brain.

He waited until the shadow passed him one more time, then counted to fifteen. He tried to count slowly, deliberately, as he slowly crept to his feet, readying himself to run. His lungs already burned.

. . . thirteen . . . fourteen . . . fifteen . . .

Michael stepped forward with his right arm outstretched, and the door whooshed open to let him pass. He jerked his head to the right to make sure the Minder hadn't seen him, then ran as silently as he could.

He was barefoot, and immediately regretted it. All night he had worried that his slippers would slow him down, and now—too late!—he wished he had the soft material between his feet and the concrete to mask his footfalls. He was running out of time, he knew, and the hallway he needed to turn down was still so far away. Any second now the Minder was going to turn around and see him, and he would be shot, and he would bleed out all over the concrete and no one would even know he had died . . .

Shaking, he reached the hallway and ducked into it, certain he had been seen. He flattened himself against the wall just past the corner and waited for the Minder to call out, to run him down. He waited for the gunshot. *Maybe* . . . Should he move down the hall? He eyed the long length of the connecting hall and dismissed the idea almost immediately. He didn't want his motion to catch the Minder's eye in case he had really gotten away with that mess of an escape.

He wanted to gasp in air, to pull the stale recycled oxygen into his burning lungs, but instead he clapped his hands over his mouth and forced himself to breathe in shallowly. It hurt. But being discovered, if he wasn't already, would hurt worse.

When he heard the Minder's footsteps coming toward him, he trembled. He was freezing.

The Minder, miraculously, walked past the hallway without even glancing to the side. There were no rooms in the connecting halls, and it must not have even crossed the Minder's mind to check that way. Michael couldn't believe his luck. Head buzzing, he slipped farther down the hall.

The map was crumpling in his hand. Michael hastily unclenched his fist and checked to make sure the drawing hadn't been damaged. In the past several months he had become comfortable with his daily route between his room and the cafeteria, with occasional detours to the Cage, and perhaps he hadn't been as careful as he should have been with the drawing. The map had been done in red wax, which hadn't adhered particularly well to the rough fabric, and now it had flaked away in places. Michael inspected his path again to make sure it was still legible. He couldn't afford to be lost tonight.

As Michael reached the next intersection of corridors, his stomach tightened. He could hear voices, and hoped they were just echoes of someone in a different arc of the bunker. He slowly poked his head around the corner to check if there were any eyes that could see him—and immediately drew back, almost cursing aloud before he could catch himself.

No, no, no. He squeezed his eyes shut so hard he wondered if he'd ever be able to open them again.

There was a whole pack of Minders standing at the end of the crossing corridor, talking quietly to each other. There was no way he could pass through the intersection without at least one of them seeing him. He popped his eyes open and stared helplessly to the opposite side of the intersection, directly in front of him. He needed to go that way to get to Mary, and three yards was all he needed to get there. But those three yards would get him spotted and killed.

He was grinding his teeth so hard, his jaw hurt. It was too late to go back—he didn't think he could avoid the Minder patrolling his section a second time, and that would lead to him getting shot, one way or another. It might be immediate, or it could take weeks or months or even—Michael shuddered—years. And even if he could somehow make it back to his room safely, he knew he would never work up the nerve to get away again.

And if he went forward . . . ? He guessed there was a ninety-five percent probability that he'd soon have a barrel trained on his chest.

He grabbed on to that other five percent and held fast. Taking a steadying breath, he shoved the map into the pocket of his worn robe and readied himself to run. There was no way for him to tell if any of the Minders would be looking his way. He was just going to have to run blind.

Sucking in a breath between his teeth, Michael dashed out from the hall and scrambled across the wide corridor. The three-yard distance stretched on for miles, and he crossed it for hours. When at last he reached the safety of the hallway on the opposite side, he was exhausted. He leaned over with his hands on his knees, willing himself to not be sick. His body ached from how tightly his muscles were wound.

He didn't hear anyone coming for him, which was nothing short of amazing. He shook with relief. Now he just needed to go down the hall and a few doors to the left—

"Hey, what is it?" A voice from the end of the corridor.

Michael froze.

"Uh . . ." The voice was high and needling, uncertain. "I thought I saw . . ."

Footsteps. Coming his way.

And quickly.

"*Shit.*" The word was out before he could shut his damn stupid mouth, and then Michael took off running. If the Minders were unsure whether they had seen him before, there would be no doubt now that they had heard that little slip-up.

He reached the next intersection.

"Hey!" A Minder had turned the corner behind him, could see him plain as day. "Archivist, *stop!*"

Screw that, Michael thought as he scrambled around the corner and ran down the next hallway toward Mary's room.

"Please be awake, please be awake." He pounded on her door, knowing that at any second the Minders would pour around the corner and see him at her door.

Mary's door flew open before him, a pissed-off-looking Mary behind it. Her eyes widened. "*Michael—*"

He grabbed her shoulders and pushed her back into her room, hoping the door would slide closed behind him before his pursuers could see it.

"Hide me," he whispered. "Mary, Mary, please help me, please."

God love the woman, she didn't hesitate at all. Michael could have kissed her.

She pushed him toward her bed. "Shirt, *off!*" she hissed.

"What?"

She shoved him down on the mattress—it was so much softer than his—and threw the blanket over him up to his shoulder.

"You're asleep. Face the wall." She was inches from his ear.

There was a knock on the door. Michael screwed his eyes shut and tried to take deep, slow breaths. Sleeping men weren't usually gasping for air.

Mary counted to three under her breath, then slowly walked to her door. Michael heard it *whoosh* open.

"What?" Her voice was sharp and irritated, tinged with sleep.

"Mary." The malice in the Minder's voice had Michael ready to bolt again. Michael hoped his shaking wasn't visible from the doorway.

"Good lord, Buchanan, what do you want now?"

A shuffle of clothing, a person shifting his weight from one foot to the other. "Mary, have you seen anyone tonight?"

She scoffed. "God, you really are dense, aren't you? Of course I have. He's sleeping, what do you want him for?"

"Uh . . ." Michael heard people shuffling into the room.

Mary's voice was all of a sudden low and angry. "Why are your friends here, Buch? Planning on starting some trouble?" There wasn't any answer to her question, which sent a chill down Michael's spine. "I'm allowed to have my visitors—and you know full well that you're not one of them." Her voice was dripping with insult.

Michael could practically hear the man's blood boil. "Listen here, bitch—"

"No, I will *not* listen here. You get the hell out of my room, you slime-covered pig. Trevor here isn't a very heavy sleeper, and he's a real jerk when he's woken up early. *And* he doesn't like sharing. Do you really want to come in here and demand something from me, with him inches away? *Get. Out.*"

"Mary, that's not why we're here. Please." Another Minder.

Cyrus, Michael thought with a start. Hell, what if he recognized him? Tension coiled tighter in his chest.

"Really, it's not?" Mary's sarcasm was palpable. "Buch is looking like he has a different story. But please, enlighten me, Cy."

"We think there's an Archivist outside his room." Michael heard Mary suck in a breath in alarm—very convincing. "We heard him, and James spotted him running down this hall."

"Oh." Mary's voice had gone soft in a heartbeat. She sounded worried. Clever woman. "Does he have weapon? Or—"

"We don't know that yet. But it could be anyone." A pause, then, "Mary, you okay?"

"Huh? Oh, god . . . yeah. Am I safe here? Are you going to go find him? Do I need to move? God, what if he has a knife from the cafeteria . . . or a *gun?*"

"Did Trevor have his gun on him?" It was Cyrus again.

"Yeah, on the table there."

"He'll keep you safe. You'll be fine."

"Wouldn't want his toy to get broken," Buchanan sneered.

Michael contemplated leaping from his hiding spot and throttling the man.

"Buchanan, *enough.* She doesn't have to like you, man. Let it go."

"She's a bitch. Why would I want that near me? Probably all worn out anyway. Plenty of Archivists left in my batch that still look like women and can be—"

Mary went from scared to furious in an instant. "Cyrus, get him out!" This was followed by a thump, as if she had thrown something at someone, and a muted grumble.

The door *whooshed* open again, and there was more shuffling as the Minders filed out, with Buchanan still muttering under his breath.

After a moment, Mary spoke. "Cyrus?" Her voice was much quieter now.

A pause. "I'll stay out here to watch your door, just in case."

Great, Michael thought, his teeth grinding again.

"Oh, thank you. Thanks."

The door closed, and Michael allowed himself a sigh of relief. But he held still.

Mary came and stood over him. "Michael," she whispered. "What the hell is going on?"

Michael sat up slowly, afraid that any excess noise would bring the Minders back. "I need you."

She scoffed. "Well, you sure do know how to treat a woman, don't you?" She shook her head, walked to a table in the corner, and leaned a hip against it, crossing her arms and studying him. "You really thought the best way to do this was to force your way into my room in the middle of the night? Have you lost it?"

Michael shook his head in disbelief. "Hell, that's not what I meant!"

The small woman just pursed her lips at him and waited. Her black hair was loose around her shoulders, free of the braid it was normally plaited in. The dark curtain around her face made her look much younger than he had previously thought. He had guessed once late twenties, early thirties . . . now he wasn't sure.

He hesitated as he gathered his thoughts, trying to frame his words in a way that would make her believe him. "They're going to kill me, and I need you to get me out of here." He could have kicked himself for the weak way his voice tossed the words out of his mouth, with none of the urgency he had meant to inject them with.

Mary rolled her eyes. "Michael, this again? Are you serious?" Her dark hands moved up to the sides of her head, as if she had to hold it together in the face of the sheer stupidity that was Michael. He could see his chances of recruiting her dwindling by the second, but he couldn't get his brain to work fast enough.

"I know you don't like this, but it's *punishment*," she said. "You're not *meant* to like it. But I swear to you, it's not that bad. I'm in the middle of my seventh project, and aside from some scrambled-up memories and emotions, I'm doing just fine when you really look at me—"

He cut her off. "I was sentenced to go through Johnny's journals, and I get that. I'm not talking about the side effects of the process here, Mary. I'm talking about a bullet in my head." Thankfully, his voice had grown stronger, and she actually stopped talking and looked at him.

"We're not going to shoot you! What are you talking about?" But there was a shake in her voice that made Michael's blood turn to icy slush.

"*You're* in on it?" He couldn't keep the hurt out of his voice. "Mary, you know what they do to these people?"

Her brows drew together and she was chewing on her lip again. "No . . . I mean—" She pulled a deep breath into her lungs, and didn't look like she wanted to be talking any more.

"How could you go along with this?" Michael asked, confused. "The tech alone already destroys our minds." Mary started to protest, but Michael kept talking. "And then when we're done, they take us out and shoot us! Are you really so cruel?"

"I never had any proof." Mary's chin was set, defiant. "Not everyone who's scheduled to be released ends up back at their compounds. But I don't know that they're *killed*." Her voice was sad, but her face was only angry.

"Coleman has them shot," Michael said. "They shot Tom." His gut twisted in anger. "I heard some of the Minders talking about it. Buchanan did it."

Mary squeezed her eyes shut and trembled. "Fuck."

Michael blinked, not realizing that she had it in her to curse. "Mary, please help me get out of here. You're the only one who can come and go without suspicion."

She shook her head, and when she looked at him, Michael could see that there were tears in her eyes. "You can't go."

"I'm going."

She actually stamped her foot at him, and let out a long high-pitched whine in her anger. Michael stared, trying to reconcile this childish behavior with the woman he knew she was. It didn't fit, and his head ached.

"If you don't help me, they *will* catch me," he said. "They'll kill me on sight. And if I don't try to escape, they'll kill me regardless. Coleman wants something out of Johnny's journals, and she wants me killed as soon as I find it."

That caught her attention. "Do you know what she wants?"

"It has something to do with the weapon that made the crater, that's all I know."

Mary groaned and shook her head. "That could be anything!"

"I know, but . . ." Michael didn't know what else to say. The truth was, he didn't really have any reason why she should help him. His head was buzzing again. "You're not going to help me, are you?"

She stared at him for a long time. With each second that ticked by, Michael knew he was losing ground, and losing time before they discovered him out of his room. How long until breakfast? He didn't know. His sense of time had been shattered by being so long in the bunker, where he couldn't look to the sky for the normal cues of day and night. It had crippled him.

A cold thought struck him all of a sudden, and he sucked in a breath. God, would it even be night when—*if*, he corrected himself—he got outside? He had structured his whole plan on the idea that he could get away from the Archives under cover of dark. But what if the buzzers weren't timed to a normal daily schedule? He had never seen any sort of clock in the building, not even in the cage. The buzzers—and consequentially the schedule that all the Archivists followed—could be timed exclusively to the whims of Coleman or some other military figure. What if he got outside and it was midday?

A wave of nausea crashed over him. He was going to be shot. There was no way for him to avoid it. All paths led to a bullet in his head.

Mary watched the thoughts flit behind his eyes with something like pain on her own face. Slowly, she crossed over to the door. Too late, Michael realized what she was doing.

"Mary, no!" But it was done. Her arm was out, and Michael could only watch with horror as the portal slid open. He was screwed.

The Minder was standing in the doorway with his back to the room, the great blue fatigues taking up all but the smallest space.

Maybe he could push past? But no, he wouldn't make it ten feet. *Damn, damn, damn.*

Michael whipped his hand out and snatched the gun off Mary's table. He couldn't think why she would have it, unless she really had entertained a visitor earlier in the night and he had left it behind. Shaking, he raised it up in front of him and prepared to fire if needed. He had no idea what he was doing.

"Cyrus," Mary called, placing her hand gently on his shoulder. The man turned to look at her, and his eyes widened when he caught sight of Michael. She pulled him in, and the door slid shut behind his back.

"*Michael*, god, I knew it was you!" Cyrus made no move to raise his weapon, even though Michael's hands were shaking wildly and the barrel was trained somewhere in the vicinity of his chest. Cyrus seemed unconcerned.

"We need your help, Cy."

Michael's eyes flashed over to the woman, the words taking a second to register in his head. "You're . . ." he said. "We're getting out of here?"

She nodded, her mouth a thin line. To Cyrus she said, "Can you get us out of here before breakfast? Michael needs to leave. Life or death."

Cyrus narrowed his eyes. Michael tried to imagine whether Cyrus could be one of the men who executed the others. After a few seconds of indeterminate speculation, Michael decided he didn't want to know.

"Hey, Cy?" Mary's head was tilted, her dark eyes wide to get his attention. "Trust me? This is important." Cyrus continued to hesitate, and she grabbed his hand. "*Please*, Cyrus. Please trust me. We need to get out."

"Coleman will kill me."

Michael sucked in a breath. She would, too. Michael didn't want Cyrus to have to face that. He lowered the gun in his hands slowly.

"If you get us out . . ." he said. "If you can get us out of the building, we'll get to the shoreline on our own."

"The *shoreline?* Are you nuts?" Mary almost shrieked.

Michael ignored her, focusing instead on the Minder in sky blue.

Cyrus chewed on his lip. Michael felt awful. This kid shouldn't have to deal with this nonsense.

"What do you need from me?" Cyrus asked.

Michael exhaled shakily. "Do you have a key to the cage?"

29

Mary had almost cried when he'd told her that he wanted to steal Johnny's journals. He had to explain that he only wanted to take them so that he could find out what Coleman wanted—on his own time, as soon as he got out and away from this awful place. That calmed her down only a little bit, but it was enough to get her moving again. She asked Cyrus to go get a copy of the key to the cage, and he only hesitated a moment before following her orders. Mary didn't speak to Michael while Cyrus was out, but occasionally she shot him nervous glances. He was still holding the gun.

Cyrus returned nearly an hour later with the key, shaking. He said he'd stolen it from one of the librarians as she slept. The young Minder looked sick, like he couldn't quite believe that he had done such a thing. Mary rushed to him and talked to him quietly for a long time, leading the young man to sit on the edge of the bed with her. With her soft voice, she reassured him and thanked him for helping her, stroking her hand across his shoulders. The closeness between the two made Michael look away; it felt like he was intruding on something private. Eventually, Michael could no longer see Cyrus's shaking out of the corner of his eye, and Mary stood and signaled that they were ready to go. Michael was more than happy, for now, to let Mary run the show. He slid his stolen weapon into the pocket of his robe.

As Michael, Mary, and Cyrus made their way through the last few hallways to reach the cage in the center of the complex, Michael started to think that he might be able to pull this off. Cyrus looked at Mary with stars in his eyes, which meant he would do whatever she asked him to, with little hesitation. That was useful, because it meant that all Michael needed to do was explain vaguely what he needed, and Mary would figure out the rest and order Cyrus to follow through. A few times, Cyrus was sent ahead of them to relieve the Minders that were keeping watch. All of them went gladly, happy with the promise of a few extra hours of sleep at that early hour.

Michael kept waiting for some sort of alarm to go off. But it never came. He asked Cyrus why, in a strained whisper as they crept through the bunker. Mary all but rolled her eyes and answered for the young Minder.

"Buchanan's such an ass, he probably doesn't want anyone else to find out there's someone out past curfew, because he wants to be the one to shoot you. So he's going to keep prowling around the building until morning comes. We'll be out by then."

Michael nodded, understanding. Buchanan was a sadistic bastard to everyone, not just to Michael.

When they reached the cage, Cyrus turned to gaze down at Mary. "Are you sure?" he asked quietly, eyes wide.

"Yes, Cyrus. I'm sure. We need this."

Michael could see that Cyrus didn't fully understand. Hell, Michael wasn't sure *he* understood. But Cyrus clearly held a great deal of love for this woman, and he nodded and handed her the key. It was a small cylinder with notches cut into it, fitted around a beaded chain. It reminded Michael of a small silver dog whistle, though what exactly that was he couldn't say for sure. Something Johnny had mentioned in one of his journals, surely.

Mary rewarded the Minder with a brilliant smile, and in that moment Michael wasn't sure if she was acting in order to ensure the

Minder's cooperation, or if she really did have some affection for the boy. She certainly didn't seem to have any issues with using her charm to manipulate men, but still . . .

Michael thought back to all those times he had watched her in the cafeteria, leaning against tables and doorways, sauntering around. She *wanted* to be looked at, or at least part of her did. There was no doubt that a good portion of her movements were executed solely to get into good graces with the male Minders. The fact that she seemed to be on a first-name and nickname basis with all the men she interacted with only supported the theory. As she worked on unlocking the cage, Michael idly wondered if any of her previous projects had been a woman who had needed to control the men in her life. That would make more sense than sweet, innocent Mary secretly being a seductress. The thought was almost laughable. Almost.

When she opened the cage and led Michael inside, he was filled with apprehension. Where did he start? The shelves stretched far back into the dim room and high above him. Each shelf was filled with boxes, and each box was in turn filled with aging journals. He had no idea where Johnny's journals were kept.

"Come here," Mary whispered to him, tapping him on the shoulder. To Cyrus she said, "Sweetie, could you please keep watch?" And she walked away without another word, leaving the poor boy at a loss.

Michael shook his head, feeling sorry for the young man, and followed after her. It was obvious that Cyrus was completely love-struck. Michael didn't have the heart to ask if it was really Mary he was in love with, or one of her projects that she housed within her.

Mary was looking straight up, her lips moving as she moved between the rows, fingers trailing behind her over the boxes. Each of the boxes had a little paper label affixed to the front, on which a name was written in a delicate scrawl. The labels were old and faded. *J. Swine, T. Simon, R. Anders, E. Hart, L. Johnson, R. Smith.* Each name was repeated on at least four boxes, clustered together, and some names had even more. To Michael, the names didn't seem to be arranged in any particular order, but Mary seemed to know exactly where she was going. After a few minutes, she stopped, her index finger tapping a box labeled *J. Gregory*.

"Here you go." Mary smiled at him fleetingly. "You have to be careful with them."

With dismay, Michael noticed that there were seven boxes that housed Johnny's journals, each with *J. Gregory* written on the label in that thin, spidery writing. He slid the first one off the shelf and, grimacing, felt the weight of it in his weak arms. He peeked under the lid and groaned when he saw that this box was only half full. The other boxes would be even heavier.

Mary started wandering off. "I want to go find . . ." Her face had taken on a quality that looked a bit like she was dreaming, and she ignored him when he called her name. She rounded the corner, and Michael was alone in the row.

"Mary!" he hissed again, waiting for her to come back to him. She didn't.

Michael huffed and let out a low string of curses as he lowered the *J. Gregory* boxes from the shelves onto the floor. The thought of him needing to carry all of these out to the room where the carts were kept—a good fifteen-minute walk—made his back ache. His arms started to tremble, already protesting against the strain he was about to put them through.

He really needed Mary's help with this. Even as tiny as she was, she still looked much healthier than the grey ghost Michael had turned into, and he had no doubt that she could lift one of these boxes. *Where did she go?*

There was a shout from the front of the room, and Michael froze. It hadn't sounded like Cyrus.

"Shit," Michael breathed, his eyes wide. He crouched down and stayed low to the floor, listening for any more noises that would signal they had been discovered.

Slow footsteps echoed in the cage. Michael couldn't tell which way they were coming from, and he held his breath, squeezing his eyes shut in an attempt to concentrate. That didn't last more than ten seconds before his imagination got the better of him. He needed to be able to see.

Come on, Michael, think!

He felt glued to the floor, painfully aware of the seconds ticking by. His heart was hammering in his chest, which felt like it was going to explode if he didn't inhale soon. Michael had few choices left. He chanced a breath, and nearly jumped out of his skin when someone rounded the corner.

"Oh, hell!" Cyrus yelled, just as startled as Michael. The poor kid looked like all the blood had drained from his face. The Minder had his gun out and was shaking. "Where the hell is Mary?" he whispered, eyes bugging out from his head.

Michael opened his mouth, but no sound came out. He was too panicked. His eyes couldn't leave the barrel of the gun, which was pointed right at him. The Minder followed Michael's gaze and hastily holstered the gun, muttering a low apology.

Cyrus leaned down to better see Michael, and spoke quickly. "We need to get out of here. Another Minder was sent in to do a sweep, and I had to knock him out. When he doesn't report back, people are going to know that we're here. *Where's Mary?*"

"I don't know!" Michael finally spit the words out of his mouth. "She walked off a few minutes ago!"

Cyrus growled and took off, leaving Michael alone again. Michael cursed, his eyes roaming over the boxes at his feet. He was only going to be able to carry one. Which one to pick?

He had no way to tell which journals would hold the information he needed, and if he picked wrong this whole thing would be wasted. He was wasting time staring at the boxes, expecting the answer to magically leap out at him. It wasn't going to work that way.

A children's game drifted into his head. *Eeny meeny miney moe* . . . and, exasperated, Michael picked the third box up, hefting it onto his hip with a wince. Then he took off as fast as he could in the direction Cyrus had taken, his atrophied muscles screaming in protest. "Mary!" he hissed. "Cyrus!" There was no answer to his calls.

The caged room was huge. Michael almost laughed when he thought back to his first impression of it, that it was only slightly larger than the airplane hangar—the one that held the motorcarts—had been. He saw now that this room dwarfed the hangar. It was at least three or four times as large.

"Damn it, where are you guys?" He wasn't even sure if he was going the right way anymore.

All of a sudden, Mary appeared underfoot. "Jesus!" she shrieked, scrambling backward to get out of the way. "Watch it!"

He shushed her, waving his free hand to quiet her. "Is Cyrus with you?" he asked urgently.

"No, he should be back at the front." She frowned at him. "What's wrong?"

Cyrus appeared at the end of the row, running toward them with relief in his eyes. "There you are! Let's go!" He tugged Mary up from the floor by her arm.

"Wait!" the small woman cried, leaning back down to grab a box of her own.

"You have *got* to be kidding me!" Michael hissed at her, furious. She had left him to go find her *own* journals?

"Hey!" she snapped, "I'm helping you get out of here, and I'm going to have to play it off like I'm taking my break early. I am *not* taking a whole month off without reading because of you. You are not that special." She glared at him, her dark eyes challenging.

"Mary, we don't have time for this. We need to leave now," Cyrus whispered, shaking her arm a little so that she would look at him. When she did, her eyes became afraid and her lips trembled. *Definitely an act,* Michael thought bitterly.

"What's wrong?" she whispered again.

"Someone found us. We need to get to the cart if you're going to get out of here." Cyrus was like a puppy around her. Michael could almost see his tail wagging.

Mary nodded and reached out to him. *"Thank you,* Cy. He would have caught us if you hadn't been here." Cyrus melted and smiled awkwardly. Michael rolled his eyes.

"All right, let's go. Go!" Michael ushered them away, toward where he guessed the entrance to the cage was. Thankfully, he was right. The three of them stepped over the unconscious guard gingerly, Mary having to hop over his body awkwardly, her legs too short to make the distance when hindered by the box she carried.

They hurried down the hallways, Cyrus moving ahead of them to make sure they wouldn't be spotted. Michael had no idea how long it would take for someone to notice that the unconscious Minder back in the cage hadn't returned. Or how long until the Minder simply *woke up.* Michael almost wished Cyrus had killed him instead of just knocking him out.

As they headed toward the motorcart room, a thought seemed to strike Mary and her face paled. "Blankets!" Her eyes widened, and she stopped, calling Cyrus over to her with panic evident in her voice. "I need my rucksack and some blankets! The guard at the tower is going to think it's weird if I'm leaving to go on break without any of my things." She held out her box of journals to the Minder, her eyes wide, and waited for him to take them.

Cyrus was eyeing the box with terrified eyes. This, Michael mused, he would not do for her. Cyrus thought the journals were too sacred. He would help them steal the boxes, but he wouldn't touch them himself. Interesting.

"I won't take that, Mary. I can't."

Mary frowned. "I need to go get my things, and I can't carry this with me!" Her voice was high and urgent.

"I'll go get your things," Cyrus countered, his eyes begging her. When she made no move or sound of assent, he whispered, "Please don't make me do this. They'll shoot me."

Mary sucked in a breath harshly. From the dark that tinged her eyes, Michael could see what she was thinking: that they might shoot Cyrus anyway, and she was the one who'd brought him into this. Her eyes grew sad.

"Okay." She removed her key from around her neck and handed it over. "Please hurry." Cyrus was gone in seconds, running down the corridor and around the curve. Mary gazed after him, her face a mask of worry.

Michael thought that they had probably wasted two minutes with that little exchange, and they were running out of time. He reached out to Mary and touched her hand, which was white from its intense grip on the box, and tried to keep his face as calm as possible.

"We need to move or someone could see us."

Mary nodded, tears pooling in her eyes. She really was concerned for Cyrus. Michael couldn't figure her out.

They continued their frantic pace through the remaining corridors and halls, and Michael was relieved not to encounter anyone else. Michael was sweating from all the running about, and his arms shook with exhaustion. Finally, they came upon the cart room. He thought he might collapse with relief. It took all the strength he had left to make it to the first cart.

Mary walked to the back of the cart and opened it up, looking at Michael with concern. "You all right? You look half dead." She gestured for him to get in the back.

"Heavy," was all he was able to wheeze out, his chest tight and aching. He felt useless. He tried to remember a time when he had been strong, able to throw seed bags back and forth and heft up a stray sheep or pig if he needed to. It seemed like lifetimes ago. His head spinning, Michael climbed into the back, and Mary shoved the boxes in after him. He collapsed on the floor of the old cart. Sand from the outside world swirled around his face as his breath puffed out in short gasps, his cheek pressed against the gritty floor of the cabin. His heart was thudding in his chest, each pulse making his head feel too small, like his brain was trying to find a way out of its constricted prison. He was aware of Mary's voice, maybe asking him a question or maybe just muttering to herself. In any case, his head was too far away to focus on what she was saying, and it all just became slush in his mind.

Several minutes passed as Michael struggled to regain control of his lungs and buzzing head. Mary sat in the passenger seat, and if he opened his eyes, he could just barely make out her face from his position at the bottom of the cart, her gaze alternating between his sorry body and the back window. Her eyebrows were drawn down in worry.

Where is Cyrus? Michael wondered idly. He had been gone for too long. He became aware of Mary tapping her foot impatiently, could see her worn boot drumming the floor through the empty space underneath the seats.

"Where is he?" Michael croaked. The woman flicked her eyes down to him and made a face that let him know they were running out of time.

"Thirty seconds," she said quietly, before focusing again on the view out the back. She started muttering under her breath, but Michael couldn't make out what she was saying between her low voice and his ringing ears.

Michael exhaled slowly and squeezed his eyes shut tight, counting as slowly as he could to thirty. On thirty, he cracked an eye open, but she was still staring out the rear window with her wide, dark eyes, her lips moving frantically. Michael closed his eye again and kept counting.

He was on eighty-three when he heard Mary curse softly and sniff, and the door to the cart opened then closed quickly. A few seconds floated by hazily in Michael's brain, and then the driver's side opened up and Mary slid inside.

"We can't wait anymore. We have to go now." Michael wasn't sure if she was talking to him or just trying to reassure herself, so he didn't reply.

The key should already be in the ignition, as always, he thought, but still he crossed his fingers and waited with a tight chest. He didn't know if he'd be able to handle moving the boxes (or himself) into another cart if this one didn't start for some reason. But then the engine did start up, and a deep, sickly rumble erupted around him. With his ear pressed to the floor, the sudden cacophony made Michael wince.

Breathing deeply to calm herself, Mary reversed the cart out of the row. The movements of the cart were jerky and rough, and Michael's companion groaned, slamming her hand against the steering wheel in an attempt to make the machine submit and run smoothly. It didn't work. The cart continued to sputter and shake as Mary coaxed it from the cart room.

We won't even make it out of the building, Michael thought darkly, wanting to scream at Mary to just shoot him now.

"It's still dark out," Mary said after a few minutes. "With any luck they won't be able to see you or the boxes. You need to stay down, and don't you dare make a sound. The guard is going to shoot first, ask questions later." Her voice was shaking. "Do you understand, Michael?"

"Yes," he rasped out, and tried to shove as much of himself as he could under the rear seat. He had no doubt that if the guard looked, he'd be spotted in an instant. He wished Cyrus had come with the blankets so that he had something bigger to hide under.

Michael's heart felt like it was in his throat. He tried not to breathe in the sand on the floor.

The cart slowed to a crawl with a screech of bad brakes and a shudder of exhaustion. This machine did not want to be running.

Mary reached across to the passenger side to roll down the window. A beam of light came in, just beside Michael's right boot. He kept his eyes on the beam, making sure to stay very still in case the light touched him and he was discovered.

"Hi!" Mary chirped happily to the guard. Michael couldn't hear the words in the Minder's grumbled reply over the rumbling of the engine, but Mary laughed tightly and said, "Yes, it's way too early. I agree." A few moments ground by as the Minder said something else to her, and Michael inhaled deeply. His throat tickled. *No, don't you dare,* he scolded himself. He needed to cough. Of course he did. He held his breath.

"God, you know," Mary started talking again, sounding wistful, "this latest project is really taking it out of me. I just needed to take my break early. Don't want to turn into a grey zombie." She laughed again and Michael bristled. His lungs were screaming for air, but he refused to cough. The Minder was talking again.

"Yeah, yeah," Mary said, "of course. I'll let her know, no problem at all. Your mother still works at the bakery, right?" A pause. "No! Oh, dear, I'm so sorry to hear that. When I get back we'll sit down and talk all about it. Are you okay?"

Come on, come on. Michael was impatient. Every second that ticked by while Mary made small talk was another second he could be discovered. It was taking a tremendous amount of strength to stay still and not breathe, and it was strength that he just didn't have. He slowly moved his hand down to the pocket of his robe to check that the gun was still there in case it came down to him having to defend himself.

Then he checked again.

Dread crept over him as Michael realized that his pocket was empty. He had dropped the gun somewhere. His eyes darted around, and he spotted it down near the back door of the cart— directly in a beam of light, dust motes swirling around the cold metal. Michael was going to be sick. If the guard saw it glinting in the corner of his eye . . .

Michael buried his face in the crook of his arm and tried to cough as quietly as possible, unable to avoid it any longer. Mary immediately began speaking louder, trying to cover up the noise that Michael knew she could hear.

"Oh I know! That's why I'm driving now, my driver never showed up! He overslept! Imagine, I'm going to have to make the drive all the way to four-one-five in the dark on my own. And you *know* I'm not a very good driver. I mean really, it's going to take me an extra hour at least and—"

Michael tuned her out while he waited for the guard to glance back and see him. He was hoping against hope that the rumbles from the engine and Mary's shrill voice had kept the guard from hearing him, but Michael didn't dare breathe again until Mary bid the guard goodbye ("I'll send another Minder back with the cart— be sure to pick me up next month!") and at last drove the beat-up cart into the dark of the morning.

"What the hell was that?" Mary snapped at him after a few moments of tension, both of them waiting for the guard to call out or sound an alarm. There was nothing.

Michael picked up the gun before sliding from under the rear seat and crawling up into the passenger seat beside Mary. "I couldn't help it. I'm sorry. It was an accident, I swear."

She turned her head to glare at him, then let out a shaky breath and turned back to the barren hills that they were flying over in the dark. Headlights attempted to light the way, but they weren't very helpful. The sky was pinking up behind them, the sun starting to wake but not yet releasing its light. Michael's plate blinked underneath the thin fabric of his robe, throwing out a dim red flash in the otherwise shadowy cabin. They sat silent for several minutes. Mary broke the quiet first. "Where are you headed, Michael?"

He frowned, not having really thought about it. He hadn't truly believed he would make it out of the building, after all. "I guess . . ." He wanted to go back to 441, to see Lily, give her a hug and see how big she'd grown. His stomach hurt. "I heard once that there are fishing villages dotted all along the coast. The Republic didn't bother putting up fences on account of the water, supposedly. If I can find someone to take in a visitor, I'll be able to read what I've got in peace." He frowned. "I don't even know if what I'm looking for will be in the box I grabbed. I wish you'd helped me carry out more so I'd have a better chance." He didn't mean to sound so petulant, but the words were out and they hung accusingly between them in the dark. Mary didn't try to defend her actions, just pursed her lips and kept her eyes on the dirt before them.

The noise started out low. Michael thought he might have been imagining it. But as he focused, it grew and grew, a high wail that sent horror crashing over him, flooding his brain for the millionth time that night.

"Mary?" He hoped he was hallucinating.

"I hear it!" Her eyes were round, her knuckles white as she clutched the steering wheel. He could see her chest rising and falling rapidly. She was panicking too.

"What do we do?" he wheezed, his mind racing. Already Mary was accelerating, her foot pressing the pedal all the way down to the floor.

"Shit, shit, shit!" Mary cried. "Those goddamn fucking alarms shit fuck bitch!"

Michael just gaped at her, this uncharacteristic display of curses stunning him into silence, making his brain sputter as badly as their cart.

"Where do we go?" She had crazed tears in her eyes. "Where do we fucking *go?*" She flicked the headlights off, plunging them into almost total darkness. The sunlight hadn't yet reached the ridge they were careening along. The blinking red light on Michael's arm barely illuminated the cabin every other second. Bathed in the red light, the small woman looked crazed.

"Mary! Turn them back on!" Michael made a grab for the switch but she pushed him back.

"Sit still!" she snarled at him,. "The sky is bright enough, but they'll see the lights if we keep them on, and they'll catch us."

Michael groaned and dropped his head into his hands, trying to brace himself against the door of the cart as the uneven terrain jostled them around. His sleeve fell down to his elbow, revealing the plate.

"Ohhh," Mary whimpered. "Oh, god, they're outside. They've got the carts outside."

Michael snapped his head back to the rear window. He could see them, headlights in the distance. They were just pinpricks for now, traveling over the hills Michael and Mary had crossed just minutes before. They disappeared from view as Mary drove the cart over a crest and into one of the valleys, then raced inside the trough of earth to try to put more distance between them and the Archives.

"What was I thinking?" Mary shrieked, causing Michael's eyes to water. "All because I didn't want to see her grandson shot. God damn it all, Michael Driftveil!"

"Shut up, Mary," Michael snapped at her. He vaguely took note of exactly what she'd just said, but pushed it away for review later. If he lived to see noon, he'd deal with it then. "Think! Are there any complexes nearby?"

"Not that we can get into without a Minder noticing and calling the rest, oh god oh god." She was falling apart beside him, terrified, tears falling from her eyes. He didn't believe for a second that she could see where she was driving.

Michael couldn't pull air into his lungs fast enough, and he was starting to get dizzy. Then a thought hit him.

"The crater!" he gasped, wanting to reach out and shake the woman driving.

"What? No! We can't go in there!"

"We have to. Mary, drive to the crater!"

They were driving within one of the ripples in the earth; to get to the epicenter they'd need to go up and over the undulating earth. Mary let out a strangled, animalistic sound and jerked the steering wheel to the side, the cart careening over rocks as it struggled to obey. They started to climb uphill.

"Just please, don't drive into it," he begged her. He couldn't see the earth in front of him, but imagined Mary leading them right up to the edge, and then just that little bit further, sending them screaming to a death of twisted metal and crushed limbs.

The chances of that happening were chased from his mind as Mary crested yet another hill and Michael could actually *see* the crater laid out before them. Or rather, the total absence of everything else. While the night was pitch black, the crater was even worse—the blackest thing he had ever seen. Chills raced across his skin as he gazed into it. He felt insane. Just looking at the void in the earth was ripping his soul away from him. Michael wanted to sob.

Johnny had been in a magnetruck accident once. The strips that ran underneath the city had failed, and the vehicles on the road had collided into each other violently with too much inertia, screeching across the road with no tires to act as a buffer or brake. Johnny had been terribly frightened.

Because of that story, Michael understood what was happening to him and Mary right at that moment. A hundred years ago, it would have been called a horrible accident.

The cart slammed into something hard, halting it immediately. Mary flew forward into the windshield, the glass spider-webbing from the impact of her skull. Michael was slammed into the dash, his chest immediately blooming into a wreck of fiery pain. The sound of twisting metal scraped and screeched in his ears.

It took him several moments to pull himself together, for the pain to subside into a hazy blur. *I'm in shock,* he thought—calmly, which was part of the problem. He hoped he wasn't dying. "Mary?" he croaked, unable to speak any louder. For a minute, he was sure she was dead.

But then she shifted, and groaned. She cracked her eyes open. There was a gash on her forehead, blood pulsing from it and coursing down her face. Michael had never felt relief like that before. All the air was sucked out of his lungs when he realized she wasn't gone yet.

Suddenly the passenger door beside him was wrenched open. *They found us.* Michael waited for the bullet to come as he was dragged out of the cart and onto the hard dirt. He didn't have the ability to fight them; he could hardly move. It was over. There were men standing over him, shouting loudly, but Michael couldn't understand what they were saying.

Mary was dropped onto the dirt beside him, looking straight into his face. Blood was in her eyes now, but he thought he could see, in the growing sunrise, that one of her pupils was blown, the black of it completely eclipsing her light brown irises.

Michael smelled gasoline.

There was a loud bang. Michael had expected there to be more pain, and wondered where they had shot him. Heat bloomed over his body. Would that one shot kill him, or would they have to shoot him again?

Michael closed his eyes. *At least it doesn't hurt.*

Part Three

The Void and What Was Inside

30

The first thing he knew was that he wanted to cut his arm off. That was it. If he cut it off, surely it would hurt less. That made sense.

When Michael opened his eyes he was surprised to find that he was buried. He was looking straight up at black dirt. He tried to lay very still, worried that if he breathed in he would choke on the earth. He could feel the weight of it pressing down on his chest, his abdomen screaming in pain. He reached up with his left hand and tried to push the dirt off his face—his right arm wouldn't move—but found with some confusion that the dirt wasn't actually on him.

There was a noise somewhere off to the side, and Michael startled, swinging his head toward it so fast the world spun. There was a woman there, in the dirt with him, and she let out a little yelp of surprise when she saw his eyes on her.

"You scared me!" she scolded him before rushing over, something in her hands, silver hair falling in her face.

He tried to scramble back from her, remembering the last time an older woman had come at him while holding something, but he couldn't move. The woman tutted at him and pressed something cool against his arm, the pain deadening almost instantly.

"There, better now?" She smiled at him, already so much kinder than Coleman had ever looked. Through the haze in his mind, he thought this woman and the senator might have been the same age, but it was hard to tell because the dirt surrounding him swallowed the light.

He had to ask her, his confusion too much: "Dead?" His throat felt drier than he'd ever felt it. "Buried?"

She looked at him with sympathy. "No, dear. Not dead. Though you may wish you were, with how you look." She shook her head, wincing toward his arm. "You almost drove straight in. You're lucky you crashed into one of the rain reservoirs. We heard the crash and dragged you both out of the cart."

There was a knock from somewhere, and the woman looked up. "Captain, he's awake. I just put a new salve on." She didn't sound like she was smiling anymore.

"Thank you, Talia. A moment, if you could." The voice was deep, full of authority, and Michael saw the woman nod and move away.

Suddenly there was a man peering down at him, his skin as dark as the earth that surrounded them. Michael felt very small, but he stared up at the man in a way that he hoped conveyed confidence. From the man's unimpressed look it didn't work.

"I wanted to speak to you before the funeral. It's good you woke when you did."

Funeral! Michael's heart sank. "I . . . what? She didn't—she's not here?" He hadn't even thought of Mary in the few minutes since waking up, but now she was all he could think of. His throat seemed to swell up and he felt his eyes burn. Another friend, gone. He had a brief flash, just the smallest glimpse of a memory, of blood on her face and the rising sun hitting her just right so that a beam fell on her unresponsive eye. Had she been dead even then? He felt sick.

"What were you doing driving toward the crater?" The man's words were clipped, his voice firm.

"We were running away. I asked her to come with me, to help me." *And it killed her, oh god.*

"Running from what?"

"From the Minders, the bunker, the Archives." He tried to focus on forcing air into his lungs, but it hurt so badly. "They were going to kill me."

"For what?"

"For knowing too much. Even though I don't know it yet."

The man studied him for a minute, then said gruffly, "And all of those books? How did you come by those?"

Michael looked at him strangely. "We took them from the Archives, to read them. Where else would we get books like that?"

Captain twisted his mouth to the side and moved on. "We had to rip the plate off your arm so they couldn't see where you are." He must have seen the surprise on Michael's face, because he tried to explain, "There's a device inside that lets them track you. We have a man whose father taught him about the others' electronics before he passed on. He recognized it and told us we had to remove it, but it had to be done quickly, so we had to . . . tear it from you. We tossed it back into the cart with the body to make it look like you had burned when they found you. With any luck, they'll think you died."

"You *left* her body in the cart? What the hell is wrong with you? You have to go get her!" Michael felt manic, furious that Mary had been left to burn. "I have to go get her!" He started to sit up, forgetting how much pain he was in, but the man pushed him back down.

"Not your woman's body. The man you killed when you struck him. Stay down."

Michael stared back in confusion, not quite willing to let his anger drain yet. "We hit someone?"

"Michael!" There was a cry from the side and then Mary was there, rushing to lean down beside him. "Talia told me you woke up, I needed to check!"

She clung to him, and he let her even though it sent his muscles and bones screaming in pain. If he could have, he would have clung harder.

Mary was grinning and crying all at once. "We made it, we both made it, oh god thank you."

Michael looked up into the man's face above him, saw with no small amount of uneasiness the narrowed eyes and twisted mouth. He hurriedly looked away, and asked Mary quietly, "Where are we? Mary, who are these people?"

She squeezed him again and he had to bite back the pain. "We're in the crater. They came to save us from the Minders, they've been . . ." She raised her head to look at him, her face red from the tears. "People have been living in the crater this whole time. There are hundreds of people here." She was staring at him with a question in her eyes, as if he would be able to clear up her confusion. "They've been living here and no one even knew. How is that possible?"

Michael slid his eyes back to Captain, the man's frown growing even more pronounced.

"We've been told our whole lives that the crater is toxic," Michael croaked at the man. "That it would kill you if you got too close."

"But it's *not*, Michael. Captain was born here, there are healthy children here, I've *seen* them." Mary had grown pale, biting her lip. "The Republic told us it was toxic . . ." she trailed off, searching Michael's face for confirmation.

He shook his head at her, then had to stop because the room started spinning. "This doesn't make any sense."

Mary's jaw tightened. "Michael, what if . . . they lied? On purpose?"

He blinked. "Who?"

Mary sucked in a breath, her eyebrows drawing together tightly. "They could have lied to keep us from seeing anyone here, to keep us away." She chewed on her lip.

"I think the senators know about the people living in the crater."

31

After promising her that, yes, he was fine, and no, he wasn't going to die while she was gone, Mary agreed to go with Captain and Talia to the funeral. Captain tried to assure her that he didn't blame her for the man's death, to keep her from crying, although Michael noticed that he received no such kind words himself.

"It wasn't you, little one," Captain promised, before his words turned cold. "You wouldn't even have been out there if your friend hadn't asked you to help him escape."

Michael's mouth dropped open. He hated the man almost immediately.

"What was his name?" Michael asked, trying to keep his words civil, but failing.

Captain ignored him. Michael glared at the other man for a moment before turning his eyes to the packed-dirt ceiling high above him.

"I'd like my books now," he declared, not bringing his gaze down. "Would someone please bring my box of books to me?"

"I'll have someone send it in." Talia's voice chimed out, though he couldn't see her.

"Thanks," he mumbled, and tried not to listen to Captain comforting Mary before telling her it was time for them to go.

He was awoken by a noise. Loud, echoing in the dark room. Voices, he realized after a moment. *They're singing. That's what it sounds like.* He had to catch his breath. No one in the Republic sang. If it weren't for Johnny, he wouldn't even know the word for it. His heart pounded as he listened. The voices sounded impossibly sad.

Someone had lit a candle, and placed it in a little dish on the floor beside him. It illuminated the box of journals beside it, and with some difficulty Michael was able to swing his left arm over to pluck one out at random. *I want to read it,* he thought, laughing at himself. Michael had thought he'd never want to read another book again after escaping the Archives. Yet here he was.

Surrounded by song, Michael opened the journal and began to read.

32

There's a man inside the bunker. An old man.

He came to us last night, right up to the door, bold as you please, and waited. Waited for us to open the door for him, I guess. He looked right at the camera and tilted his head, like he was asking permission to be let inside, that's what Jeff said. Jeff was the one who was watching the screens when he came up. Poor kid must have had a heart attack. We've been watching those screens for so long with no movement, I was actually starting to think the camera didn't work anymore, that a loop of the same day outside over and over had been playing just to make us feel safe. It wouldn't be the first time the people who designed the bunker had put things in place to keep us in the dark.

Anyway, he came right up to the big metal door and waited. Jeff freaked out and ran out of the monitor room, flying through the halls like a screwball, from what I've heard from people. Rock stopped him first (go figure) and demanded to know what was happening. Becca said that when Jeff told him there was a man sitting outside, Rock just about fell over. She said his face went totally white, then green, then he started swaying like a sheet under the heat vents! I would have liked to have seen that.

So then Jeff, Rock, and Becca start running through the halls, hollering and waving their arms like there's a national emergency, which of course draws everyone out of their rooms and out of the kitchens and whatnot. A big mess of people all panicking and running around was bound to get someone hurt. One of the Jessicas (blonde) tripped on someone and twisted her ankle pretty badly. It was already starting to bruise by the time someone found me in the storeroom cataloguing the canned food for the millionth time. I know that someone has to be taking extra food, but I haven't been able to figure out how they're getting into the room. As far as I know, I have the only key, the one Mr. K gave me. Has someone else had one all along? That thought annoys me more than it should.

While I was wrapping Jessica's ankle (I have to remind her to give me the bandage back when she's able to walk so that I can wash it and use it again . . . we're running scarily low on bandages), Jeff hovered over my shoulder, hopping on one foot and then the other like he had to pee. The other people in the mob were whispering to each other in small clusters, but at that point I just wasn't interested in eavesdropping on them. I was too focused on making sure Jessica hadn't broken anything to listen to what people were whispering about. It's a miracle no one's broken anything this far, and I really don't know what I'm going to do when someone *does* break something. Jessica put on a show of being very very hurt with tears and the whole thing so that some of the other boys would fawn over her.

When I was done and looked up from the bandage, Jeff may as well have been a ghost he was so pale. I snapped at him, "What?"

I really shouldn't have yelled like that, but I was pissed about the mob in the halls. I don't know how many meetings I've had to have with everyone about how dangerous it is for us to be careless, what with how limited our supplies are, and a big panicky group is definitely careless. Jeff shrank back from me suddenly, and looked like he was going to throw up. Poor kid. I felt terrible. *Feel* terrible.

Trying to make it right, I sighed and bit the inside of my cheek to calm down. When I wasn't angry anymore I looked back up at him and spoke more gently. "What's this all about, Jeffy?"

I shouldn't have called him Jeffy, either, because that makes him feel like a little kid, and I could see him draw himself up and try to look grown-up, his eyes suddenly a little bit brighter and more angry than scared.

None of us are grownups, you know, not a single one of us. Not that anyone else agrees with me.

"There's a man!" he said. Only he didn't really say it like normal, he more growled it out like he was trying to sound like . . . what? Like his father? He doesn't know what his father sounds like. There's a nature holo in the film room that has a big brown bear in it. The sound file sounds a little bit like how Jeff was trying to sound, but humans don't make that noise, so it came out weird. Maybe that really was what Jeff was trying to sound like. Maybe he thinks that's what adults sound like. Anyway, it was absolutely ridiculous, and I started laughing before I actually heard his words.

"Wait, wait, wait," I said, wiping a stray tear out of my eye from laughing too hard. Little Jeffy was PISSED that I was laughing at him, let me tell you. I thought he might punch me. Sometimes I'm a real ass. "What did you say? A man? A man where? Not here!"

Jeff growled again, and actually bared his teeth at me. Definitely trying to imitate the nature holo, then. Hoo, boy.

"There's a man," he ground out, his hands fisted at his sides. "There's a man outside the freaking bunker, you shithead! He wants in!"

That stopped me. Wow. So I'm looking at him, squatting on the ground next to little Jessica as she's holding her ankle and pretending to put on a brave face, boys flanking her and making sure she's comfy on the cold smooth concrete floor (what a freaking joke), and Jeff is glaring at me, his face all red, barely containing his anger, and everyone else is just looking at the two of us like it's a ping-pong match, only there's no ball. It's quiet for about a minute and a half, and then someone screams like a moron and everyone starts panicking *again*. I don't even know who it was, but if I ever figure it out I'm going to wring their scrawny little neck, and then I'm going to use what little first aid we have left to make sure they don't die so I can do it all over again. Freaking idiot. The two guys on either side of Jessica and me leaned over her so that no one could step on her while everyone else bolted from the hallway, scrambling away to their rooms like the end of days had come. I'm sure more than a few of them must have thought that one of the Bubblers had come to get us, but the Bubblers don't look like us so I wasn't too concerned with that. I just kept trying to picture *how* a man could be outside, and how he could have found us, and what he wanted, and what should we do?

When everyone else had gone it was just me and the two other boys crouching over Jessica, plus Rock and Jeff. Jeff had gone pale again, no red anger left in his face, and Rock looked just as sick.

"What are we supposed to do now?"

I don't know if it was Jeff or Rock who said that, but I looked up and sent Jessica away with the two boys, making sure they didn't let her bad foot hold any weight. Then I told Rock and Jeff, trying to sound braver than I really felt, "We go see what this man wants."

33

A wood piece had been embedded into the burnt earth by the alcove. It wasn't a door, just something to knock on, a way for the crater people to let each other know they wanted to come in. There was a knock on it now. The sound jolted Michael away from Johnny, and he glanced up, wondering who it could be.

For several days, the two Archivists had largely stayed away from the people who lived in the crater. The medicine woman, Talia, came by a few times a day to tend to their wounds (with the exception of Mary's eye, her injuries were coming along quite nicely; Michael had thus far not been so fortunate with his arm), and sometimes the big man named Captain came by to ask briefly if they needed anything. Captain's visits made Michael unhappy, often leaving him in a sour mood for hours. The dark man's eyes always lingered on Mary, his smile for her a million times warmer than the terse curve of the lips he reserved for Michael, and Mary smiled back at him warmly and laughed at the poor jokes he made that neither of the Archivists actually understood. Michael felt small and emasculated, bed-ridden, unable to sit up without retching. He could feel each rib underneath his skin as he breathed, and he hated. He hated Captain, he hated Mary, and he hated himself.

Eventually Mary had begun leaving Michael to go venture out into the crater, to meet the people there, she said. In truth, she just didn't want to be around his bitter mood. He knew it even if she denied that was the real reason. She told him that she felt cooped up, which didn't serve to make Michael feel any better. He wanted to get up and walk, too. He was growing lonely, and with the loneliness came an irrational anger that blackened his heart. It scared him.

"Hi, Michael," Mary chirped, holding a bundle in her arms. She looked happy, happier than she had been in weeks.

Michael inclined his head to her in greeting, just a little bit. He watched her smile falter for a second before she could plaster it back in place.

"I brought you something. It's really cool!" She beamed and presented the bundle to him, a packet about the size of her torso wrapped in some sort of fabric. Michael took it wearily.

It was heavy, and tried to fold under its own weight before he was able to lay it on his lap.

"Careful!" Mary hissed, jumping to help him so it couldn't crease. She started to unwrap it for him, taking the weathered twine carefully in her hands so that the brown cloth surrounding the package could be removed and set aside, and then she grinned at him. "Ta-da!"

Michael let out a breath, slowly. "Oh, Mary . . ."

She had brought him drawings, dozens of them, on great sheets of paper. Some were of landscapes, some of people or animals, and others still of designs that didn't seem to be anything in particular. They were done in different hands, with a different level of detail in each, and all of them breathtaking.

"I know you liked when Johnny drew . . ." Mary was looking at him hopefully, her eyes wide. "The people here draw all the time, with bits of charcoal and the dirt from the crater."

Michael ran his finger over the line of a stranger's cheekbone, a child peering up and laughing at him from the paper.

"Talia said that when the refugees came here to get away from the Republic, they started using simple drawings to communicate since they didn't have a common language between them. Eventually they all learned, and almost all of them can speak the mixed language they have now, but they kept drawing, because they liked it. They use it as wallpaper to cover up the dirt." She laughed a little.

"Where did you get these?"

"You like them?" Michael thought Mary's face might split open from the breadth of her smile. She truly beamed. "I asked around, although that went over like a lead balloon because most of the crater people hardly understand me. But then Captain brought them up to my room, after I told him they might help you."

He felt his stomach clench, and he drew his hands back from the paper. "You got them from Captain?" His voice was harsher than it should have been, but he didn't care.

Mary's face fell.

He swallowed thickly, trying to stave off the frown that was creeping on to his face. "These are beautiful. Thanks." He turned his eyes to the wall beside his mattress.

She blinked at him, biting her lip, and waited for him to say something else. When he didn't, she sighed quietly and deflated. "Okay, well . . ." she moved to go, "I'll let you get back to your journal then . . ." She gave him a chance to call her back, but Michael only nodded and picked up the worn book again, dismissing her.

34

"Are you crazy?" Rock shouted at me, "We can't go TALK to him! Then he'll know we're here!"

"He already *knows* we're here." I tried to stay calm, I really did, but Rock just rubs me the wrong way with his stupid face and stupider name. "If he didn't know, he wouldn't be waiting by the door. He wants us to let him in."

"What if he hurts us?"

I whirled around, and Angel was standing there, listening to us. I kissed her and Jeffy made a gagging sound, which I ignored.

"He won't hurt us. He's been in the wastes for, what, how long is it now?"

"Eleven years," Jeff muttered, while Rock shouted, "Ten!" I guess they're both right. I think I worked it out that it's been ten and a half years since it happened, eleven years since we got here. Crazy to think it's been that long. It doesn't feel that long.

Anyway, I told them that we'd be able to take on an old man that had been starving for years and years, and Jeffy and Rock took off to go look at the monitors.

There was a tugging on my sleeve, and then I was looking into green eyes deeper than anything else in this world. "What if he wasn't starving? What if there are more people out there?" Angel said. "More people than in here?"

I kissed her again and we followed the boys to the watchroom.

When we got there, Jeffy was hopping up and down, pointing frantically at the monitor on the far side of the room. Sure as hell, the old man was there. He had an old cloak on, which he had pulled up around the back of his head to keep the whipping sand off of his face, but we could see the white hair underneath. He was looking straight at the camera, waiting for us.

"All the adults are supposed to be gone." Rock's voice was shaking. "They all died. They're all gone."

"Apparently not," I murmured, and Angel was clutching at my hand so hard I thought she might break it.

"What if he's not an adult?" Jeff squeaked. "What if he's one of the monsters that the soldiers were talking about? What if the Bubblers figured out how to look like us?" Angel squeezed my hand harder, and I told Jeffy to shut it.

"Does anyone remember how to open the door from this room?" I asked, but they just looked at me with big round eyes. That was a no.

"All right, I'll go up."

"Me too," Angel said immediately, and I wanted to kiss her again.

"We'll take radios. Rock, Jeff, you guys *stay here* and watch the monitors. I'll go through the gate and see what he wants, and Angel will shut it behind me. Once it's good, I'll radio to open up." I was trembling like crazy, hoping she couldn't see it. "If something happens," I looked at Angel for a long time, her face ghost white, "radio to Angel and let her know. She won't be able to see me from the other side. And Angel, if that happens, you don't open that gate back up again."

She nodded at me, her eyes firm.

I grabbed four radios off the back wall where they'd been charging, tuned them all to channel 3 (when was the last time they had to be used? I remember playing with them when we found them, but I don't know if anyone else has even looked at them since then), and tossed one each to Jeffy and Rock. I pressed the third one into Angel's hands, which were shaking worse than mine. The last one I slid into the front pocket of my shirt, then thought better of it and clipped it to my waistband. The shirt I was wearing was big enough that the radio wouldn't be immediately noticeable there, which for some reason I thought would be best.

Jeffy's voice made me look up. "Are you going to bring a gun?"

Angel and Rock looked at me expectantly.

"I—" I tried not to let my voice squeak too bad, but I know it did. "I don't know how to use one. Do you?" Jeffy shook his head. I took a deep breath. "Right, well, as soon as this is over, we're going to go back into storage and everyone is going to learn. All right?" It's stupid. I can't believe none of us even thought to practice before. I'm sure all of the guns are sitting in the storage room, just like they have been since the soldiers came back, so long ago.

I miss David.

"Ready?" Angel asked me, being brave. I nodded, swimming in her eyes again, and we left the monitor room.

The walk up to the gate was long and quiet. Angel held my hand the whole way. The hall is so big up that way that our footsteps were bouncing around the concrete, making it seem like there were more than just the two of us heading up. It was comforting.

When we made it to the gate I started to move forward, but Angel tugged my hand back to her lips and kissed it. She told me she loved me. I could see how scared she was, and I leaned down and kissed her back, and then I let go and stepped away.

"As soon as I'm through, you close it," I reminded her, and then pressed the green button on the wall panel so Angel could start to turn the big wheel on the gate. After a minute we both heard the *snick* of the big lock releasing, and my heart started pounding so much I didn't hear what Angel said to me then, even though I saw her lips move.

The gate was much thicker than I realized, and it took both of us to get it open once it was unlocked, me prying at the edge and her tugging at the wheel. Finally it swung out just enough for me to force my shoulders through, and I twisted and pushed until I could move the rest of me out, into the world I haven't seen for a decade.

The first thing that hit me was the smell. We've been breathing the same air for years, and it wasn't until today that I realized how stale it is. The air out there is sweet and new, at first. I breathed it in deep before I knew what I was doing, and it flooded my lungs beautifully, and I was happy. Until I gagged, coughed, and spluttered. Underneath the sweet there's something acrid, terrible, and the sand that was swirling around the air got into my mouth and stuck to my teeth and tongue. After that I breathed much more shallowly, which helped, a little.

The next thing was the sound again, *snick*, as the lock clicked back into place. Angel had closed the gate—apparently it was much easier to close it than to open it—and I was stuck out there until I signaled it was safe. The fear that rushed through me at that moment is not something I want to feel again.

The last thing I noticed was the old man, who had backed away from the gate and held his hands up so I could see he wasn't holding anything. He was ten feet from me, and I froze, struck dumb. I hadn't really thought this far ahead.

After a minute or two he tilted his head to the side. "They sent a kid out to meet me?" He sounded surprised, his voice a little rough, but not threatening.

I rounded my shoulders and tried to stand up straighter. "Who are you?" I barked at him, then winced just a little. The sand in my throat scratched when I spoke.

"My name isn't important. I'm just an old man."

I stared at him. He stared back.

Sad to say, I broke first. "If you don't tell me who you are, this conversation is over. And you can choke on all this sand."

"Judah." He smiled at me, his leathery old face crinkling up. The wind whipped up around us, and sand flooded our little alcove. I coughed, but Judah didn't even flinch.

"They told us there was a bunker here. I didn't really believe them." He cackled, and I took a step back until my back collided with the heavy concrete gate.

"Who told you?" I was cold suddenly, worried. People knew about us. Judah had found us, and he was going to go back to wherever he came from and tell those people where we were. I thought I might get sick.

"The senators." He said it so simply, but it was like a million volts to my chest and I jumped.

"Our government still stands?" I've read about the government thousands of times in our textbook, and I was excited to hear that there was still a senate.

"Well," Judah said, "*a* government, surely."

I deflated.

"Oh, son," he sighed at me, and I made a face at my shoes, "I'm sorry. Have you really been locked up since it happened? The Loss?"

"We didn't think it was safe," I said carefully. "We were told we needed to stay inside."

There was a crackling by my hip.

"Is he human?"

I glared at the camera up at the corner. Stupid-ass Rock and his big stupid mouth.

"Rock, you asshole, shut up!"

Angel this time. I groaned and pulled the radio off my hip.

Judah looked amused as I clicked the volume on the radio down. "What did your friend mean, am I human? Don't you think that's an odd question?" He was laughing at me.

"He meant," I was growling now, so pissed at Rock (and a little annoyed with Angel, too, actually) that I could hardly open my mouth with how badly I was clenching my teeth together, "are you human or are you one of the monsters?"

The old man blinked at me for a few moments before hooting with laughter. "Monsters!" He cried, guffawing like one of the nature holos we have of monkeys. "What monsters?"

I frowned at him. "The ones that attacked us. *The* monsters." But he was laughing still and I was starting to get embarrassed.

"There ain't no such thing as monsters, kiddo!"

"But they told us—they saw it when they went out!" I was insisting now, sure that this guy had lost it.

"Did *you* see any monsters? Any of you?"

I clicked my mouth shut. Did they really not exist? Had David lied? My stomach flipped.

"Look, son. It wa'nt no monsters that attacked us, just an accident. Let me in, and I'll explain all about it. Do you have water?"

"Why should I let you in? Why are you here?"

He looked at me, not laughing anymore. "Because, kid," (I hate that word! I'd forgotten how angry it makes me) "I'm here to tell you all that it's safe to come out."

I studied him for a minute or five, grinding my teeth together while I thought. If I let him in, he could hurt someone. If I let him leave, he could come back and bring more people with him.

I looked up at the camera, but it didn't give me the answer. Taking the radio again, I clicked up the volume and pressed the transmit button. "He wants to come in. Says he knows what happened."

No one said anything for a while. "You read me?"

"*Wait a minute. Angel, switch to channel 5.*"

We waited, much longer than a minute, the old man and I just looking at each other. He was smiling, a little, but his eyes were very serious. I'm sure I didn't look too pleased myself. I didn't know it right then, but Jeffy and Rock were letting Angel know not to open the door until after they had rounded everyone up in a safe place, just in case. Jeffy's smart like that, and Rock was the one to run around and tell everyone to get over to the cafeteria because we were going to be bringing a stranger in. Apparently no one gave him too much trouble, which is nice. As of today there are thirty-seven of us.

Finally I heard the lock click again behind me, and I could hear the grind of the wheel as Angel turned and pulled. I didn't help her. I wanted to keep my eyes on Judah, and I didn't want to turn my back.

I glanced back for just a split second when the gate opened enough for me to see Angel. Her face was red and sweaty, but I swear she's never looked so beautiful. I thought I could just collapse into her right then, given how exhausted I suddenly was.

"Let's get out of the sand," I said to Judah, but he shook his head solemnly.

"Oh, son. It's not sand."

I shuddered and my blood felt cold.

I backed into the bunker and motioned for the man to follow me, which he did, eagerly. Inside the long hall were not only Angel, but Jeffy and Rock as well, and even one of the older boys, Stephen. He must be, what, twenty-six, twenty-seven? I've never really talked to Stephen too much since the classroom, which seems silly since there are so few of us. I remember being told that his brother was in the bunker with us, but he was a soldier, and he was too old. His brother went just like the rest of the adults. We almost lost Stephen, too, because he was so miserable without his brother.

Stephen nodded at me, and I dipped my head back at him. Stranger or not, I was happy he was there.

Everyone was looking at me expectantly, even the old man. "This is Judah," I said quickly, my throat still scratchy from the sand. "He said, um, that he would tell us what happened."

Stephen stepped right up to Judah and stared him down. "How did you find us?" His voice was very calm, but intense, like he was only seconds away from flying off the handle. I stepped back and looked at Angel nervously. She shrugged.

Judah didn't flinch. "I walked. Lots of people are looking for this place. Couple thousand healthy people locked away and kept safe? It would be nice to have those numbers on our side." His eyes shifted back and forth between the five of us, carefully, assessing. He must have seen it in our faces, although I tried to keep mine as neutral as possible.

He sighed. "How many do you have? A couple hundred?" He peered around our heads and over our shoulders, down the hall, hoping to see someone. He muttered, "We could still use a few hundred, I suppose."

"Who's 'we'?" Rock spoke up, not nearly as intimidating as Stephen, even though they're about the same age. His voice shook.

"The Republic of Coastal Territories. We're the largest, safest group out there right now, and we're trying to put the country back together." He sounded earnest, if slightly rehearsed. "There are smaller groups out there who want to take over, but they're violent and cruel. We've got around fifty thousand to our number." He looked around at us again. "We're good people," he insisted.

"Shitty name," Rock muttered, and I sighed.

"Do you have weapons on you?" Stephen asked.

"Yes."

Angel moved to stand behind me.

Stephen straightened up. "If you want to come any farther, you're going to have to leave them. I won't risk the chance of anyone getting hurt, accident or otherwise."

Judah studied Stephen for a long time as the rest of us watched, holding our breath. Finally, Judah nodded, and he shrugged out of his cloak. He took two long knives from the back of his belt, and a trench knife from a pocket in the cloak, and laid them all out on the floor. The clothes underneath his cloak were worn, but mostly clean. His button-down shirt read *Yankees*. His pants were canvas, and loose on him, and his shoes were falling apart, although he had fixed that with quite a lot of silver tape. Sheepishly he pulled a plastic baggy out of his back pocket and placed that on the floor with the other weapons, a bright green powder shifting inside.

"Rat poison," he said. "Just for keeping them out of my hut."

"Mind if I check?" Stephen waited for the man to nod before patting him down. Judah made no protest.

Satisfied, Stephen folded the man's cloak and placed the knives and poison neatly on top, then scooped the whole thing up into his arms. "We'll lock these up," he said firmly. "You can hold the key to the locker. One of us will hold the key to the room. Agreed?"

Judah nodded. "Sounds great." He smiled, charmingly. My stomach still felt (and feels) uneasy. I don't like that he's so accommodating. Although, I wouldn't like it if he *wasn't* accommodating, I suppose.

We walked all the way past the cafeteria, where everyone else was huddled, and straight to the monitor room. Jeff keeps the key to the room most of the time, but he handed it over to Stephen without a word when we drew close.

The second locker in the back was cleared out—the other one's door is busted open, it's been like that since we started using the room—and Stephen put Judah's items inside. The little rectangle key was passed to Judah, and he mumbled a thank-you.

I looked at Angel, and she looked as exhausted as I felt. I took her to our room not long after that, after checking that Stephen was okay with making sure Judah would be settled for the night. Stephen said he'd listen to what Judah had to say, and if he approved we'd all gather in the cafeteria to hear him out. I was more than happy to pass on responsibility for the night.

Angel is giving me grief about staying up writing. But I couldn't sleep, even with how tired my bones feel. And besides, I need to write this down. It's too important not to. I don't think anyone else writes nightly anymore. Angel calls me crazy, even though she smiles. I don't think they're thinking about you, whoever you are. They're not thinking about making sure you understand what's happened to us. They're not thinking beyond today.

I'm thinking about you. I'll keep writing. I'll let you know what happens tomorrow.

Goodnight.

Day 3908

We all gathered in the cafeteria this morning, as Stephen told us to. He liked what Judah told him last night, and figured it would be all right to share with everyone. I'm still not sure I believe all of it, but I'll write it down for you anyway.

Judah sat down at a table in the center of the room, and we all sort of clustered around after Stephen introduced him. The man had taken a shower, and combed his hair, and I almost didn't recognize him without the covering of grime and grit.

"Now, what happened out there," he began, and we all watched, rapt, "was terrible. And you kids were probably right to be afraid at first. But," he held up his hands and smiled at us with yellow teeth, "you don't need to be afraid anymore."

"Come on," Rock complained. "Just tell us what happened!"

Stephen glared at him.

"Okay." Judah shrugged. "It was an accident, that's all."

We stared at him, waiting.

"An accident?" Jenn prompted, when it didn't look like he was going to continue.

"Oh, yeah!" he cried. "Just an accident. Someone hit the wrong button and *poof!* Cities go missing."

Angel squeezed my hand.

"See, what they had done"—he paused for effect—"was create a device that could *erase* bad things."

"Who's 'they'?" I asked.

"'They'! You know—scientists and doctors, smart people." He waved his hands in the air. A collective sigh of annoyance went through the room.

Stephen tapped Judah on the shoulder, and the old man swung around to look at him. "We need to speed this up. Tell them what you told me, quickly."

Judah pouted, but complied. "They wanted to use it on this big ball of trash. It was massive, just swirling around in the ocean out in the middle of nowhere, half the size of the country." He snorted. "And they didn't want anyone to remember that something so ugly had ever been created by man, some eco-hippy agenda or something, I don't know, yadda yadda yadda."

Stephen winced.

"So they made this *bomb*," Judah held his hands out in front of him, as if he were holding a ball, "and they were gonna nuke the shit out of this trash monster, *blammo*." He opened up his hands and made them fly apart in an explosion. Then he frowned. "But something went wrong, and they hit a couple of cities instead." He looked down at his old shoes.

"Why did everyone go nuts, though?" Jeffy asked, his voice small and quiet. "They all killed themselves. Why?" And I heard the other question in there too, even though he never said it.

Why did they leave us alone?

Judah shrugged sadly. "Don't know. It happened everywhere, like a virus. People got depressed and couldn't handle it." He held his hand up to his head, like a gun, and I had to look away. I was remembering Ms. Maggie, and David. "They couldn't handle not remembering anything. And looking at the crater just made them crazier."

"No monsters?" Rock whispered. "No one attacked us?"

"Nope. You can all come out now. Go see the crater if you like. It's perfectly safe." Judah was smiling now.

I looked at Stephen, and Stephen looked back at all of us. "What do you think?"

People were scared, torn right down the middle between wanting to stay where we knew it was safe and wanting to see the world we'd been away from for so long.

I raised my hand. "I'd like to make a team to go out there, to make sure it's safe." Jeffy and Rock raised their hands immediately, then Johnson and Chris and a couple more boys, and finally Stephen. The girls kept their hands down. Scaredy-cats, all of them. Even Angel, who was making a face at me.

"But," Stephen said, "only if Judah goes with us. He says it's safe, so he shouldn't have any problem. Right?"

I watched as Judah's face oscillated between surprised, uncertain, and then flat. I didn't like it, but no one else seemed to have noticed.

"Okay," he chirped, shrugging.

"We'll need masks or something," I said. "It smells real bad out there, and the sand in the air hurts."

"Oooh, yeah," Judah said, nodding. "That's the, uh," he made the explosion motion with his hands again, "the city bits."

I shuddered.

"Let's take a couple of weeks to get everything in order," Stephen said. "Judah will stay with us until we're ready to go."

Not much room to negotiate there.

I can't believe we're going outside.

35

Michael felt excitement and fear and exhaustion all at once as he closed the journal, unable to take the emotional overload anymore.

He began studying the ripples in the packed dirt walls, lying on his left side so as not to hurt his arm, nose pushed almost to the wall. If someone walked by the entrance to his alcove he would shut his eyes quickly to pretend to be asleep so no one would speak to him. In truth, it didn't matter; not one person in the whole colony wanted to be around him. His foul mood was palpable, radiating off of him in waves, making the sensitive citizens of the Void rush to be away from his cell.

And it *was* a cell, more so than his room in the Archives had ever been. He could feel himself dying, wasting away to a shred of all that he could have been. As he gazed at the tiny ridges in the black earth, Michael wondered if the medicine woman was poisoning him, if Mary and Captain and the rest of the crater people were plotting to destroy him, just to rid themselves of his darkness. Then he wondered if he would care at all if they succeeded.

The ripples in the dirt were hypnotizing, and he found his anger slipping away from him, though the dark veil of paranoia still clung to his mind thickly. Michael shifted a little so he could pull his left arm out from under him, then reached out the few inches to drag his fingertips over the grooves. The wall was hard, solid, and didn't crumble beneath his hand. Unsatisfied, Michael took a fingernail, or what was left of one at least, and gouged at the surface viciously, determined to see the ridges marred. After much effort, he'd made a small gash in the wall, and he smiled maliciously—then felt guilty. His chest felt tight as he thought about what this place had once been, and he hoped the people who had lived here in the before had been incinerated, not compressed into the edges of the Void as he had dreamed. Solemnly, Michael collected the dirt that had fallen into his quilt and pressed it back into the wall, pleased when the most of the soil didn't fall again.

"What are you doing?"

Michael jumped, hissing in pain when his arm was jarred too roughly. He twisted his head to find Mary standing in the doorway, one hand pushing aside the curtain that stood for a door. She didn't look like she wanted to get rid of him, she looked only concerned, her brows drawn together slightly and her head tilted to the side. Still, he couldn't keep down the feeling of jealousy that started up at the sight of her, and he turned back to the wall almost immediately.

There was no sound for a few moments. Michael, thinking she had gone, felt glad (and then a little disappointed) that he was alone again. Then he heard her sigh heavily as she entered his alcove, crossing the tiny room and settling herself beside him. She waited.

Cautiously, Michael turned so that he was lying on his back, and turned his head. She was sitting on the dirt floor, her legs folded in front of her.

"Use the rug, you'll get dirty," Michael muttered, feeling like he was correcting a child.

Mary looked around for a moment before spotting the lumpy, blue, circular rug that was sitting in front of the chiminea that Michael never used—he had no use for the light, as he'd started feeling too sad and ill to read after the sun set. Mary slid the rug under herself to humor him even though her dress was already marred by the black earth. "Happy now?" she teased him quietly. Michael said nothing.

She fiddled with the hem of her dress a bit where it covered her knees. "I haven't worn one of these since I was a kid. You can't work in them very well, you know. Though they are pretty, I guess." She shrugged a little, mostly to herself.

"What were you before you were an Archivist?" Michael asked quietly, realizing with some surprise that he didn't know. Months and months spent with this person, and he knew not a damn thing about her. He shook his head in wonder.

She furrowed her brow a little, as if it took great effort to remember that far back. "Hatchery," she said finally, wrinkling her nose. "I hated the way the chickens smelled though. It was miserable." Mary shuddered, and Michael let out a tiny smile in sympathy. He himself had tried to avoid that section of the complex as much as he could. "How about you, Michael?"

He wasn't sure he wanted to tell her, but the words spilled from his mouth before he could stop them. "I worked on one of the farm plots. It was nice, kept me busy." He sorely missed the sun on his skin, but he wasn't going to tell her that, didn't want her to have that over him.

Mary was still looking at him curiously, expecting more, but he didn't have more to tell. He slid his eyes back to the grooves in the wall beside his head.

"Why aren't you talking to me? I thought we could talk about what we've been reading."

Michael sat up suddenly and glowered down at her, and she made a face at him. His words were icy when he spoke. "Now you *want* to talk about it? Isn't that against your rules? Never talk about the Before?"

She frowned at him, her eyes worried, and he felt a worm of regret start to wriggle through him. "Not *my* rules, Michael. The Archive's."

Michael wanted to lie back down—his head was spinning—but he hated the thought that she would see that weakness in him.

"Archivists who talk about what they're reading have bad things happen to them. I don't know why, but they don't like it when we talk about the journals. I was protecting you."

Michael snorted, not buying it. Mary's eyes were tearing up in some strange emotion that wasn't quite anger, her nose turning red beneath her dark skin.

"I didn't want you to get hurt—or killed. But we've already broken all the rules they have, and if they found us now . . ." She sucked in a breath shakily, unable to say it. She was frightened, and it was his fault for dragging her out here where she wasn't safe, wouldn't ever be safe again.

"The rules don't matter anymore," Michael muttered, and slowly eased himself back onto the pallet, blissfully horizontal again. He saw Mary nodding at him out of the corner of his eye. He sighed, weary and wanting to close his eyes. "I don't want to talk about Johnny. I'm too tired to try to make sense of it all." If only there had been enough time to screen the journals before he had stolen them. He looked back to the dirt. The grooves on the wall were evenly spaced, but tight together, huddled, afraid to be too far away from their own kind.

"All right." Mary stretched out on the rug, gazing at the ceiling with her arms tucked under her head. It seemed she wasn't planning on leaving him any time soon, and again he couldn't decide if he was grateful or annoyed.

36

Angel's sick. She won't eat a thing in front of me, and I know she's been crying from how red her eyes are. She tells me it's just a headache. I don't believe her. I hope she doesn't have the flu or something like that.

A few of the other Recorders have gotten pretty sick over the years, and we've lost three from my class—four if I count Ms. Maggie, who wasn't really *in* the class but was certainly a part of the group. That number isn't so bad in the grand scheme of things, I know. But the thought of Angel being the fifth makes me want to curl up and scream.

She won't let me kiss her in case I catch it. When I'm sitting next to her I can feel the heat rolling off her body in waves. Normal headaches don't come with burning fevers. Normal headaches aren't contagious. I'm worried that some lingering form of the virus could have been let in when the old man came into the bunker. I haven't seen anyone else get sick lately though, and I haven't noticed her start to forget anything important. Just little things, like where she put her pen or what we've planned to cook for dinner that night. Each time she does forget something, I panic a little and reach my hand out to check her fever. She always scowls at me and pushes my hand away.

I keep asking her to go to medical so I can use the machines (if they still work—it's been a couple of years and I don't think anyone maintains them like we were told to), but she won't. She says she'll be fine if she rests. Stubborn girl. All I do is worry about her. I can't think about anything else.

I should be prepping for the trip into the crater. I won't be able to leave if she doesn't get better. I can't leave her like this. I hope she gets better soon.

Day 3925

Angel's still not eating much.

We're supposed to be leaving next week. Stephen's been raiding the bunker for instruments we can use to take measurements out there, to see if we can figure out exactly what the bomb was made out of. He's found lots of little sample jars and microscopes and slides and things. And there are suits with oxygen tanks hooked up to them in a room that we broke into—it had been locked all the way in the back of the seventh hall. No one knows what happened to the key, and none of the keys we'd found on any of the adults' bodies could open it. In the end, Rock ended up torching the door down, getting it really really hot until the metal glowed bright orange and he was able to hammer a big section out of the middle. It just kind of melted apart, like how I remember butter melting. Real butter, not whatever the hell it is we have now. He told us he saw someone do it in a movie, before we came here. I think he's crazy, but it worked.

It worries me that the people who set up this bunker thought we'd need oxygen suits. Did they really think things were going to get that bad?

Of course, nothing we find comes with instructions. No one thought to pack those when they stocked this damn building. I'm guessing they didn't count on the operators going crazy and offing themselves, leaving us behind to try and figure this mess out.

With as many people we have right now, we're estimating that we have about five years of food left. Eight if we start rationing right away. The thought is frightening.

I keep having these nightmares that we'll go out there and the world won't be ready for us, that we're going to be buried miles and miles under earth or water, and that as soon as we open the locks, everyone we've kept alive these past ten years will all be killed instantly, drowning in flood or suffocating with black dirt filling our mouths and ears and eyes. I'm glad Angel hasn't been around when I've woken up from those dreams. She'd think I was crazy.

Now, when I'm awake, of course I know that those things aren't going to happen. If I could get outside to bring Judah *in*, then of course we aren't underwater. I get that. But I still don't know what we're going to find, and that terrifies the hell out of me. I keep trying to remember if I ever overheard any of the adults talking about what was left of the other cities after they were destroyed. I can't remember. Maybe I knew about that once, and that's one of the memories that got eaten away. I know that at least ten cities were obliterated before home was hit, and the actual number was probably a whole lot more. I don't even know how many cities were destroyed in that last wave of attacks. Hell, we don't even know if that *was* the last wave of attacks. We're operating under assumptions and guesses based on half-baked information.

If Judah is telling the truth, five hundred million people died because of a little mistake. My brain hurts thinking about that many people gone in an instant—a flash and they're history. It's crazy. But I know that that's what happened. It happened to my family. All of our families. And I want to know why.

Day 3930

We're delaying the trip again, because Angel is *still* sick. I can't go with her like this.

Day 3945

I think I know what's wrong with Angel. I can't even put all of my thoughts together in an order that makes sense, but I know. I don't want to push her to tell me. And I certainly don't want to be wrong.

Day 3947

Still nothing. I'm leaving in a week to go see the crater. A week. That's it. And she still hasn't said anything to me? Why? Maybe I shouldn't go on the trip . . . If I'm right, I'm not going. They can go without me, I know they want to. But why hasn't she *told* me?

I'm not sleeping well. I keep coming up with reasons why she's not telling me, why she's let me go weeks without saying anything to me. All of the reasons make me angry with her.

Day 3951

I'm leaving tomorrow. I can't stay, not now.

I asked Angel if there was anything she needed to tell me. Immediately, she looked guilty, so I knew my guess was right. It's not an illness. But I still have to leave.

I'm furious. I can't even begin to accurately describe how I'm feeling right now. If I sit still for too long my hands start shaking and I want to hit something. I want to hit *her*. Which just makes me feel worse. I'd never hit her. Never in a million years. Not even now.

I thought I loved her. I thought she loved *me*. She let me hold her as I asked her, and she began shaking. She was her own personal earthquake. At first I wanted to shelter her, keep her from shaking herself apart. But as the minutes ticked by without her offering any sort of explanation, I just grew angry.

"Your clothes are tighter", I snarled at her, furious. It would have been better if I had been able to stay calm, but it hurt so much.

"You're sick all the time. You won't eat. You won't let me touch you. *Why won't you say it?*"

And she looked up at me, damn her, with her green eyes that used to make me melt and want to swing her around just to hear her laugh. Angel looked up at me and she cried. Her nose got red, and her face crumbled in pain.

My heart ached for her. It did. But, feeling sick, I unwrapped my arms from around her and stepped back. I wanted to tear my hair out. I knew then that there was another question I needed to ask her, one that I knew was going to kill me, but I couldn't stop the words from rushing out of me and jumping between us.

"Is it mine?"

She couldn't even force herself to say it. This woman I'd fallen in love with—she didn't have the courage to voice what she had done. She destroyed me. All she could do was shake her head "no."

Maybe if she had been able to talk to me about it, I would have been able to forgive her with time. But not now. I don't know her now. And I certainly don't know the baby that's growing inside her.

37

Michael felt sick. There was an anger burning inside him that he didn't know how to bank or diminish, and it was all aimed at a woman he didn't know. He stared at the words on the page, written with short angry strokes that betrayed just how much pain Johnny had been in when he wrote them. Johnny had been completely crushed, and though Michael was far removed from the Archives and from the chair that slipped its tentacle into his brain and made him feel, there was no running from the raw emotion Johnny had poured into those last entries. Michael felt the heartbreak as if it were his own. Furious tears burned the back of his eyes and made his head feel like it was being squeezed in a vise.

All sorts of words came to Michael's mind, none of them pleasant and all of them meant for Angel. The vile lot of them were housed right on the tip of his tongue as Michael tossed the journal down onto the bed. He wanted to pace angrily about his small, packed-earth room, but he couldn't muster up the strength to do it, so he just seethed with his arms thrown over his face. The air was cold outside, and neither the curtain over the open doorway nor the blanket he lay under did anything to keep the wind from ripping right through him, making him shiver. It seemed that no matter where he read, he was destined to feel frozen at the end of it.

He let out a harsh little laugh, more a bark of pent-up energy than anything else, and ran his hands through his hair.

Mary looked up at him from her spot on the floor beside him. "Michael?" she cooed. "What's wrong? What is it?"

He didn't move his hands, preferring to wallow by himself.

They stayed that way in silence for a few moments, but a thought started to gnaw at him, and it didn't want to let his brain go once it had grabbed on. He felt sick.

"Who did you pick as your Recorder?" He was afraid to hear the answer.

Mary sighed, he could hear her brain turning. "I . . ."

"Tell me."

"Angel. It's Angel."

He had known. Her answer didn't surprise him at all, but he still felt his chest swell with anger.

"She's *pregnant*," he spat. Mary cringed.

"She . . . um." Mary sucked in a breath, shaking. "She has a little girl. A healthy one."

"I don't give a shit."

He watched as her face fell.

"He tells Angel later that they can work things out. That he'll raise the kid with her. He wanted a baby."

"Johnny didn't want that kid. He didn't. I know it."

Mary was shaking her head. "You're not in the chair. You don't know that for sure. It's just not possible for you to feel that."

"You told me once that it was possible; you told me that before. You said some people get too connected and they don't even need the spike once the initial connection's made. You said it."

"That only worked before, Michael. If volunteers were reading their parents' journals. They had to be related to the Recorder. That doesn't happen anymore." Her lips thinned and she looked away.

"I *feel* it," he insisted. She didn't argue with him again. "Do you think she knew she wasn't wanted? Felt it?"

"Angel? She knew. She knew as soon as she told him. She knew he wouldn't love her again." Her face had gone terribly sad.

"Not Angel." Michael shook his head slightly before he could think better of it, his head pounding as it was. "The baby. Do you think she grew up knowing she had ripped two people apart?" He was feeling morose, thinking of a different baby's face. "I don't want Lily to think that, even if she wouldn't know why that feeling was inside of her. I hope you can't feel something like that if you aren't told . . ."

"Who's Lily?" The question hung between them, heavy, as Mary studied Michael.

He debated for a long time how to say it, the words caught in his throat, unwilling to come loose easily. Finally he just had to force it out, the words knifing him. "My daughter, back in 441."

She scowled suddenly, the quick change in her features jarring. "Bullshit. Don't lie to me, Driftveil. You wouldn't be an Archivist if you had a kid." She shook her head. "You had me feeling bad for you. I thought you'd left behind a girlfriend."

"I'm not lying to you," he said. "She's ten, and she's brilliant, and she's real. Not a lie." Mary wasn't buying it; he could see it in her eyes. "They told us we were too young and denied the parentage application." His heart hurt. "I would have turned eighteen a month before she was born, and they still denied the application."

Again, that pause between them. The empty space was starting to make his head pound.

"They reassigned her?" Mary's voice was quiet.

"Her mother didn't want . . . When they denied the application, they told us Rachel had to go get it taken care of before term, and she told them to go fuck themselves. And then the Republic denied her any medical treatment for being difficult." His eyes burned and he blinked furiously. "I was working when she was born. I didn't even know her mother was gone until I went to go check on her at the end of the day and found that her hut had been scrubbed and reassigned. She gave birth on the floor, and then the parentage committee was called in, and they took the baby away. They took Rachel to the west hill immediately. No one even sent a runner to come get me or let me know."

Nothing had felt real in the weeks after that. Michael frowned at the ridges in the wall.

"The couple who got her, they named her Lily, after their other daughter who died the year before." He hated that, hated that his daughter had a dead girl's name. It was too morbid for a kid to handle, and besides that, Rachel would have hated the name. "They were nice enough to start with, but they didn't like me trying to be around her as much as I was. I used to see her every week or so." Would he ever see her again? The way his arm was holding up, he didn't think so. But at least he still knew exactly who she was. "Rachel wanted a house with red brick. We were trying to get one." His voice was unexpectedly rough and low.

"*Bastards.*" Mary's dark eyes flashed angrily.

Michael nodded.

She inhaled for a long time, until Michael thought her tiny lungs might burst, and then she held it for a time, debating with herself.

"What?" he prodded, closing his eyes. His arm was throbbing in hot fire in time with his headache.

She bit her lip, looking at her knees, covered by the green dress. "Do you know why Sonicrete is pink?"

Michael wrinkled his face up. "Because they don't take the time to cure it all the way."

When she didn't say anything, he glanced at her. She was shaking her head.

"They dye it."

"What? Who?" He didn't understand her, couldn't assimilate the information into his mind.

"The Republic. When they ship the Sonicrete bags out to the complexes, there's a dye in there that turns it pink. And the

Sonicrete has a compound in it that makes it break down faster than regular concrete, so it has to be replaced or recoated every few years. That's why none of our buildings last, but the bunker is still around. The bunker is made out of concrete."

He frowned, deeply. "That doesn't make any sense. Why would the Republic design our buildings to fail?"

"To make you hate it."

Michael stared at her for a long time. Mary started squirming, uncomfortable under his gaze. She started to babble under the pressure, her hands twisting nervously in her lap. "The Republic's population was too low fifteen years after the virus started offing everyone who thought too much about what happened to them. If their statistics are right, they had something like one baby born for every four deaths, and that's not sustainable for a group whose whole goal is to take control of what's left of the country. So they started opening small sections of the land again and forming new complexes, so people could spread out and have their own houses. They tried to grow the population that way, except everyone was still too depressed to make any more people for the Republic to control, so we just had adults holing themselves up and going to sleep in cold beds.

"So Angel comes along, and suggests that they pass a law that you have to apply for housing, and the determining factor would be if you were having a baby. You could apply for parentage, pay the fee for the house, and raise your kid in the house until they were adults themselves, and then you moved back into the hut you started in unless you were having another kid. And then to make it worse, the committee decided that the huts should be as repulsive as possible. They made them so they'd degrade and they're cold—and they're pink. And they make the Law Building pink, too, to try to jam it into your brain that pink is a terrible color, the color of total failure, the color of having no one care about you. And then you hate the hut so badly that all you want is to have a baby so you can get away from the horrible pink huts." Her face was angry. "And then the population crisis wasn't a crisis, just a concern. And then it was just a distant memory." She looked straight at Michael. "There's no reason they should have denied your app. That's bullshit."

Michael was furious. "They do it all on *purpose*? And Angel came up with it? Are you fucking *kidding* me?" His anger with the woman grew, suddenly white hot again.

"She didn't ever dream that it could affect you, Michael. She thought the system was a good one."

"Angel?" He chuckled darkly. "Why would she give a shit about me?"

Mary jerked her head back like he had slapped her. "You haven't figured it out yet?"

His brows knitted together. "What the hell are you talking about? You talk like everything should be obvious to me. It's *not*."

"My Recorder's name is Angel Phillips."

He blinked stupidly at her. "I *know* that. I know who Angel is."

"She named her daughter Samantha. Samantha Phillips."

That name . . . so familiar. It jangled around in his head. "Who is . . ." And then it came to him. His chest grew tight as he realized how close the Archives had come to taking her away from him. He could only hold her face in his mind for a few hazy moments before she flitted away. "That's . . ." He cleared his throat with a great deal of difficulty. "That was my mother's name."

Mary looked at him quietly, her eyes showing concern. She was always looking concerned for him, at him.

When he only stared, she reached out and touched his elbow. "Michael," she said, her voice very low, "are you okay?"

He didn't know what to tell her.

38

Day 3952

We're spending the night right on the edge of the crater, which is terrifying. But it's beautiful, too—we're sleeping out under the stars. Just like camping. Except that we're all sleeping in our suits so we don't suffocate on the "city bits," as Judah calls the sand.

Even though I know he's nuts, I'm starting to think Judah was right. There's nothing here.

We walked out in the morning, bundled up in our suits with three days' worth of food and water on our backs. We're going back tomorrow morning, but Stephen wanted to be sure we had enough.

It took a couple of hours to get there, but I think it could be a faster trip if we weren't so loaded up. It was also made worse because there are all these *hills* in the way—dozens of them just to get to the thing. Rock complained and asked if we could go around the hills at all, because there were too many and he was out of breath after three.

Judah said that there was no "around" the hills; they surround the crater like ripples. What caused that?

We took samples of the dirt along the way, one at the top and bottom of each hill—I didn't really know what I was doing, but Stephen seemed to know—to see if we'd be able to measure anything changing the closer we got to the bomb site.

The crater is MASSIVE, and hard to look at. It swallows up all the light around it and it's just huge. I don't like staring at it. I don't think we'll find a damn thing with those little tubes of dirt, to be honest, but I'm not going to tell Stephen that. It's empty out here. There's nothing.

Day 3953

A noise woke us before sunrise. I don't know what the noise was exactly, but it scared the shit out of me and I sat up immediately. The other boys were sitting up, too.

We listened, silently, and I was hoping I was imagining it, but it happened again, and then again. Like a howling, but not.

"Look!" Jeff cried, and I could just barely make out where he was pointing in the dark.

Reader, whoever you are, there were *lights*. Tiny lights, in the crater, moving around.

People started freaking out before Stephen could hush them up.

"The monsters," Jeffy sobbed. "It's the fucking monsters, the Bubblers found us."

"Judah, what are those?" I called out, hoping he would know.

We all waited for him to say something as we listened to the growling, howling noises.

"Judah?"

He didn't answer.

He didn't answer because that bastard up and left us in the middle of the night, just like that.

Stephen started cursing. Powerfully, colorfully. I won't put down all he had to say because it would make you blush, but it was kind of scary to see him lose it like that.

We sat very close to each other, in the dark, huddling and trying not to listen, until the sun came up enough for us to try to find our way back. We were terrified.

As soon as it was light enough, Stephen got us up and we started back, double time. We got lost. It took us hours longer than it should have, and we didn't get there until late afternoon.

When we returned, the heavy door at the front of the bunker sat open and unattended. We all froze.

"What do we do?" someone asked. I'm not sure who, maybe Johnson. The blood was pounding in my ears, making it hard to concentrate.

Jeff started walking forward first, slowly, and then he took off running toward the gate. No one said anything else. We just followed him.

Judah was just inside the gate. I thought Stephen was going to kill him.

"What did you do?" Stephen screeched, pushing the old man against the wall.

Judah had the nerve to look innocent. "There are people here to rescue you. That's all."

I was taking off my suit when I heard it, the crying. I turned around, and there she was, sitting on the floor, sniffling and sobbing. She looked ugly.

"I opened it," she said. "Judah came to the door, all upset. I couldn't hear him, so he wrote a message in the dirt. It said you were hurt. I had to let him in to get help."

Judah winced. "Sorry about that. They wanted me to open the door quickly. Hope you don't mind the lie." He looked sheepish. I wanted to throttle him.

She called my name, but I didn't look at her. So she started crying harder and I thought I would die.

"Who's 'they'?" I asked Judah, and he laughed.

"They! The senators!"

"They" were waiting for us in the cafeteria. Seven of them.

As soon as we entered, a woman with a pinched face ran up to us. "Oh, you poor, poor *dears*!" she cried. "To be locked up here all alone! You poor *babies!*" I hated her.

The other Recorders were in the cafeteria, too, looking terrified. Two of the strangers stood in front of them, holding nasty-looking guns.

"We'll leave in the morning," Pinchy Face said. "We've got homes set up for each of you." She beamed.

"Who *ARE* you?" Rock demanded, trying to look menacing. He looks like nothing in the face of a machine gun.

"We're your senators, dear." Pinchy looked offended.

"We didn't vote for you," Jeffy said, sticking his chin out.

She laughed then—cackled, really. "Oh," she said, "oh little love. Of course you didn't *vote*. We choose our own. That's just how it works." She giggled again, fanning herself as if Jeff had just told the joke of the century.

She's awful, and the other six are mean-looking.

But they have guns. So we sat down with the rest of the Recorders. They told us not to talk too much, because Pinchy gets headaches. And I guess now we're leaving the bunker in the morning again.

39

"Why did you leave the hatcheries?" Michael's voice was so quiet Mary almost didn't hear him. She was stretched out on her stomach on the dirt floor as usual, reading one of Angel's journals for the tenth time and enjoying the heat from the chiminea, the flames only a foot or two from her legs, the warmth pleasant.

She looked up at him after a minute. She almost looked guilty, and hemmed for a long while, shutting the journal she was reading without even noticing that she had folded and creased the corner of the page. Mary hated when pages got creased; it made her so angry she would cry. Michael didn't feel like enduring another emotional outburst, so he didn't mention it to her. *Strange woman*, he thought as he watched her roll over onto her back to look at the ceiling.

"I wanted to help people, I guess. I was tired of my job and of feeling worthless. There are *so many* people who work with the birds, you know how that is, it's not like I was really making a difference. And I was lonely." She smiled a little, sadly, tilting her head back so that she was peering at him upside-down from the dirt.

"You're getting your hair dirty," he murmured, but she waved him off and kept talking.

"So one morning I'm sitting in my hut and . . ." She trailed off, trying to remember. Her face screwed up in concentration and Michael's chest felt tight just watching her. "And I had . . . a neighbor, I think? He was being sent off, and I heard the truck coming, and I just . . . got on. I don't remember what I was thinking when I crawled in, but the driver didn't care, he was fine with it. That's not allowed anymore—they started guarding the gate and ID checking everyone after that little stunt—but at the time I was home free." She blew out a breath that made the fringe of hair laying on her forehead flutter. "When I saw the crater for the first time, I threw up all over the back seat." She smiled ruefully, and he laughed a little.

"Was the driver pissed?"

"Oh yeah," Mary chuckled. "She marched me straight up to Coleman's office and claimed I was a stowaway, just to try to get me yelled at, I guess. But that ended up being exactly what I wanted anyway because then I knew who was in charge. I told her I wanted to help people and my aunt Liddy—or aunt Lisa . . . ? No, it was definitely aunt Liddy—she had been a volunteer Archivist a long time ago before I was born, so I said I wanted to do it too."

"I didn't know that. What ended up happening to your aunt?"

Mary frowned. "She went totally insane, just like all the other volunteers did back then."

Michael winced.

"Anyway . . . that was probably eight or nine years ago now, and Angel's my seventh project." She sat up and looked at the fire. "I'm certainly not lonely anymore, since there are so many memories to keep me company." She tried to laugh, tried to make it a joke, but all that came out was a choking sob. Michael wanted to hug her, but didn't.

They were quiet for a few more minutes, listening to the popping of the dry sticks she'd used to feed the fire. When Mary next spoke, her voice was so dark and so angry that Michael thought for a moment someone else must have replaced his friend. Someone furious and wretched.

"I don't think a single thing I've read has helped anyone," she said. "It's all been unimportant, semi-political people spiraling into depression before getting sick and dying. That's why I was so looking forward to being allowed to pick one of the kids. I'd never had a kid Recorder available to me before. But I knew that she had to be brighter, and I knew that the kids were always the ones that bounced back the most." She looked at Angel's journal, sitting on the floor beside her, and she grew quiet again. "I don't think anything in here is going to help people, Michael. I think the journals can only hurt."

"Mary." He didn't like hearing her so upset, but he didn't know what to say. The journals had certainly hurt *him*, and they had hurt Thomas, too. But they had also brought good things, like the drawings. "It's not the journals' fault. It's Coleman's."

If Mary thought he was right, she didn't say it.

He watched her watching the fire, listening to the hushed voices of the crater inhabitants echo through the empty space that lay just feet from them. If Michael could find the strength, he could walk out, just past the edge, and he could fall into the dark. He wouldn't die, not immediately. He would just fall in the dark, forever, until he fell asleep and didn't wake up again. No one would be able to hunt him down and hurt him, or poison him, or smother him in his sleep.

He sighed. "I think I was a better person before they started rehabilitating me." His voice was bitter and tight. "I was happier. I was healthier." He barked a laugh, and it hurt his chest. "I didn't have anyone but Lily, but I didn't feel alone so often."

Mary looked back at him with pity in her eyes.

"I should be dead," he said, his voice very small and quiet.

"Stop that." She was scolding him, but her voice was just as small and quiet as his.

"You don't understand," he said, unsure if he wanted to confess to her but doubting he could stop now that he had started, "I'm . . . I was arrested for . . ." The words clung to his throat and he couldn't lodge them free. "I was meeting up with some people, Mary. On the west hill. They were looking for jewelry. I brought the shovels."

Mary grew very still, and he knew that he had made a mistake in telling her.

"You *what?*" Her voice was incensed, and Michael studied his arm, tried to count how many areas of rot he could see through the spoiled bandages.

"You stole from the west hill? Are you kidding me?"

Eight spots so far.

"How could you *do* that? That's *disgusting,* do you have no shame? *Jesus!*"

Fourteen black splotches. Michael shuddered. "I was going back for her ring." His heart hurt worse than his arm. "I thought they might have buried her with it. I was going to keep it for Lily, when she got older and would understand."

Mary didn't yell anymore, and when he looked up again she was biting her lip with tears in her eyes.

"Oh," she said. "Oh, Mikey Moose." She was impossibly sad.

"My grandmother used to call me that." There was a lump in his throat, and he fought to clear it. "I didn't get to the ring before they caught me. I thought for sure . . . I was gonna be shot." He rubbed his hand against his face. "But they didn't end up charging me for grave-robbing. Just . . . theft." He coughed and rolled over onto his side, facing the black rippled wall so he wouldn't have to look at Mary cry.

40

The senators' meeting was today. They're worried about the population dip, especially in this sector. Apparently it's not as bad in the south, but they're still losing five people for every birth.

We're dying out. After all the shit we've been through—making it through the attacks and then the virus, rebuilding the country, putting up the barricades, making sure we had enough land to grow the food we needed to support our complexes—we're going to die out because people are still too depressed to have sex. It's ridiculous. It makes me angry. Not that I'm exactly helping the fight.

It was a closed meeting, but they wanted me there anyway. I almost refused because I didn't want to listen to the recruitment speeches again. I will not be a senator. I don't want that responsibility or that power. Hell, trying to keep track of less than forty kids in a confined bunker nearly drove me crazy. Why would I ever want to be responsible for over forty thousand citizens?

I went to the meeting, in the end, because I wanted to torture myself. Angel always goes to the meetings. When the senators recruited her a few years ago, she didn't say no. Realistically, it was a smart choice for her, because of the food bonus she'd receive for her and the kid. What's her name? Sam. I try not to think about that kid, although she has a way of weaseling into my thoughts just to make me miserable and bitter.

Like now.

Anyway, the meeting was held in the central house, which meant that it was a real event, a big forum. They actually scheduled it weeks ago, sent runners all over the sector to let the senators know to gather, and the building was packed. I'm not sure I've ever seen so many senators in one place. It would be inspiring if I didn't think the majority of them were righteous assholes.

Stephen sits at the head table now, which is nice. I'm not sure when that happened, but I'm sure his being there was the main reason I was invited to sit in at all. He wants me to join. For him, I almost would.

They didn't get to the main point right away. I sat in the back of the big stone building, by the door, in case it became too much and I had to leave quickly. My temper hasn't gotten any better over the years.

The first item was on new laws that were being called for in the complexes. The chaplains wanted a uniform place in each complex to bury the dead, as a last rights sort of thing. Apparently some of the less-developed complexes had taken to burying the bodies of loved ones in yards to be close, or they interred them too close to the farms. The head chaplain—Whitehall, I think his name is?—made a very empathetic speech about *why* burials needed more regulation, regardless of the best intentions of the families of the recently deceased. Food was becoming contaminated. People were becoming sick. He proposed that burials take place outside the complex fences, on hills to the west, away from the food and houses.

"Won't the families miss their loved ones, though? You can't suggest that we allow citizens outside the fences to visit?" I don't know who it was that spoke, but once it was out in the air, murmurs of doubt peppered the room.

"Well, of course," Whitehall said dryly, "this would mean no visitation." His voice was strong and clear above all the others. "But being buried in the west means the dead could watch the sunset, and the families may take solace in knowing that they watch the sunsets together."

The other chaplains in the room nodded eagerly.

I frowned, watching the glitter of gold and gems against throats and hands as the chaplains moved. It seems odd to me that the majority of all jewelry I've seen since we left the bunker winds up bedecked on the fingers and throats of the church. How much easier will it be to lift the valuables people are buried with if no one is around to watch over the burials?

"I also would request that the crime of grave-robbing be escalated to a tier one," Whitehall said, meaning the punishment would be death, "to ward off any unsavory characters that may attempt to take advantage of the new burial regulations and lack of supervision." Again the chaplains were all nodding, their jewelry shining like hundreds of gross little beetles. This reclassification would ensure that if any grave-robbers discovered that the valuables of the deceased had already been taken . . . well, they would be silenced soon enough. I looked away from the front of the room, shaking my head in disgust, but I kept my mouth shut.

My eyes met Angel's. She was looking right at me, and I could see in her face that she knew what the chaplains were doing, too. We each waited for the other to stand up, to oppose Whitehall.

The vote passed 27 to 9.

Angel gave a tense little shake of her head as she looked down at her notes, her mouth set into a frown. How much she's changed. Her hair has faded, and she wears it short now, tucked behind her ears. It reaches a little bit longer than her chin. Her face is lined. She looks tired.

I don't feel angry when I look at her anymore, which is good, I suppose. Being angry with her doesn't change anything. Now it just hurts, just a little, when I think about how young and happy we used to be.

Now we're old and miserable.

Oh, there are those in their forties, sure, and every once in a while we get a report that someone in some complex somewhere just celebrated fifty years on the planet, but there are so few of those now. Our oldest citizen is in Complex 17, sixty-one years old and gone batty. She was forty-one when the country went to hell, and she was locked up—this is what I hear anyway—for going nuts and trying to have a tea party in the middle of the highway. Word is she's never ever sad, just happy as all get out all the time. That's how she made it through. Nobody's that happy anymore. That's just the way it is.

I think Judah, before they shot him, was in his thirties when he came to take us. Funny how much older he looked. We all *look* so old. My hair's even greyer than Angel's.

The head table asked who would be willing to be on the population committee. There wasn't much to the request; seven senators raised their hands almost in unison, which meant that it was really just a formality to begin with. The committee had been formed prior to the forum.

Angel was one of the ones with her hand raised. She was looking at someone else, a man also with his hand raised, across the room. They were smiling at each other warmly. I don't know what to think about that.

The next topic made me sit up and pay attention. The senators want to start going through the journals that were found. This part was interesting.

They called a man up to stand in front of the head table. He had stacks of photos that he handed out to be passed around the room. Beaming and excited, he introduced himself as Jim Gillimond.

"We've done it," he grinned, bouncing on his feet. "We've figured out the Mnemosyne!" He nearly giggled with glee, then pouted when it became clear that we had no idea what the hell he was talking about. He has a face like a loaf of bread that's been stepped on.

Mr. Gillimond sighed and spelled it out for those of us who were taking notes. "We found the schematics for it in the bunker when we were first investigating it, but there was no prototype or any explanation of what it was for."

A photo was passed to me. It was a wicked-looking chair with our very own Mr. Breadface standing beside it, smiling. There's an uncomfortable-looking spike near the top, and a tube where an armrest should be.

I arched my eyebrows at Stephen, but he just shrugged. He hadn't known about it either.

"It's taken *years,* but we've finally learned how to use it. It lets us go *inside* the minds of the Recorders!" That silly, high giggle again, and he turned around to show us the terrible wound on his neck. The room cringed.

"The Mnemosyne sends electrical pulses into the brain to let readers experience the memories of the Recorders based on what has been written down." I watched as the other Recorders in the room shifted, uncomfortable, wincing. Even Stephen. Even me.

"We'll finally know reliably what happened in that bunker. This is great news!" Breadface beamed at us, then fielded the few questions that popped up.

It's weird to think about someone intentionally trying to experience what we experienced . . . I'm not sure Mr. Gillimond has thought that through all the way. There was a lot of pain in that bunker.

I'm still writing, but I'm not sure many other people are, at least not consistently. There are journals from people like us, in the bunker, who wrote for those months and months when we were told it was illegal *not* to write. The estimate for those is somewhere around ninety-five thousand volumes, which is incredible.

But then there are the other journals, the ones that normal people kept before the virus got them. Apparently they were found all over, in the homes the Republic tore down to build the barricades up and down the territory.

I haven't seen those barricades, and I have no desire to. As far as I'm concerned whoever made that decision should be shot. How stupid do you have to be to order millions of vacant dwellings razed to the ground so we can clear the land and start over again? Just to build some junk barricade to keep out refugees that may or may not exist. Stupid stupid stupid.

Anyway, these people kept journals while they were living, and so we've been setting them aside and stockpiling them with the bunker journals. There are even *more* of the journals from outside than there are bunker journals.

A woman stood up to take the floor, and after a couple of catcalls (the senators are all assholes, I'm telling you), she asked if we would be going through the outside journals, too. It got so quiet I could hear someone tapping their foot across the huge room.

Finally, Jenkins, the man that sits beside Stephen at the head table, stood from his seat and cleared his throat. Jenkins is in his fifties, and was on massive doses of anti-depressants when the Loss came through. He worked with the old government, from before, and was instrumental in forming the Republic. This guy should have been ecstatic to have a chance to learn what happened to the previous government, if only to keep it from happening to his own, so what he said next surprised me.

"The people that were put away in that bunker were carefully selected as this country's best chance at survival." This isn't really news to us—Judah told us as much when he came to take us out of there. "Their temperaments were tested. Their problem-solving skills were tested. They were handpicked to be compatible with the memory technology we're just now starting to figure out. There were hiccups along the way, yes." His eyes traveled the room, landing on the youngest senators and invitees, all of whom were kids in that bunker so many years ago. "There were supposed to be many, many more people around to guide us through this time after. But unfortunately that's not what happened, and we're forced to work out this technology on our own."

Already I didn't like where this was going, but I kept my mouth shut—again. I was invited there as an observer, not to make my opinions known.

"If we introduce these outside journals into our program, we risk unintended and unknown consequences. The journals from those people outside the bunker are not guaranteed compatible with the Mnemosyne." (God, what a terrible name.)

Mutters were starting up around the room again. It sounded like an angry hive of wasps, buzzing and bumbling, trying to decide what to do.

In the end, Stephen proposed the vote: risk unfiltered and possibly counterproductive memories to be introduced into the country we've been building? Or focus solely on the sanctioned journals and forsake the others? The head table never votes, and I couldn't tell which option Stephen supported. But when the tally was called out his shoulders sagged, from relief or disappointment I couldn't tell.

The Republic of the Coastal Territories will ignore the writings of the common citizen. 20 to 16.

41

Days later, Mary came to see Michael in his room. He was lying in bed, reading back through a journal he had already finished days ago, to make sure he hadn't missed anything. She came in without knocking and lay down next to him.

Michael carefully set the journal aside and shifted to give her room. She said nothing, so after several minutes he hazarded a rather sad joke: "Could a nice necklace make it up to you?" He tried to snicker, but it sounded like a cough.

She winced. "I'm not ecstatic that you kept it from me for so long. I understand not saying anything in the bunker, but we've been out of there for weeks." The look she shot sent a wave of guilt over him.

"But you're here, though. So you don't hate me."

"Yeah."

They looked at each other for a very long time. He didn't touch her, couldn't touch her, wouldn't touch her. He wanted to, though. Badly.

"How's your arm?" she whispered, trying so very hard not to disturb the calm that had fallen between them.

"Terrible." He didn't even think about lying to her. He flashed her a grin he didn't feel when a deep line appeared between her eyes. "It should heal. It just hurts. Don't worry about it."

She nodded and fell silent again. Something was bothering her, and Michael waited for her to speak.

He was stuck, unsure what he was supposed to do. Rachel used to do this to him, too: refuse to tell him what was wrong.

Pain stabbed through him at the thought of her. He hadn't thought of Rachel so much since right after she died. Mary noticed the pain in his eyes.

"What's wrong, Michael?"

That was the question he needed to be asking *her*. He shoved thoughts of the dead girl aside and made sure to clear his face before answering. "Arm," he grunted. "I moved it wrong." Again with the lies? Already? He could have kicked himself. "What's up with you, Mary? Something's bothering you?"

He could see the relief in her face immediately, and knew he had said what she wanted him to. Now she could tell him without feeling like she was burdening him. Women were strange creatures.

"I feel so guilty."

She went no further than that.

"About?" he prompted, a little agitated by this game.

Her eyes shined with tears that all of a sudden she couldn't hold back. "I abandoned her. I feel like I did, anyway. I should have grabbed more of her journals. I just left her there."

Michael blinked. "Angel." It wasn't a question, he was just trying to follow her train of thought.

Mary nodded at him vigorously, chewing on her lip.

"Mary . . . Angel was already dead. You can't have abandoned her."

Mary shook her head furiously. She sat up and stared down at him. "She's in there. In everything she wrote. That's *her*. I can feel her."

"But it's not. That's just the chair simulating what she felt. It's not real, you know that." He tilted his head to see her better. "Don't you?"

"She's not *gone*. I left her there, and she's stuck, unfinished."

"Christ." Michael sat up and swung his legs over the side of the mattress, holding his head in his hands. How could he make her see? "Look . . . my grandmother died happy. She had a daughter and a grandson whom she loved immensely. We didn't visit her too much, which meant that when we did she was that much happier. She died of malnutrition when I was fourteen years old." That memory actually did send a burn of angry pain through him. That damn elder rationing disgusted him. "She slept around when she was young, which meant that she didn't have a husband to take care of her when she needed him to. But she was strong, and ended up just fine without one."

Mary's eyes were burning, and Michael knew he had made a mistake.

"How *dare* you?" Her words were almost inaudible, she spoke them so quietly, but they were filled with fire. "That woman was your family. You wouldn't *exist* without her. How could you *ever* say that about her?"

"Because she's dead, Mary. She's gone! It's just the truth." His head ached, and he could feel his own anger threatening to bubble over in his chest. He wanted to shake Mary and make her understand.

"You didn't ever love her, did you? If you had, you wouldn't say something like that. You didn't love her!"

Michael struck her before he knew what he was doing. The fury he had felt with her evaporated into horror as soon as he heard the loud *crack* of the back of his hand on her cheek. The noise seemed like it would never end, echoing in the packed-dirt room.

The force of it had knocked her back to the mattress. She was staring at him, shocked, her hand on her cheek.

"Shit," Michael breathed, his eyes wide. "Mary, I didn't mean to . . . oh, shit. I am so sorry."

Mary's eyes brimmed over, but she kept herself from crying out. Her face set in anger, she rose from the bed and left him there.

Michael watched her go, loathing himself.

Michael Driftveil, you are a monstrous sonofabitch.

42

Michael closed the last journal and sat staring at the soft blue back cover in his hands. The answer wasn't in there. Emptiness and disappointment washed through him.

His arm ached. The bandages he wore had been soaked through with a brown, seeping liquid. Although he knew he shouldn't, he lifted the destroyed bandages from his arm and looked at the wound. He gagged, tried to hold down the vomit, failed, and held the book away as he retched terribly onto the cool earth beside him.

Disgusted with himself, he looked around for the long rake-like tool he knew he had seen leaning against the wall of his little alcove. He didn't know if this was its intended purpose, but he didn't see another option. It was like a wooden push broom with no bristles, and he grabbed the handle—well-worn and smooth under his hands, but old, cracked, and splintering in places—and pushed the soiled earth away, out of his alcove, out to the very edge of the walkway, then pushed further. The evidence of his sickness plummeted into the dark. Michael shuddered.

He needed to see Mary, he decided. When was the last time he had spoken to her? Days ago. When he had shut her down after she reached out to him about Angel. When he had hit her. Guilt flooded his stomach. Would she see him still? *Probably not*, he thought bitterly.

He walked back to his dark alcove and sat down on the old straw mattress, thinking. His arm throbbed with each breath he dragged into his lungs. These people had no true medicine. They said they did, but Michael knew it was just a mixture of plants that grew in the deep. Now that he could get up and walk around some, he was supposed to go visit Talia each night so she could change his bandages and spread the same thick green paste onto the wound every time. "To ward off the bad spirits that can get inside", she said, bobbing her head up and down to agree with herself, oh yes. She reminded him of a chicken.

But Michael had been avoiding going back to her. Stupid, he knew, but Mary frequented the healer with her own wounds and Michael hadn't wanted to risk the chance of seeing her, not after how terribly he had treated her. And now he was going to pay for his little act of cowardice. His arm was more infected then anything he had ever seen.

Hell, he might even lose the limb.

A crazed laugh tumbled from his lips, and he couldn't stop it or call the sound back in. What would surgery be like with these people? Would they just take an old steak knife they'd scavenged from the time before and hack his arm off? Or would it be more artful? Would they carve a picture into his arm before they mutilated him?

It still floored him that people actually lived here, even after all these weeks of living alongside them. Days ago he had decided that these people were the reason all the complexes had fences around them. The senators must know about them. If not them, at least the higher-ups did. There had been other people on Johnny's research trip, and surely they had written in their own journals about the lights they had seen in the distance. That Johnny hadn't realized the lights belonged to a human colony was inconsequential; the information was still there for any reader who was paying attention.

So yes, the senators knew about it, and they didn't want anyone else to have that same knowledge. That's why they spread the rumors that nothing could grow within a hundred miles of the crater: so that no one would stray from the established farms and run into this lot.

But why allow them to live at all? If Michael had learned anything from his life, it was that the Republic didn't tolerate people who didn't fit the mold; that's why the punishments were so strict. Michael thought that the Republic's military could easily come and wipe out this small colony if they concentrated their forces. There were only a few thousand or so in the crater, from what Michael could tell. So why ignore them?

A thought floated around his mind, far off at first, but growing steadily closer and clearer. He sat up straight and sucked in a lung full of oxygen that still smelled of scorched earth.

The crater. The pieces clicked in Michael's brain, slowly, solving the problem Michael hadn't even known he was pondering. His efforts to find the location of the weapon by stealing the journals had failed, but now he knew *why* Coleman wanted to find it so badly.

This crater that he and Mary had escaped into wasn't the only one. There were at least three others in the country that Johnny had known about, possibly more. And those craters could have colonies in them as well. They had weapons, and knowledge, and things the complexes didn't have, simply because they had taken the time, two generations ago, to scavenge enough to survive without the Republic's help.

The refugees that had fled into the arms of the new Republic had done so because they were dying without order—but these people had no such predicament. They hadn't just survived; they had *thrived.* They had their own currency, their own government, and their own laws. They were a country within a country—and wouldn't that just drive the senators crazy?

Coleman wanted to use the weapon on these outsiders, these people who had refused to assimilate. The crater people had been too strong to eradicate when the Republic had first taken control, and now . . . well, the Minders couldn't very well stage a war against an enemy they had spent the last three decades denying the existence of, could they?

Coleman was going to use the weapon on the craters again. No one would notice the disappearance of something that wasn't supposed to be there. At most, the people in the complexes would feel something like an earthquake, and it would be talked about for a time and then forgotten.

He got up from his mattress and paced, trying to decide what to do. This wasn't his fight. These weren't his people. There weren't any complexes within a hundred and fifty miles of the crater, either, so there would be no one to catch the virus Johnny had written about. The Republic would be virtually unaffected.

Michael stepped out of his alcove and looked at the candles burning in the other dwellings. The walkway these people had built into the side of the earth spiraled down around the crater. Seven levels of rooms had been carved out around the west side of the crater, tucked in so that no one coming to or from the Archives could see it. This structure had been dug out, and perilously, by humans with amazing ingenuity, creativity, and perseverance; and with none of the tools or chemical mixes, like Sonicrete, that his Republic had relied upon. Pure hard work surrounded him.

He heard a group of children squealing with laughter somewhere down below him. He stepped out into the path and leaned against the rail, trying to see them. He ignored the pain in his arm.

The children were on the level below him, several yards to the left, rolling small round stones down the slope of the path. Down at the end of the path, a boy held a scrap of cloth to serve as a finish line, and he declared the winner of the stone race with a mock trumpet noise. (Michael shook his head in wonder—he had no idea what a trumpet was, but he knew that was close to the sound it made.) The winner jumped up and down in victory, while the other three, looking defeated, trudged down to collect their stones and reset the race. They were children, and deep down Michael knew this is how children were meant to live. Inventing games and laughing, not locked underground and forced to write. Not growing up in constant fear of a Minder sending them away.

In that moment, Michael made his decision.

He wasn't going to let Coleman burn this all away.

43

Mary had built a small fire in the chiminea by her window and was sitting in front of it, knees hugged to her chest, when Michael knocked on the wooden frame of the entryway to her alcove. She looked surprised to see him.

"Hi," she said, quietly. Her eyebrows drew together in worry, as if she were expecting him to go ballistic on her again. Guilt gripped Michael's lungs, and he struggled to return her greeting. He felt like utter garbage.

He walked over and sat next to her, gasping when he saw the purple mark on her cheek. "Who did that to you?"

Mary looked at him with her dark eyes, and he knew it had been him. The pain in his chest multiplied. For the bruise to still be there after a week and a half . . . He shuddered. *I'm a monster.* How could he ever have hit this woman? "Mary, I had no idea. God, I am so, so sorry." He reached out to touch her face, but she flinched, and he drew his hand back immediately. He understood at once that their relationship was no longer one of closeness, and he felt like a fool for even trying. He had destroyed that, had no right to it.

"Please don't ever touch me again." Her voice was icy. Michael nodded, not even pretending to be surprised. He shifted a few inches away from her, giving her more space. He waited until he saw her shoulders relax before he spoke again.

"Coleman wants to use the weapon."

Mary smiled bitterly. "Of course she does, the witch. If she could use the weapon, she'd have so much power her head would explode. She'd love it. We already knew that."

Michael shook his head. "No, I mean . . . I think she wants to use it here. To get rid of the colony. That's why she wants the Archivists to find where it is. She *knows* there are people living here, and she—along with the Republic—wants to destroy all of this." He waved his arm, indicating the whole structure that had been carved into the charred earth.

Mary's jaw dropped. "My god, Michael, your arm looks terrible! What did you do?"

"Aren't you listening to me? They're going to bomb the colony!"

Mary chewed her lip. "So we just make sure she never knows where it is, that's all. Once you figure it out, let's go and destroy it."

"No," Michael said, his shoulders sagging. "Johnny didn't write it down in the journals we grabbed. If he wrote it down at all, it's back in the Archives." He paused. "We need to go get the rest of the journals and bring them back."

Mary's eyes flashed. "You want to go back there?" Her voice was a whisper.

"And we don't need to destroy it," Michael continued. "If we know where it is, we can keep it—just the threat of it will be enough. We can get her to leave us alone forever. As long as we have the weapon, they won't be able to touch us. They wouldn't dare. And if they do . . ." He let the end of that sentence hang in the air in between them, heavy with anger and promise. He felt a little giddy at the thought of Coleman being crushed into a hole of nothing.

Mary was frowning at him. She wanted to say something, though. Michael could see it sitting behind her eyes.

"What is it?" he prodded, not as gently as he had intended. He wanted her to be happy with him.

Finally she looked away from him. "We can't go back. We almost died getting out of there. No way are we going to get back in."

He groaned in frustration. He saw her jump, but ignored it. "We have to!"

She turned back to him, her eyes set, the purple mark on her cheek staring at him like an accusation. "And what if they capture you? Do you think she'll let them kill you? No! They're going to put you right back in that chair and make you read every line until she gets what she wants. And your brain will be fried in the process. This is a stupid plan you've cooked up."

He looked at her sullenly. "So what do you want me to do? Nothing? You want me to just sit here and wait until someone else finds it?"

She looked like she was going to cry. "You were Coleman's best bet because of your relationship to Johnny. It'll take someone else decades to get even a tenth of the understanding you've pulled from the journals. No one will find the weapon in our lifetime." She seemed to notice that she had said too much, and shut her mouth tight with an audible *clack* of her teeth.

"My relationship to Johnny?"

Mary was back to gazing at the clay chiminea, silent.

Michael's jaw tightened. "Do you have any proof?"

She actually laughed. Michael tried very hard to not be angry with her, but he was failing. "What proof would there be to give you, Michael?"

He felt a throb in his chest, the dull memory of a heartache. "But—why would she lie to him?"

Mary gave him a solemn look. "I wish I could tell you."

He was quiet for a very long time. Mary turned back to the fire, yellow light from the small flames dancing over her face, the heat putting a light sheen of sweat on her brow.

"I'm going back." When he spoke next, his voice was rough with emotion he knew was not his own. "Are you coming with me, Mary?"

"I need time to think about it. Will you at least wait a few days?"

Michael nodded, then stood, and left her staring at the fire.

44

Mary and Captain were standing at the edge of his bed when he woke. It was a weird moment of déjà vu for Michael, and he started, looking around him in a panic.

He was not in the cold grey room of the Archives, but in the dirt alcove, the burned and packed earth surrounding him on all sides. And it was not a Minder who stared back at him.

"What's happening?" he asked when he had shaken off the fear. Sleep still clung to him like a veil. "What's wrong?"

Captain's eyes were vicious. He glared at Michael in a way that said Mary had told Captain exactly what happened to her face. Mary looked at her scuffed brown shoes, hands on her hips.

"Do you think it's funny to beat down on little things like her?" Captain snarled, stepping forward with his hands balled up into fists. He would kill Michael if he had the chance—Michael could see it.

"Stop that," Mary warned. When Captain started to protest, she grabbed his arm and pulled him back toward her. "That's not why I brought you here. Now stop."

"There are laws." The bigger man's growl sent Michael's stomach turning.

"I appreciate that, Captain, I do. Michael made a mistake." She eyed him for the first time, and Michael felt the heartache kick up again. "A really shitty one that I *should* let you hurt him for. But he's not going to do it again, so you can just leave it alone."

Mary gnawed on her lip, then turned away from Michael. "Get dressed. We need to talk to you," she said to the wall. The tone in her voice stung. More than ever before, he felt like a criminal.

He scrambled out of bed and pulled on his pants, eyeing the other man warily. Captain was still seething, and Michael could practically see the fire shooting from his eyes. Not that he could blame the man in the slightest. *Was it me who hit her, or Johnny?* The question had played over and over in his mind for days, but in the end it didn't matter. Whoever's anger it had been, it was *Michael* who had hit her, Michael's hand which had given her that awful wound.

"Okay, Mary," he said when he was fully dressed. She turned around and took a deep breath.

"We want to go back to the Archives with you."

Michael's eyebrows leapt up his forehead. "We?" He looked back and forth between Mary and the large man who hovered over her protectively. "You told Captain? Why?" Even though he knew he had no right to be, he was angry with her. This wasn't what they had discussed.

"Because this is Captain's colony. And he's got more of a stake in this than either of us."

Michael didn't agree, but he tried not to let his face show it.

"I've got men," Captain said, his voice no less angry with Michael than it was before, "and they can fight. They'll be able to get us in if you can show me where the bunker is." His lips pressed into a thin line, and he growled, "Can't believe they've been right beside us the whole time and we didn't even know. Stupid."

Mary looked sheepish. "We took great pride in staying hidden. Haven't had an intruder in seventy years. No one's even gotten close. Even our own compounds don't know where we are."

Michael looked at her grimly. "You're not a part of them anymore. You're a convict, like me." He snorted a laugh.

Her eyes narrowed at him; she didn't find it funny. Michael could have kicked himself.

Or, judging from the other man's steely look, he could just let Captain do it for him.

Shit, he thought, *he's going to kill me as soon as the fighting starts.*

"We're going." Captain's voice was firm.

"Now? I'm not ready, I have to—"

"Now."

Michael blinked, then looked at Mary. She was inspecting her shoes again.

"The raiding party's outside," she whispered. "Let's go."

45

Michael looked around him at the men and women who were ready to storm into the Archives to protect their home. Anger burned behind their eyes, and they were rowdy, cheering, building themselves up. They chattered in what sounded like a hundred different languages, and Michael was unable to decipher any of it.

Surely, some must have known that this would be their last living day. The weapons they had were little more than sharpened farm tools, all of them handmade. It was like fighting with sticks and stones when put up against the guns and other war tech the Republic had at their disposal.

Michael wished he knew what Captain had told them to get them all so ready to die. Michael suspected that not all of what they had been told was entirely accurate. No doubt some of them would have been ready to fight regardless—threats to one's home could do that—but this group seemed to contain every capable adult they had, plus many of the older children, which made Michael believe that Captain's explanation may have been embellished to a certain degree.

In any case, they were ready, and within hours the thrown-together army was snaking its way up the narrow pathway out of the crater, Captain at the front, leading the men closest to him in a sort of war song. Michael and Mary were a few yards behind him, listening quietly to the harmonies the men created. Michael shook his head, still amazed at the sounds these people could make.

Mary stared straight ahead as she walked. Michael wanted to hold her and tell her not to be afraid, that he would protect her, that nothing bad was going to happen to her, but he couldn't. He couldn't bring himself to lie. So he walked beside her without saying a thing.

The sun beat down on the convoy, and Michael was starting to worry that they had walked right past the Archives, when suddenly the people in front of him stopped walking. Michael peeked out from behind the line of men to see Captain in the front, his dark hand in the air to make everyone still and silent. Behind Michael, the marching line dissolved, and the army gathered into a crowd, an amorphous blob that awaited Captain's instructions. As if on cue, everyone except for Michael and Mary crouched down as low to the dusty ground as they could, waiting patiently. Michael scrambled to follow suit, but Mary remained standing.

Captain had in his other hand a piece of scrap fabric, and was studying it intensely. Michael frowned at the familiarity of it, and then it struck him: it was his map of the Archives. Michael turned his head to stare up at Mary, unhappy. She had the grace to look down at him guiltily and shrug in apology.

Behind the heavy steel and concrete gate, the outer hall that led down into the bunker was only ten or so feet wide, which meant the crater's army would have to pack themselves in tightly once they made it past. But if the guard at the tower shut the gate down first, no one would be getting in at all. Mary must have warned Captain about that ahead of time, because Michael could see him gesturing to a small group of men. After a few moments of hushed discussion they went ahead on their own, crouched low with their weapons out, toward the guard tower.

Frowning, Mary marched over to Captain, hugging herself from the cold. Michael scrambled to get off the ground and follow her, brushing the dust off himself hurriedly.

Mary walked right up to the tall man, her head reaching only a little past his elbow, and stared him down. Michael would have laughed at the absurdity of it if she hadn't looked so determined.

"You remember what I told you?" Her eyes were blazing.

Captain didn't even try to hide his amusement; his white teeth flashed in a wide grin. "Of course, little girl. No one will be hurt if they don't cause any trouble."

Michael frowned. "Of course they're going to cause trouble, though. You're trying to break into a secure facility."

Captain shrugged. "It won't be so secure if my men get to the tower and keep the gates open."

Mary's eyes narrowed. "Those Minders are my family. You remember that."

"And no one in grey." Michael stared at Captain for confirmation. "Right? They've been ordered not to hurt anyone wearing grey?"

Captain sighed and planted his hands on his hips, glaring at Michael with an intense hatred. "I told my people not to harm anyone unless it was necessary to the mission. Trust me."

Michael didn't. He felt sick. He touched Mary's elbow and moved a few yards away from the crowd, out of earshot. He ignored the startled look Mary shot his way, a direct result of him touching her, and waited for her to follow.

She walked over to him cautiously, chewing on her lip. He thought about the way she used to walk, bouncing along through the Archives, her enthusiasm palpable. Now she walked woodenly, dragging herself to meet him. She was afraid of him.

"I don't like this," he hissed when she was close enough to hear him. "Captain's not doing this for the same reasons we are."

Mary sighed and held her head, closing her eyes. "I know."

"We need to get Captain to send them back home, or way too many people are going to die."

"I know."

"Then what are we waiting for?" He stared at her. "Talk to him! He won't listen to me—you have to tell him."

Mary only shook her head, her eyes still closed. Michael gaped at her.

"*What?* Mary, come on. You have to stop this."

She gazed at him sadly. "I can't. Or won't. Or both. I don't even know."

"Why, damn it?" He couldn't believe what he was hearing.

She fixed him with her stare. "Because I know where it is, Michael. *I know.* And no one else can ever find out. We're going to destroy the journals. They're too dangerous now." And without waiting for a response, Mary turned to walk back to the group.

She knows? Michael's mouth had dropped open. How could she know? The answer came to him even as he formed the question in his mind. Angel had figured it out, and Mary had read about it. Why hadn't she told him? *What the hell is she thinking?*

"You can't destroy them!" Michael's hand shot out and grabbed her shoulder before he could stop himself.

"Don't touch me!" she shrieked, whirling around on him and batting his hand away, sending a shooting pain up his injured right arm. She was furious, her eyes black and huge, her face red and distorted. Captain was there within seconds, standing in front of Mary like a shield. His eyes were murderous. Michael shrank back.

"I'm sorry," he gasped. "I'm sorry, I'm sorry." Captain towered over him, an angry mountain that could flatten Michael in an instant.

Mary let out one more frustrated cry, stamping her foot. She had tears in her eyes. Michael was breathless with shame and confusion and hurt.

"I hate what they did to you in there!" she screamed, eyes wild. "The Archives *destroyed* you. They made you dangerous and angry, and I *hate that*!"

"Mary, please, I'm trying to help—"

"You want the weapon so you can use it on the senators, don't you?" Her voice was challenging, but her eyes were suddenly pleading. "Tell me I'm wrong, Michael. Tell me you don't want to use it for revenge."

Michael's mouth moved, but no sound would come out.

"I'm sorry this happened to you. You used to be a good person. But you're not anymore, and you're going to stay away from me."

"*Mary*—"

"Don't you *dare* get in my way!" she spat, tears threatening to fall, before she whirled away and hurried back to the rest of the group. The crater people had been watching the exchange with interest, and Michael balled his hands into fists.

Captain stepped up very close to him, and spoke in a low voice. "I would advise you to stay far, far away from Mary and me when we get inside. Otherwise, I will burn you alive."

Michael was furious. "You turned her against me! She was my friend." The words tore from his mouth in snarls. "You got into her head and made her hate me, tried to get her to kill me. You've been poisoning me through my arm! I know you have."

Captain's finger was suddenly poking him very hard in the chest, but Michael refused to step back this time. "She told me *not* to kill you," Captain said, his voice a growl like stone grinding against stone, "because she knows you've gone crazy. I didn't believe her, but I see it now."

Michael ground his teeth together.

"But I don't like you, and it would make me so happy to make you hurt for the hell you're putting her through. So either you stay away, or you're fucking dead." The finger gave one final stab before its huge, menacing owner turned away and rushed after Mary.

Michael stayed rooted where he was, the feeling of betrayal sitting hard in his gut. Mary and Captain had hatched a plan without him. Even worse, Mary had known the information Michael needed all along, and had decided not to tell him.

His mind spinning with the implications, Michael kicked at the dust underneath his boots, trying to decide what to do. He had no weapons. He was already weakened by his arm, which was now on fire from where Mary had pushed it away. He'd never be able to get into the bunker on his own. He wouldn't even make it past the guard tower.

He stopped pacing and whipped his head around to look toward the bunker. The men Captain had sent ahead earlier were now returning triumphantly, grinning from ear to ear. Even from here, Michael could see the red on their clothes and faces. He almost vomited when he saw how pleased they looked. There was no doubt that whichever Minder had been watching the tower was now dead; Michael just hoped that death was the worst they had done to the guard.

Michael turned back to see Mary being held in Captain's huge arms, cradled as she shook with anger. Anger directed, he realized with ice in his blood, at Michael, not at the men who had just come back to the group with blood on their faces.

He caught Captain's gaze, full of wrath, and watched as Captain released Mary, clapped her on the shoulder, and bellowed to his people in a language Michael didn't understand. The people of the Void straightened up, the air around them bristling with power. And then they started to march toward the bunker with murder in their eyes.

Michael turned to go back to the crater. *I need to get Angel's journals.* The thought of making the trek all the way back was already making him dizzy.

But the men who had gone first, the ones who had disposed of the guard at the tower, were already coming for him. They quickly formed a circle around him, cutting him off. One of the men stepped up, just inches from Michael's face, and grinned with sharpened teeth.

"You'll come with us. We'll make sure nothing happens to you, small man." The other men laughed, eight feet tall and ruthless, red glistening on their skin.

Michael's blood boiled, but he didn't try to run. He felt his death hanging over him.

46

The men dragged him along, laughing crazily. They babbled to each other in a weird language that Michael couldn't follow, only every fifth or sixth word of it Republican. He started to wonder if they weren't just making sounds to make him uneasy. The words he did recognize made Michael cringe, though—like "blood" and "kill"— and as they chattered excitedly their grip grew tighter and tighter on his arms.

They were at the back of the makeshift army, jostling him about as they hooted, shaking their weapons.

"It's been too long since we had a raid!" one of them cried, in perfect Republican, and Michael knew it was so he would hear and understand and be afraid. The man flashed his teeth at Michael and then the group of them started to make a noise, like a beast but more vicious, a deep growling in their chests that shook Michael's bones.

"We protect our own." "Nous protégeons nos gens." "We keep our own safe." "Protegemos nuestro propio." "Wir halten einander sicher." "We'll keep our families protected."

It was a buzzing chant, muttered underneath the growling of the people in front of them, a war call, in that mash of languages again, as the people of the crater moved forward toward the gate. Their noise grew as they all pushed to make it into the narrow concrete shaft. And as the growling from the men eclipsed the fevered chants from the women, as the noise became so deafening Michael thought he might never hear anything again, Michael realized something: he knew that sound.

This was the sound of the mighty beast that had slaughtered all those sheep outside his hut on that cold winter night, years ago. The beast that had departed without eating any of the carnage left behind, causing so much confusion and fear around the complex. Michael had cowered in his hut that night, listening. The beast—it was an army of people from the Void.

Because they were so loud, Michael almost missed it, but then he saw the amber lights flashing on the wall and his blood ran cold. The buzzer was going off.

"Hey." He couldn't even hear his own voice, but he pulled against the men holding him and tried to get their attention. "Hey! The Archivists are going to start coming out!" The men ignored him and continued their crazed chanting.

They were in the halls now, having made it through the choke point of the entry door. Michael's boots slipped on something, and he looked down. The floor was coated in red. He vomited, sick splashing down his shirt.

There was less chanting all of a sudden, and then more screaming. The army around him was drawing their weapons, too many people choking the hallway as they surged against each other in the tight quarters. Pops of gunfire, and more screaming, and the screeching of the buzzer, all battering Michael's ears. He watched as an Archivist was cut down with a long knife the size of his arm, and he cried out. A flare was tossed into the middle of the crowd by a Minder, blinding him momentarily, and he smelled the smoke pouring off of it. The men holding Michael yelled and brought their hands up to cover their eyes.

Michael tore away from them and ran.

"Mary!" he screamed, searching desperately. He had to find her. *This is all wrong, we have to get out of here.* "Mary!"

He was pushing Archivists and Minders and crater people out of his way just the same, trying to stay low to avoid the swinging blades and flashing guns. His arm, bandaged but bleeding through again, was on fire. Something warm hit his shoulder. He kept running.

There!

He had seen her, and Captain, standing at the far end of the corridor, so very far away, and separated from him by hundreds of people. He jumped up and tried to see them again, pushing up to see over the heads of those around him. Mary was bouncing on her feet, visibly shaken and furious. Captain was trying to calm her.

"Mary!"

She couldn't hear him; it was too loud and too far. He watched helplessly as Mary nodded, pointed down the hall behind Captain at something Michael couldn't see, and then tore off running the opposite way. By the time Michael had made it to the end of the hall, shoving people out of the way viciously, both of them were gone. Michael screamed in frustration, feeling the blood drip down his arm.

47

The gun was shaking in her hand.

"Mary . . ." Coleman was blinking at her, her mouth open, afraid. "I thought you . . . What are you doing?"

Mary tried not to let her voice shake too badly. "I'm not going to let you find it." She didn't want to cry, but the tears were coming. She was angry. Anger had never made Mary cry before she read Allysan Murphree's journals, and now she was regretting having taken that project on. Now she could barely stop the tears.

Coleman, to her credit, kept the confused look on her face, though her eyes grew colder. "Find what, Mary? God, I'm so glad you're safe. When I heard Driftveil was missing I was *terrified*, you have no idea how dangerous he is—"

"No!" Mary screamed at her. "No! You weren't worried about me. You weren't." She watched as Coleman blinked slowly at her, her face tight. "But you were mortified that you lost *him*, weren't you? I bet that must have been embarrassing to explain to whoever you report to, that you had lost the most promising Archivist you had. That even though he was starving to death, he escaped all of your Minders." Mary's eyes were burning. "But you were never for a moment worried about me."

"I don't know what you're talking about, Mary. I don't! Put the gun down, *please*."

Mary raised it higher, aimed it at the old woman's face. She didn't know if she was holding it right, or what it would do if she pulled the trigger, but she saw Coleman's eyes widen to the size of eggs, and her teeth clicked together audibly.

"When I showed up you promised me I could help people." The tears started. She couldn't stop them now, and she felt ridiculous. They weren't really her tears, but Coleman didn't know that. "I would never have come to read if I had known you were trying to bomb the goddamn crater, *damn* you!"

Mary couldn't help but think of all she had lost of herself so far. She couldn't remember her own brother's face, or the house she had grown up in, the house her mother had almost died to qualify for. Instead, she had love inside her for a daughter she had never known, had never met. She had love inside her for a man that had stopped loving her when she was twenty four years old, and she'd never met that man either.

"I thought I could help people," she said, her voice shaking. "I thought reading would serve the country, make it a better place for people to live. But reading *destroyed* Michael. You made him violent and sad. You absolutely *ruined* him just so you could get the information you wanted and then kill him."

Coleman frowned. "We *are* helping people, Mary. We're keeping the complexes safe, protecting the Republic. Those living in the crater don't belong with us, and we can't be safe until they're gone. They threaten everything we've built in the last hundred years."

The tears ran freely now. "You ruined him. You've ruined others, too, the ones that are useful to you, you hateful bitch."

Mary saw Coleman's eyes flash, but the old woman kept her voice gentle and friendly, although still tinged with fear.

"I wish I had realized who you'd picked out. If I had read Angel's file more closely, I could have realized that we'd be bringing Michael in soon and I would have stopped you. I didn't want you to feel so close to him. I am so, so sorry, Mary."

Mary felt her jaw working angrily, waiting for Coleman to confirm what she had suspected for weeks. "You would have stopped me? You knew Angel's connection to Michael? You would have kept me from feeling this way?"

"*Yes.* Oh, god yes, I didn't ever mean for this to happen. Angel's journals were supposed to be separated so they couldn't be accidentally assigned. They've been kept separate for a decade because I didn't know when we'd be bringing him in—"

Mary made a noise then, a disgusted sob, and Coleman's head snapped back as if she had been slapped. Coleman realized her mistake as soon as she heard that noise.

"You planned all of it." Mary's voice was shaking.

And just like that, the old woman's face switched from earnest pleading to white-hot anger. "You," Coleman hissed, "you *manipulative* little—"

"Did you deny his parentage application?"

Coleman's eyes were full of hate and fire, and fear, too.

"Coleman," Mary tried to dash the tears away from her face with her shoulder, "*listen* to me. If you tell me, I won't let them hurt you." She lowered the gun—it trembled in her hand—but she kept her eyes trained on the old woman's face.

The air seemed to rush out of Coleman. Her shoulders sagged and she looked impossibly small. "Mary . . ." she whimpered. This was a woman who was terrified, who knew that what she had done was terrible. Mary almost pitied her.

"*Tell me.*"

"Yes." It came out as a broken whisper.

"And you denied his fiancé's maternity care so she would die and the baby would be taken away." It wasn't a question, but Mary still watched, horrified, as Coleman nodded. The woman planned the whole thing from the start.

"He *was* arrested for a very serious crime," Coleman pleaded, her eyes wide.

Mary felt the cold gun in her hand, the weight of it, as she thought about what a nice young man Michael used to be. Her heart ached. "You would have put him in the Archives no matter what he had done, because you needed him."

Coleman started to smile weakly, her eyes watery. "There you go. You understand."

"How could you *do* that to someone? He was a good kid before you started messing with his life. *You put him here.* How could you do that?"

"There are people, like Michael, who can contribute far more to our country as Archivists than they could in any other way." She was starting to recover her composure. "We're only trying to keep our people safe, and for that we need the weapon. And to find the weapon, we need Archivists."

"How many people have you done this to?" Mary eyes were hollow, horrified.

Coleman looked repentant, and stood slowly from her chair, her arms stretched out with her palms open and empty. "Oh, Mary, darling," her voice was sickly sweet, and Mary retreated a step, "I know how strong you are. I know you'll understand when you hear all about it." She made a move to hug the younger woman. "We *needed* him."

Mary bit the inside of her cheek as Coleman's arms wrapped around her. She felt sick.

"I know where it is."

She felt Coleman freeze at her whispered words, felt the stiffening of her spine and the transformation of her arms into iron bars.

"Where?" Coleman hissed. "Where is it?" She gripped Mary's face between her hands and shook the girl.

Mary raised the gun to Coleman's temple and shot her.

48

When she made it to the cage, Coleman's key in hand, she found Captain growling at the librarians behind the wire. They had locked themselves in, and he paced in front of the barrier. Mary imagined a great beast, with teeth like knives and paws as big as her head, pacing back and forth behind a glass window, its shoulder blades raising sharply as it walked, its tail swishing in agitation.

"Captain?" she whispered, not wanting to startle him.

He rounded on her just the same, the flame from his torch blazing a trail behind her as he spun. Mary shrank back, but she watched as Captain's body changed, relaxing, his face smiling, though his eyes still burned hotter than his torch.

"Mary!" he sang to her. "Did you manage the key, little one?" His teeth flashed white.

She nodded, but her face crumpled and she began to cry. Coleman's blood felt sticky on her face, and the tears ran some of the blood onto her lips. She fought the wave of revulsion that coursed through her.

"Oh, sweet girl." He came to her, gathering her in one arm, holding the torch far away so he wouldn't scorch her. "No tears today. You've done such a great service to us today, little Mary." She sobbed into his chest, smearing blood and grime that had collected on her face onto his shirt.

"Better?" he sang, when she had begun to calm. There were sounds of gunshots and screaming beyond the door behind her, but she nodded anyway.

"I'm so sorry, your shirt's dirty . . ."

He waved a hand at her dismissively. "Oh no, I've already got blood on it." And she saw that he did. A pool of red was on his side.

Mary looked at him sharply, worried. And he smiled at her, his eyes sad now.

Before she could ask to see the wound, or to try to tend to it, he plucked the key from her hand. "My people thank you, Mary. Go on, find your way out of here. Take your gun." He hugged her briefly and made his way to the cage.

The librarians, about a dozen of them, were huddled tightly beside one of the tall shelves. They watched Captain draw closer, their eyes wide and fearful. He unlocked the gate and slipped inside, stepping up very close to them before bending down to look into their eyes.

"Give me the keys," he growled, and they scrambled to comply. Twelve keys were removed from twelve necks and tossed hurriedly at the tall man's feet.

"Thank you." He scooped the lot of them up and looped the chains over his hand, then crossed back over to the gate and stood to the side of it. He looked back at them expectantly.

The librarians looked at each other with relief before detaching themselves from one another and moving toward the gate, eager to be away from this madness.

"*Thank you,*" one of the women cried to him as she moved to escape.

Captain smiled and slammed the gate shut with them only inches from their escape, locking them all in—himself included.

"Captain?" Mary stared, her eyes flitting between the group of librarians, the closed gate, and the man on the other side who held the keys. "Captain, they have to get out."

He ignored her.

"Please!" one of them cried. "Please, let us out!"

He met the plea with a cold glare. "You're responsible for this, too. This horror. You allowed it to happen. You deserve to meet the same fate as your journals."

He bent down and thrust his torch against a box, the flames licking eagerly.

"Captain!" Mary screamed. "Stop it now!"

The librarians were looking at each other frantically, confused and frightened. As the flames started to take hold, one of them—it was Jacqueline, the tiny old woman who manned the front desk—drew herself up and ran toward Captain to rend the torch from his hand.

"You can't burn them!" she squawked. "You can't! It's important!"

Captain brushed the ancient woman aside easily, and she tumbled to the ground, yelping in pain as her head struck the concrete.

"Stop it!" Mary screeched, running to the gate and shaking it, trying fruitlessly to wrench it open. "You have to stop it! Let them out!"

Captain ignored her and dipped the torch down to another box.

A sound welled up inside of Mary, starting low in her stomach and building up, up through her chest and throat to tear forth violently from her teeth, the scream louder than the crackle of the fire as the journals burned, louder than the terrified cries of the librarians. She'd been betrayed. Again. Mary couldn't stop screaming.

49

Michael could smell smoke once more. It was in his mouth, choking him, choking the halls. The Archivists were running away, screaming and sobbing.

"No," he whispered. "No, please." He started running faster than he thought possible, shoving the Archivists out of the way with his good arm. He hoped he was going the right way, prayed that it wasn't too late. He didn't have his map, but then again he was too panicked to be able to see the numbers on the doors anyway. He had to jump over bodies. He had to jump over the bodies of children, children who had been trampled while trying to escape. A sound ripped its way from his teeth, a strangled horror. This wasn't supposed to be happening.

Several gunshots. Michael pushed his body faster, his lungs burning, trying to stay as low to the ground as he could. The smoke was thicker here, the only indication he was going the right way.

All of a sudden there was a Minder in front of him, previously shrouded by the thick smoke, but now he was here, and pointing his muzzle directly at Michael's chest. He had arrived like a dream, fading into existence, seeming simultaneously real and imagined, but all dangerous.

"What the hell have you done?" the Minder snarled at him. His eyes were wide and crazy, tears running tracks down his face from the smoke and the rage that was fueling him. "What did you do? You bastard!"

Michael raised his hands slowly in front of him, gasping, shaking his head. "No, I swear to you I didn't do this. Please let me past, my friend is—"

"I thought *I* was your friend, damn it! Why are you killing us?"

Michael's mouth dropped open. He hadn't even recognized the man standing in front of him. "Cyrus!" Michael's body was suddenly wracked with a fit of coughs, and he doubled over with the force of it. Every second spent coughing was another second Michael should have been finding Mary and stopping the fire. When he forced himself to straighten, pained and smoky tears streaming down his face, Cyrus looked to be no closer to lowering his weapon. "Oh god, Cyrus, please. Please believe me." More coughing. "This wasn't the plan. You have to let me through."

Cyrus walked closer until the muzzle of the long rifle was pressed against Michael's sternum. Michael tried not to flinch away, instead looking straight into Cyrus's grimy, tear-streaked face, hoping.

"I watched them cut down everyone they could reach. Archivists and Minders just the same. How could you let them in?" Michael almost didn't hear it for how softly Cyrus spoke. But the anger in his voice was unmistakable, the betrayal and hurt just as clear as anything Michael had felt himself.

Michael didn't move except to say, "I'm sorry."

Whether it was the apology or the effects of the smoke, Cyrus lowered the gun and squeezed his eyes shut, his whole body shaking with grief. "They're burning it all. Everything we have. They're burning it."

Michael grabbed his friend's shoulder. "I'm going to go. Please leave, get out of the bunker. Please!" And he was running off again, diving deeper into the ever-thickening smoke. He didn't look back to check if the Minder had moved, but he prayed despite himself. *God, don't kill Cyrus. Please let him live.*

Blood was everywhere. He slipped in it, falling to his knees and getting covered in the slick red. He tried so very hard not to disturb the bodies, but he felt the sickening *crunch* again and again as he stepped on fingers, limbs, skulls. Within minutes, he was hearing screams again. They were coming from the Cage, he knew. He could see it through the haze at the end of the hall, the doorway belching smoke into the rest of the facility. Michael felt his stomach turn.

"Mary!" he yelled into the smoke, hoping that she was still alive. And then, on a level much deeper than that, he hoped he wouldn't hear her voice at all. Michael hoped that sweet Mary hadn't been a part of any of this, that she was in a different part of the bunker entirely, far removed from this madness.

"Michael!" She appeared out of the smoke just before he reached the room, grabbed him fiercely around the middle, and clung to him. "Michael I didn't mean to kill them." She was covered in blood, and sobbing terribly.

"What did you do?" He shook her, and she sobbed harder.

The heat radiating from the concrete box around the cage was unbearable. Michael could hear the screams from within the room. Mary's hands were over her ears.

He shook her. "Where is the key? Mary, where is it?"

She looked up at him, coughing, more tears streaming down her dark face. "Captain took it inside, Michael. It's gone. I can't unlock the cage. He's burning. The librarians are burning. It's all gone." She dissolved into gasps and shakes.

Horror washed over Michael. He left Mary outside the room, shaking her off as she tried to hold on to him, her nails biting into the skin on his arm.

He felt his skin start to blister as he walked into room 0001. There were people pressed against the cage, huddled near the floor to avoid the smoke, screaming at him to help them. Their hands reached through the bars, outstretched, begging for him to come closer.

He stared at them for a moment, his eyes watering in pain from the smoke, then ran toward the inferno to grab onto the bars and tug. The metal burned his hands, the skin crackling in searing pain. The bars didn't budge.

One of the librarians took hold of his hands. The skin on the right side of her body was black and charred, her clothes were burned away, and yet she still fought for life, desperately. "Michael," she cried. "Michael Driftveil! *Get us out.*"

The woman at the front desk, he realized, stunned. He hadn't recognized her.

He shook the bars a few more times, the heat making him dizzy even though the flames were yards away. The sound of the fire roared in his ears. Screaming, Michael began to kick at the gate, draining himself. His efforts weren't doing a damn thing.

He was going to die in here with them if he didn't move.

Hating himself, Michael tore away from the woman. His skin stuck to the bars.

"No no no, don't leave! Let me out! Oh god, let me out!"

Michael turned away from her and ran. He grabbed Mary from where she had fallen to the ground outside the room, pulling her hair in anguish. He was going to save *someone,* damn it.

He tossed her tiny body over his shoulder and ran away from the fire. Mary was kicking and screaming, telling him to take her back to the cage. He tried not to listen to her insults, to her calling him a coward for running away, calling him a pathetic mess of a man.

He was going to save someone. He couldn't get the terrified voice of the librarian out of his head.

There were more bodies than he remembered in the hallways. He was disoriented and exhausted, and all at once he knew he was going the wrong way. He stopped, whirling in place, trying to figure out from which way he had come. The yellow numbers on the doors here were in the lower 500s. He had no idea where that was.

"Mary, I'm lost," he gasped, spinning in circles. Mary had gone quiet on his shoulder, no longer fighting him, no longer begging him to put her down. *She's dead*, he thought. *We're both dying here today.* He knew he was going to die in the Archives. He had always known it. He just didn't think it would be this way, asphyxiating to death, covered in blood that wasn't his. The world was spinning without him moving. He was dizzy. He was tired . . .

Michael Driftveil fell to his knees, and his eyes closed. Mary fell from his shoulder with a hard *thump*, landing in a pool of red. He reached out, felt for her hand, smelled for the last time the terrible smoke that signified his failure. He would never know what Angel had figured out. He had failed . . .

Michael slipped away into the dark.

Epilogue

Mary opened her eyes, and wished she hadn't. The lights were too bright, and her eyes stung with an irritation she couldn't blink away. Memories of fire flooded back to her again, as they had for years.

Michael . . . She willed away the tears, but they ran from the corners of her eyes down to her ears anyway. That was the thing about tears: they didn't listen, and they certainly didn't do what you wanted. Especially not guilty tears.

There was a man sitting in a wooden chair on the far end of her room, as always.

"Hey," she croaked, making no move to wipe the moisture from her face. She was too tired.

"Hey yourself," he said gently. "How are we today?" He smiled at her, his eyes crinkling in the corners. She watched him for a moment, thinking back to how young he used to look. He'd grown into a man right in front of her eyes.

Bracing herself, Mary swung her legs out of the bed with a little difficulty. Her left leg felt wooden and heavy, which still surprised her even after all this time. Finally, she pushed herself into a sitting position, wincing as her bones creaked. "Good, I suppose. Today's the day, right?"

He nodded. "Yeah. You excited?"

She didn't feel excited. Mary knew she ought to be. Today had been a long time coming. "Of course." She lied, and faked a smile for him.

"They'll come in a bit for you. Where are you heading?"

Mary looked at him pointedly, sadly. "Oh, Cy. You know I can't tell you that."

He snorted a laugh. "Yeah, I know. But I have to ask, you get me? They only ever let me watch you in the hopes that I could gather intel from you."

She really did flash him a grin then. "They're not getting anything out of me."

He smirked. They sat there for a long moment before his eyes grew sad, and Mary's chest ached. He still loved her, even after everything. "You gonna be okay?" he asked, his voice quiet and rough like steel wool.

She shrugged. "I'll manage. I'll ask for help if I need it." Truth was, she was terrified. But she wasn't going to let Cyrus know that.

"You'll come back if you need us." It wasn't a question.

"Of course." Another lie.

Cyrus wanted to ask her another question, but hesitated.

"What is it, hon?" She threw out the pet name easily, and was pleased when he didn't balk. He really didn't see her as the terrible person the Republic had tried to make her out to be since the fire. Her heart hurt.

"Are you going to find him?"

Mary thought a moment before shrugging. "I don't know if he's alive."

"He wasn't with you when I found you." Like she didn't know. Like he hadn't pointed that out before.

"Well... maybe someone else dragged me out of there. He could have burned."

He looked doubtful, but let it go. He stood and walked to the bars that separated them, reaching his arms through the spaces in between. She stood and crossed over to him, letting him embrace her. "Glad they're letting you go, Mary." He squeezed her as tightly as the bars would let him.

"Thanks for testifying for me." She grinned at him with a joy she didn't fully feel. She knew he had lied for her. That was the only possible explanation for why she was still alive. He must have told them that she had been kidnapped, or brainwashed, or something. In any case, after almost three years in this cell, they were letting her out. The thought took her breath away.

He peered at her. "I know that, whatever your reasons, you did the right thing."

She wished she believed him.

A few hours later, a disgruntled-looking guard gave her a cane and a rucksack that had her clothes in it. He wasn't a Minder, Mary noticed. Technically, she was free of all charges, but Mary knew that to most she was still an enemy of the Republic. The smear campaign the senators had launched against her had been wildly exaggerated, but not entirely inaccurate. She had, in fact, committed treason, although a few Minders like Cyrus had broken oath to defend her and keep her from execution. The important thing was that she had done what she needed to do to protect thousands of innocent people. If not more.

The collateral damage from the fire still broke her heart, but the intervening years had at least brought an end to the nightmares.

Would she ever find the colony? That was the question she asked herself as she was led out of her cell and into the sunshine—and oh, god, the light felt amazing on her skin! Would the colony even be there still? Had it ever really existed? She didn't know. She was operating solely on assumptions, just as she had been for the last three years. Angel had heard stories of monsters in a land far away, across the water. Monsters with long arms and flat faces.

She was farther south than she had ever been in her life—probably around Atlanta Crater, if she had to guess. All the

Archivists they had been able to find after the fighting had been taken down this way. The Archives themselves had been unsalvageable thanks to the flames; thousands of journals, from all the conservation programs in the country, lost.

She had heard once that the government was based somewhere in the south of the country, but the location had always been fuzzy, and changed depending on whom you talked to. She was definitely in the capital now, though, no way to deny that. The Minder presence here was astounding, the Law Building and prison so much larger than the one back home, and almost as big as the Archives.

Mary knew that she would never be able to return to her home complex. Not with how the Republic hated her.

She needed to make it to the coast, if she could. And from there she needed to find a way across the ocean. That particular little gem made her tremble in fear. She knew enough about marine biology from her time as an Archivist to know that the ocean was full of beasts that could swallow her whole.

The first leg of her journey took weeks on foot—not helped by the fact that she limped something terrible. She tried to stay far away from any complexes, which meant staying in wooded areas that hadn't been cleared for settlements. Sometimes she was lucky and was able to catch small animals to roast under her miserable excuse for a fire. Most nights she went hungry and thirsty.

But somehow, some miracle allowed her to reach the coast. She smelled it before she could see it, the salt in the air clinging to her nose and skin. When she finally made her way out of the groves of thick, waxy-leaved trees and into an area where the soil became too sandy for any dense vegetation to grow, Mary gasped. It was more beautiful than she remembered. Of course, Mary had never really looked at the ocean before—those memories were not her own. But she thought it was the most beautiful thing she might ever see in her life.

For a full night, she looked out across the water, lying in the sand and enjoying the warmth that the tiny grains had soaked up from the sun during the day. She didn't see anyone else on the sand, or in the water, and though she had spent the whole trip avoiding people, Mary found herself disappointed. She had memories of people flocking to the beach in times of warm weather, splashing each other with the cool water, tanning their skin in bathing suits.

For now, she was too afraid to approach the water, although the sight of it sparkling under the moon made her throat ache in thirst. As scared as she was of the ocean, Mary wanted to run up to the waves and take a big gulp of the seawater. She knew she couldn't, but it was still difficult not to try.

The sight of the sun rising over the water made Mary gasp one more time. She had never seen a sky so red, and the reflection of the sky on the water reminded her of the fire. She couldn't tear her eyes away, afraid to blink too much in case she missed even a moment of the beauty. When it was over, the sun creeping steadily higher into the sky and the red burning off to reveal a cool, brilliant blue with hardly a cloud up above her, Mary stood and dusted the white sand from her legs and back.

She needed to find a boat to take her east, to Europe, to see if there were still Reachees there like Angel had heard.

One foot in front of the other, Mary started walking.

A HUGE **THANK YOU** TO

Amanda and Jim Davis

Angel Lee

Angela Ye

Angelos Kyritsis

Aunt Linda

Bill and Venisha Knepper

Brianne Hartnett

Cheryl Kittle

Emily and Steve Pedlow

Gary Rademaker

James, Julia and Brenden Anderson

Jay Edwards

Jim and Rhonda Swinehart

Joshua Paul Sommers

Katie Montes

Kitt Hodsden

Laura Shanae Crenshaw

Laura Smith

Mike Danylchuk

Peggy Goodale

Phillip C. Enders

Rebecca Vogel

Rene Trudeau

Rhett W. Whitaker

Roderick J. Fraser Jr

Sara Anderson

Sheila Kittle and Maurice VanZoolingen

Terrie LaRue and Keith Faison

Tye Weisenfluh

Tyler Johnson

Tyler Swinehart

Uncle Bruce

ABOUT THE AUTHOR

Corryn Anderson is a young writer who loves all things geeky and strange, and who spends her time writing, playing video games, and obsessing over board game strategy. Her debut novel, ARCHIVIST, was written at the age of 21.

Corryn lives in sunny Florida with her partner Tyler, the loudest cat around named Mau Mau, and a six pound puppy named Trogdor the Burninator.

You can email her at CorrynAiyana@gmail.com

Find Archivist on Facebook!
Facebook.com/ArchivistNovel

Like the book? Think it could have been better? Be sure to leave a review on Amazon or Goodreads!